LEAH CYPESS

DEATH MARKED

Greenwillow Books
An Imprint of HarperCollinsPublishers

Death Marked
Copyright © 2015 by Leah Cypess

All rights reserved. No part of this book may be used or reproduced in any manner whatsoever without written permission except in the case of brief quotations embodied in critical articles and reviews. Printed in the United States of America. For information address HarperCollins Children's Books, a division of HarperCollins Publishers, 195 Broadway, New York, NY 10007.
www.epicreads.com

The text of this book is set in Centaur MT. Book design by Sylvie Le Floc'h.

Library of Congress Cataloging-in-Publication Data

Cypess, Leah.
Death marked / Leah Cypess.
pages cm
"Greenwillow Books."
Summary: After killing the leader of a clan of assassins and falling in love with his heir, a young sorceress discovers she is the one person to bring down the evil Empire that has been oppressing her people for centuries, and now, in the heart of the Empire, Ileni herself is the deadliest weapon the assassins have ever had.
ISBN 978-0-06-222124-7 (hardback)
[1. Fantasy. 2. Magic—Fiction. 3. Assassins—Fiction. 4. Love—Fiction.] I. Title.
PZ7.C9972Dc 2015 [Fic]—dc23 2014030211

15 16 17 18 19 CG/RRDH 10 9 8 7 6 5 4 3 2 1

First Edition

 Greenwillow Books

DEATH MARKED

To Shoshana, Hadassah, and David

CHAPTER I

The mirror shattered into a hundred pieces, a sudden explosion followed by a cascade of jagged shards. Ileni whirled, throwing her hands up in front of her face, but nothing hit her: no sharp pieces of glass, no sting of cut flesh. After a moment, she lowered her arms and crossed them over her chest.

The broken fragments of glass hovered in the air, glimmering with rainbow colors. Then they faded back into the mirror, smoothing into a shiny, unbroken oval.

"Impressive," Ileni said. She had no idea who she was talking to, but it wasn't difficult to sound unafraid. After six weeks in the Assassins' Caves and three days as a prisoner of imperial sorcerers, false courage was second nature to her. "But since I'm the only one here, it seems a waste of effort."

The colors flattened into a vaguely human-shaped form. Before she could make out the face, the form spoke. "Absalm said this was the only spell that could get through the Academy's wards."

Ileni froze. She dug her fingers into her upper arms.

The image in the mirror sharpened, revealing a blond young man with dark eyes. His grimly set mouth curved up slightly in the hint of a smile. "You were expecting someone else?"

Ileni tilted her head. "I wasn't expecting anyone. Given that I am, as you pointed out, in a rather heavily warded room."

She almost—almost—managed to keep her voice cool. But it shook just a little, and of course Sorin noticed. The slight curve turned into a real smile. "It's good to see you, Ileni."

She pressed her lips together before they could betray her with an answering smile. "How did you know where I was?"

His smile deepened.

Ileni's jaw clenched. "You shouldn't be trying to contact

me. You might have pushed this spell through the wards, but the imperial sorcerers will know it happened."

His eyes narrowed. "Will that put you in danger?"

More danger than I'm in already? "No. I can protect myself."

"I hope you're right." He leaned forward a fraction. "I'm glad you're alive."

Ileni forced a laugh. "Why, thank you. I'm glad I'm alive, too."

"I wasn't sure you would be." He seemed about to say more, and her breath froze in her throat. He must know, now, that she had killed his master. He knew, and yet he had said, *I'm glad you're alive.*

She hadn't realized, until this moment, how afraid she had been of him finding out. Not because he would kill her—she should have been afraid of that, but she hadn't been. She had only been afraid he would hate her.

Sorin shook his head slightly. "Things have been complicated here. I couldn't force Absalm to track you down until now."

"*Force* him?" Ileni stepped closer to the mirror. She was sure he could hear the sound of her heart hammering, but there was nothing she could do about that. She didn't know herself if it was from excitement or fear. "I like the sound of that. You have been busy, haven't you?"

"So have you. How did you manage to infiltrate the Imperial Academy itself?" The admiration in his voice was genuine, and Ileni was dismayed at the thrill that ran through her. She had left him behind. She was supposed to be past this. Even if it had only been three days.

Irritation sharpened her voice. "I'm not *infiltrating* anything. I'm not on your side, Sorin. Don't forget that."

His expression didn't change. "How did you get in, then? What did you tell them?"

Nothing. I'm a prisoner. The truth twitched at the edge of her tongue. If she said it, he would save her. He would find a way.

Instead she said, "It's not important."

"Isn't it?" His mouth tightened. "Do they know—"

"That I have no magic of my own anymore?" She got it out without a tremor. She was proud of that. "Yes. It's not exactly something I could hide. Not here."

A silence fell between them, and stretched too long. Ileni was acutely aware that she was finding it hard to breathe. Sorin's eyes searched her face, looking for—what? She didn't know, and she also didn't know whether he was finding it.

He seemed different, somehow. Just a week ago, he had been teaching her to fight and making her laugh and kissing her in hidden corridors. But the face in the mirror was inscrutable and dangerous. If even Absalm was following his commands, he must have swiftly secured his position as the new master of the assassins. He had always been a killer, but now he was a leader of killers.

"So," she said finally, when she couldn't bear it anymore. "You just wanted to check on me?"

He let out a breath. "Yes. And to see if you needed help."

She almost laughed at that—or maybe it was a sob. She couldn't ask him for help. They really *weren't* on the same side. "I don't. Thank you for the dagger, though."

"You're welcome," he said, with a light bow.

Ileni had found the dagger in her backpack the first time she opened it on the mountain path. She had no idea how Sorin had put it there without her noticing, but she had immediately stuck it into her boot. It was still there, alien and heavy, yet comforting at the same time.

Their eyes met. His gleamed, like sunlight hitting black stone, and an answering spark lit in Ileni. She almost reached for him, as if she could touch him, as if he was right there in the room with her.

"Are you absolutely certain you don't want help?" Sorin said. "If you need me, I will come. Once the imperial sorcerers find out you lived here in our caves, your life won't be worth much."

She hesitated, wondering if he had seen through the casualness. He *could* help her. He had hundreds of assassins who were his to command. He had a sorcerer, who apparently obeyed him at least some of the time. All she had to do was say yes, and he would bring her back.

She made her voice firm. "They won't find out. Someone will be coming to investigate any moment now. So you had better go."

"I will. Ileni . . ."

Her voice emerged low and steady. "I'm glad you contacted me."

Something hot flickered deep in his cold black eyes. His voice, though, was as steady as hers. "It was worth putting up with Absalm's pouting, then."

Ileni stepped back. "Don't do it again."

He didn't say good-bye. His image vanished in a swirl of colors. The surface of the mirror turned black, darker than black: so dark it made the rest of the room seem dim, even though the glowstones shone bright. Then the blackness was sucked away into the mirror, and Ileni was left staring at her own reflection.

She had just a moment to note the stricken expression on her face. Then the door to the room slammed open, and a burst of magic threw her away from the mirror and across the room.

Pinned against the wall, she looked at the black-haired woman in the doorway and said, weakly, "Karyn. Nice to see you again."

Sorin stepped back from the mirror, keeping his breathing relaxed and even. Gray fog moved steadily across the glass surface, as if driven by wind. Across the black stone room, Absalm cleared his throat.

"Well done," he said.

Sorin whirled to face him. The old Renegai sorcerer nodded at him, an approving, fatherly gesture.

Sorin kept his voice cold. "If you want to reopen the portal, can you?"

"It's still there, yes. I could reopen it easily." Absalm's voice was gentle, patronizingly so. Sorin didn't *need* gentleness. Certainly not from this man. "But why would we want to? There's a reason the master never made contact with an assassin until his mission was completed."

But Ileni was no assassin. She wasn't even a sorceress, not

anymore. She could die out there, alone in the Empire, and he wouldn't know until it was too late to save her.

Sorin struggled to gain control. His feelings for Ileni were not just a weakness, but something worse: a *sign* of weakness. Among his fellow assassins—his disciples, now, at least in theory—many suspected, but few were sure. Absalm, of course, would be busy stirring their suspicions into certainty.

The best strategy would be to pass off his involvement with Ileni as a dalliance, a bit of sport. Or, better—as something he had undertaken upon the master's command, an inducement for her to play her part. He had half-convinced himself that was how it had started.

But he had let her go. She was in the Empire now, with the master's blood on her hands—and he had stood at the entrance of the caves and watched her walk away. He had no explanation for it. None that would satisfy Absalm, or the other assassins, or even himself.

He shouldn't have to explain himself to anyone. He was the leader of the assassins now. But he was not the master, who had held absolute power in these caves for nearly a century. Absalm had been the master's friend, worked with him, been privy to more of his plans than any of the assassins themselves. Absalm could undermine

Sorin's authority easily, if he chose to.

Which meant Sorin had to find a way to make Ileni's presence in the Academy work for him. To make them believe it had been part of his plan all along.

If he could do that, he might not have to kill her.

"Ileni," he said, "is a well-honed blade. And now she needs to be aimed at her target."

"Was that the purpose of this conversation?"

Sorin tried to smile mysteriously, the way the master would have; but the memory of the master made grief twist within him, and he could tell by Absalm's flat stare that the sorcerer wasn't convinced.

"It was a start," Sorin said.

"And how do you intend to continue?"

"You don't need to know that."

Absalm pressed his lips together. Sorin waited just long enough to make sure the rebuff would sting, then softened the insult with a question. "Do you think she suspected how we knew she was there?"

"No," Absalm said. His tone was surly, but there was respect in it, too—real respect, not the pretense he had been displaying for the past few days. "That was excellently done. I don't think she suspected a thing."

CHAPTER 2

Lies spun in Ileni's mind as she looked across the stone room at the black-haired sorceress. Karyn was wearing a loose white gown, and her face was even more grim than usual, which Ileni hadn't thought possible. Three days ago, right before transporting her to this room, Karyn had made a promise: *I will kill you if you don't cooperate.*

Secret communications with the Assassins' Caves likely did not count as *cooperating.*

Ileni's feet dangled a yard above the floor, and Karyn's spell pressed her hard against the rough wall. She tried to think up an excuse—an explanation—anything to buy her time, to convince Karyn she was too valuable to kill. But she, who had lied for weeks to the assassins around her, was suddenly afraid that she couldn't pull it off, that Karyn would see right through anything but the truth. As if, exhausted by the strain of constant deception, she could no longer pull up another lie.

She had told her last lie in the caves without even intending to, right before she had walked away, the black mountains a shadow on her back. Only three days ago, she had promised Sorin: *I'm not going back to the Renegai village.* She had meant it. But half a day later, as she strode down the winding trail with her pack digging into her shoulders, she had realized it was impossible.

Sorin or any of the other assassins would have known exactly which roads led to the Empire, and could have journeyed there with no more provisions than she carried in her pack. But Ileni had never been trained to leave her village at all. And that village was the only place she knew how to get to.

Even if it was the last place she wanted to go.

Ileni had a lot of practice, by then, in doing things she didn't want to do. So she had set her face toward her village, promising herself it would only be a short detour, trying not to think about how she would explain why she had left her exile in the caves. Or—even more unthinkably—why she was headed into the Empire.

Then Karyn had ambushed her.

Ileni supposed she should feel some measure of gratitude to the imperial sorceress. She hadn't had to return, to face her people after failing them twice. She hadn't had to see Tellis. Instead she had been taken—magically transported, even— straight to the center of the Empire's power: the Imperial Academy. The source of the magic that kept the Empire running, and the ideal place to discover if that Empire was as evil as she had always been taught.

To decide if she was, in fact, going to help destroy it.

Assuming the imperial sorcerers didn't just kill her, this had actually worked out quite well. The trouble was, Ileni couldn't think of a single reason why they wouldn't kill her.

She had spent the last three days locked in a stone room, and as far as she could tell, no one but Karyn knew she was there. The fact that Karyn hadn't killed her already was her one slim thread of hope.

She had only a brief memory of the encounter with Karyn, the two of them facing each other on the narrow road. Then Karyn had flung out her hand in a flash of violet light, and the next thing Ileni remembered was waking up in this windowless room. It had taken her only a few minutes to sense the wards around her and realize where she was.

Since then, food had appeared regularly on a tray on the floor, and her chamberpot had occasionally disappeared and reappeared—casual uses of magic she had once been accustomed to. But she'd had no contact with any human being. How long would Karyn have left her here if Sorin hadn't forced her hand?

The magic holding Ileni loosened, and the stone wall scraped against her back as she slid to the floor. Karyn lifted one hand, and blue-white light sizzled between her fingers. "If you helped an assassin breach our wards, I will kill you right now. So I suggest you explain what just happened."

Fortunately, Ileni had just spent several weeks keeping fear hidden. It was instinctive by now. "Don't be ridiculous. You know I have no magic left. I can't help anyone do anything."

"Every sorcerer in the Academy felt the magic coming from this room. Your presence here is no longer a secret."

So it *had* been a secret? Interesting.

"I wasn't doing anything," Ileni said. "Someone was trying to contact me."

"Someone from the *Renegai* village?"

The sneer in Karyn's voice made Ileni want to lie, just to spite her. *Yes. My people can break your wards. What do you think of that?*

But the imperial sorcerers still believed the Renegai were a backward group of ragtag exiles, no threat to them. If Ileni pretended they had the ability to breach the Academy's wards, that might put them in danger. The assassins, on the other hand, were already perceived as a threat. And besides, they could take care of themselves.

"No," she said. "Someone from the Assassins' Caves."

Karyn straightened, and Ileni was glad she hadn't lied. The sorceress was now looking at her as if she represented a true danger. As if she was someone to be reckoned with.

That might or might not be a good thing. *Reckoning with her* could very well translate into *killing her*. But it felt good, in that moment.

"What did they want?" Karyn asked.

Lies spun through Ileni's mind, some senseless, some unbelievable, some contradicting each other. But seeing Sorin again, even for a few minutes, had reminded her how to take risks. She smiled directly at Karyn and said, "I'm not going to tell you."

"Oh," Karyn said, very softly, "I think you will." The blue-white light around her hand expanded, forming a crackling ball of barely restrained power.

Fear ran through Ileni, a taut thread. Only four days ago, she had seen Karyn hold Sorin suspended over a chasm, the ugly coiling of a deathspell emanating from her chants. Karyn was an imperial sorceress. Torture came easily to her.

"What you'll also tell me," Karyn said, "is who you were *really* talking to. Now that you're gone, there is no fully trained sorcerer in the Assassins' Caves. Certainly no one capable of breaching our wards."

Ileni wished that were true. But if there was one thing she would never tell Karyn, it was that Absalm was still alive. That was the thread that could lead the sorceress to the whole tangled conspiracy—to the real reason she had been in the caves, and the real reason she had left.

Her chance of discovering whether the Empire was as evil as she had always believed—not to mention of surviving the next ten minutes—depended on Karyn believing she was no threat. She had to look at Ileni and see a naive, powerless ex-sorceress. Not a . . . weapon.

The sense of betrayal, thick and dark, rose in Ileni's throat. Absalm was an Elder of her people, someone she had trusted, and he had twisted her entire life for his own purposes.

She swallowed her hurt and fury. She was *not* a weapon—not yet, anyhow. She was not here to be Absalm's tool, but to decide for herself which side she was on.

Right now, the Empire's side wasn't looking very promising.

"I don't know how they broke through your wards," she said. "But I could help you find out."

Karyn's eyebrows went up. "Really. You *do* switch sides rather easily, don't you?"

There was enough truth in that to make Ileni flush. "I was never one of the assassins. I was forced to go to the caves, forced to tutor them in magic. And I *left*."

"So you did. To return to your own people. Apparently you are still attached to them, despite your dalliance with killers."

The slight emphasis on *dalliance* made it clear Karyn knew what Sorin had been to her. Ileni struggled to keep from blushing and failed spectacularly. "Yes. I was going home."

She hadn't planned to say *home*. It just slipped out.

Karyn curled her fingers slowly into a fist, and the blue-white light shrank into her palm. "For what purpose? From what I understand, the Renegai don't have much use for sorcerers who have lost their powers."

Another truth. *It doesn't matter,* Ileni told herself, as different kinds of shame roiled within her. As long as Karyn didn't figure out the deepest truth of all.

I may not have magic, but I have the power to kill you all. And I'm here to decide whether to use it.

Although it wasn't her power, not really. She was just the vessel—trained in magic even though her power had always been temporary. The only magic she could ever draw on, now, would come from others' deaths. A caveful of assassins would, at a word, kill themselves so she could have their power. With that much power, she could destroy the Imperial Academy of Sorcery, the epicenter of the Empire's might. With the Academy gone, the Empire would have no adequate defense against the assassins.

She could be the one to accomplish the goal both the assassins and her own people had been working toward for centuries: wiping the Empire off the face of the earth.

Unless she died here first, killed by that very Empire. Which she would be, if she couldn't keep up with her lies.

She made herself say, in a small, helpless voice, "I had nowhere else to go."

Karyn snorted. "And now that you're here, you'll just throw in your lot with us?"

"I could help you," Ileni said. "I lived in the caves for weeks. I might know things that would be useful to you."

Karyn tilted her head sideways, a pose that could have been mistaken for amusement if not for the suspicion in her eyes. A tic started in Ileni's eyelid as the silence stretched. Then the sorceress said, "All right. You can stay."

"I—" She managed not to say *what* or *why*, mostly by biting her lip so hard it hurt.

"For now," Karyn added. "But I'll be watching you."

Ileni nodded.

Karyn slowly opened her hand. The blue-white light was gone. "I'll find a way to explain the breach—say it was a mistake during your preliminary testing. And then I'll have you enrolled as a new student. Nobody has to know where you came from." She flexed her fingers. "You realize that if anyone discovers you used to be an assassin, you won't survive a day here."

"I wasn't an assassin."

"You taught them magic, didn't you? Trained them to kill us?"

The bite in Karyn's voice killed Ileni's next question.

There could be only one reason Karyn was letting her stay: because she believed Ileni *could* help her fight the assassins. But did she really believe Ileni had turned traitor? Or did she have some other plan, a way to use Ileni against her will?

Well. That would be nothing new.

Karyn crossed the room and touched her finger to the mirror. "Right now, I'll summon the nearest sorcerer. Some luckless student will be here shortly to escort you to the testing arena."

She closed her eyes and murmured a brief spell. A shimmer of magic, distant and tantalizing, brushed Ileni's skin, and she shivered despite herself.

Karyn's eyes opened just in time to catch that. She watched Ileni from beneath hooded eyelids. "I have access to as many lodestones as I want. If you had known that, I assume you wouldn't have gone to so much trouble to steal the one I had last time we met." She pursed her lips. "Though I suppose if you had managed to hold onto it, *you* could have tasted power again."

It was such an obvious, childish taunt. It shouldn't have worked.

"It's interesting, though." Karyn was practically purring. "How do you think you'll feel, being surrounded by sorcerers-in-training? Once you would have been the best of them, isn't that right?"

Ileni knew exactly how it would feel. She had left her own people for the Assassins' Caves just so she would never have to feel like that again.

She didn't trust herself to control her expression. She turned away from Karyn just in time to see two young men appear in the doorway.

Literally, *appear*: a second ago, the space outside the door had been empty.

"Good," Karyn said, still sounding like a stroked cat. "This is Ileni. She'll be—"

One of the new arrivals looked at Ileni. She froze when she recognized him, but his face remained perfectly pleasant, as if he had no idea who she was. He bent toward his boot, a smooth feline movement, without losing his placid expression for a second.

Ileni went for her dagger, but he was faster.

Assassins always were.

"Whoa," the other boy said mildly, and Karyn snapped, "Ileni!"

The assassin's hand was around her wrist, tight enough to hurt, yet he exhibited no strain. His other hand was curled but empty. Too late, Ileni realized that he hadn't been reaching for a blade. He had merely been bending to wipe off his breeches, which were marked by a long smudge of chalk.

"What are you *doing?*" the assassin asked, voice high-pitched and shaking. His eyes were wide, his breath fast, as if he was the one who was afraid. But his eyes glinted with amusement that only she could see.

Ileni's heart sank. She didn't dare look at Karyn. She forced her fingers open and heard her dagger clatter to the floor.

The assassin didn't glance down, and he didn't let go of her wrist. He was wiry and muscular, with a crop of unruly red hair, and was wearing green and black instead of the assassins' typical gray.

"Sorry," Ileni said. Her voice emerged high and scratchy. "I . . . thought you were someone else."

She didn't check to see if anyone believed her; she knew for certain that Karyn wouldn't. She kept her eyes on the assassin, to find out if she was going to die for her mistake.

A moment of silence. Two. The killer's pale blue eyes stared into hers. Then he let go of her wrist and stepped back, and she couldn't help a sigh of relief that sounded long and loud in the small room.

"I think," he said, "you know exactly who I am."

Ileni's mouth was too dry for speech, even if she had been able to think of something to say.

"Arxis?" the other boy said.

The assassin glanced at him sideways. "I traveled with a band of traders, for a while. One of our ventures into the mountains took us to Ileni's village, and she and I . . . well. Apparently, she thought it was more than it was."

"We did *not*—" Ileni began hotly, and stopped. The glint in his eyes was no longer amused. She recognized that coldness.

She could almost feel the dagger on her throat.

"I did not *think* it was more than that," she said finally. Her face burned, but she went on. "It *was* more than that. You told me it was."

"Oh, Arxis," the other boy said. "You need to rein in that silver tongue of yours."

"What I need," Arxis said, "is to stay away from gullible, romantic village girls." He swooped down, picked up her dagger, and held it out to her. "You might need this, in case you come across someone who's actually dangerous."

Ileni had to bite the inside of her mouth to keep silent. She took the dagger, wishing her hand wasn't shaking.

"Enough," Karyn snapped. Arxis glowered at Ileni convincingly. Ileni glared back. She didn't have to try to be convincing, because she meant it.

Karyn sighed. "Evin, congratulations on being in the wrong place at the wrong time. She's your responsibility now."

Ileni glanced at the second young man. His eyes were wide, his hair a mass of brown tufts fanning out around his head. He ran his fingers through his hair, leaving it exactly as disheveled as before.

"I *do* have a talent for that," he said, as calmly as if there hadn't been a dagger drawn just a minute ago. "Being in the wrong place at the wrong time, I mean. Though yesterday I was in the wrong place at the *right* time, and that didn't go much better."

Everyone ignored him. Ileni kept her eyes on Arxis, on his remorseless face and coiled body. She had seen, a dozen times over, how fast assassins could strike. Sorin had taught her some basic defense moves, but they had only worked because he had held back. If Arxis decided to kill her, she was dead.

And if he knew she had killed his master, nothing would stop him from killing her.

Finally, Arxis took another step back. Ileni's shoulders

relaxed, even though she knew he could easily kill her from all the way across the room. She forced herself to sheath her dagger.

"Interesting," Karyn said. It wasn't clear who she was talking to. "Evin, why don't you show Ileni to the testing arena. I will meet you there."

Ileni opened her mouth, then closed it. Karyn knew perfectly well that Ileni had no magic left. Ileni had grown up more powerful than any of her people, but when her power had begun to ebb, she had been sent to the assassins to serve as their tutor for the rest of her life. From future leader to useless sacrifice over the course of a few months.

If Karyn thought she had something to gain by demonstrating Ileni's powerlessness during a "test," she was making a mistake. Ileni was quite resistant to humiliation by now.

"I'm looking forward to it," she said.

"Good." Karyn seemed sincere, which puzzled Ileni.

"This way," her new guide said, and waited for her to start walking before he led her out the door and into the Imperial Academy of Sorcery.

CHAPTER 3

Having a solid wall between her and the assassin was a huge relief. Ileni tried to put Arxis out of her mind as she followed Evin through winding passageways. These corridors were narrower and prettier than the ones in the Assassins' Caves, better lit by glowstones that lined the walls in decorative, fanciful patterns. The air was filled with a faint flowery scent that struck Ileni as unpleasantly artificial, a peculiar contrast to the hulking, solid stone that surrounded them.

Magic.

And that was the key. The Empire was vast and powerful, but it depended on magic for everything from transportation to communication—and, most importantly, to win its wars, quash its rebellions, and defend itself against the relentless strikes of the assassins. Without magic, there was no way it could keep control over its vast territories. If she could take that magic away—or even cripple it—that would be the beginning of the end of the Empire.

"So," Evin said, as they trotted down a few shallow steps, "looks like things are going to get a little more interesting around here. Where did you say you were from?"

Ileni took a deep breath. Might as well get it over with. "I'm a Renegai."

Evin nodded politely. "Oh, really? From the Kerosian Grasslands?"

There were other Renegai? Did the Elders know? "No. From the Kierran Mountains."

"Oh, right! The separatists in the grasslands call themselves the Singers. My apologies." His voice was higher than she was used to hearing from men, and she realized that what she had thought was Karyn's high-pitched voice was actually the way people spoke here.

They reached a fork in the passageway, and Evin took the corridor on the left. He was tall and lanky, and walked with a loping, casual stride. It looked awkward to her, compared to the focused grace she was used to from the assassins. From Sorin.

His voice, too, was nonchalant. "What happened back there, with you and Arxis?"

He didn't sound condescending, but he did sound amused. *Gullible, romantic village girls,* Arxis had said. Ileni bristled. "It's not what he said. It was a misunderstanding."

"Do you always solve your misunderstandings with knives?"

"I find it saves time."

He looked at her sideways and grinned. "I'd better be careful what I say around you, then."

"I would advise it."

Evin's eyebrows rose. Ileni knew she sounded unfriendly, but that was all right. He was an imperial sorcerer. She had grown up hating him, even if he had grown up not knowing who her people were. "How long has he been here?"

"Arxis? Not long," Evin said.

"What does he—" she began, but then they turned a corner and, all at once, weren't underground anymore.

They never had been.

They were standing on a ledge on the side of a mountain. Below the ledge—very, very far below—a mass of tiny treetops swept downhill in a cascade of blurry green. Above, the sky unfurled, brilliantly blue. The rocks stretched up behind her, steep and craggy, with a hardy bush clinging to a crack in the cliff face above her.

"What is this?" she breathed.

"The way to the testing arena, of course." Evin was already walking along the ledge—which, Ileni realized, was actually a path that hugged the side of the mountain. His feet practically touched the edge of the ledge, but he seemed not to notice the precipitous drop. "The Academy spans a couple of mountain peaks. You can see why it's the ideal location for magic-users."

Ileni didn't see that at all. But she nodded. "Right. Of course."

Evin continued down the path, clearly expecting her to follow. Ileni wanted nothing more than to shrink back into the darkness of the cave, far from the vast space below. She couldn't make her feet move forward.

We know how to overcome fear, Sorin had told her once. She could imagine his scorn. He might have been afraid, if he was here, but he would never let fear stop him.

She set her jaw and took one step out, then another. The ledge was solid white stone, but terribly narrow. She put one hand flat on the pitted rock of the mountainside and inched forward. She kept her eyes focused straight ahead and did not—did *not*—look down.

Evin glanced back. His surprise was a prickle of heat against her skin, but she couldn't force herself to move faster. Once, she would have been as fearless as he was, but now she didn't have the safeguard of magic. One misstep and she would fall, shattered to pieces far below.

Her life was full of fears like that now, reminders of small safeties she no longer had.

By the time she caught up to Evin, her entire body was shaking, little tremors that made her legs weak and her hands unsteady. Evin waited for her at an archway that led back inside the mountain. The opening, where light shaded into darkness, was such a welcome sight that Ileni stopped caring how pathetic she looked. She lunged past Evin into the dimness, pressed her back against the rock, and took several deep breaths.

"Fear of heights?" Evin said sympathetically. His face was open and earnest, his mouth twisted slightly, but with empathy rather than mockery—another difference from the caves. "I've seen it before. It will pass."

Ileni wanted to say something nonchalant, but she

couldn't stop trembling. She closed her eyes and tried to think of something calming. It had been a long time since anything in her life could be described as *calming*, but she reached all the way back, to before Karyn had grabbed her, before she had been sent to the Assassins' Caves, before the Elders had told her she was losing her magic. She remembered sitting with Tellis in one of the Renegai practice rooms, back to back, focusing on the rhythms of a relaxation spell.

She had let her discipline go in the caves, hadn't bothered with the mental exercises designed to hone magic she no longer had. Now they came slowly and jerkily, and she forced them gracelessly through her mind. Eventually the rhythms came back to her, halting but effective, and her breath fell into the pattern. No magic accompanied the rhythm, of course, a lack that scraped sharply and painfully against her concentration. But slowly, steadily, her muscles relaxed.

She wasn't sure how long it took. When she opened her eyes, her hands were steady, and Evin was leaning on the opposite wall watching her. There was no hint of impatience in his stance, which probably meant he was very good at hiding it.

"Thank you for waiting," Ileni said. "I'm ready to continue now."

"Of course," Evin replied, his voice as neutral as hers. His brown eyes were calm and steady, shaded by long dark lashes. "It wouldn't be fair to test you when you were shaken up. The testing arena is this way."

He led her deeper into the passageway and through a doorway to the left. Keeping her newfound calm wrapped tightly around herself, Ileni followed.

When she entered the testing arena, recognition ran through her with a chill sense of inevitability. It was smaller than the training room in the Assassins' Caves, and the weapons lined up near one wall were fewer in number and far less exotic in type. But otherwise it was the same: round, cavernous, and sparse, lit by glowstones that covered the walls and the high arched ceiling. There were no stalactites here, though. The ceiling was a smooth, polished curve stretching from wall to wall.

"All right," Evin said, and she forced her feet to move. In the center of the chamber was a simple raised rock, the perfect height for sitting. Evin stopped next to it and faced her.

Whatever expression was on her face, it made his brow furrow. But all he said was, "Do you want to get in some practice before Karyn gets here? We can start with something simple, like . . . can you call up fire?"

Ileni had called fire dozens of times a day, once. Nothing would explain a sudden fit of crying, so she pushed down the stab of loss and said, "That's all right. I'll wait for Karyn."

"Are you sure? It's not as if I have anything important to do right now."

"Then go do something unimportant," she snapped.

"Well. I do have a lot of *that* to do," he said. "All right, then. Good luck."

"I won't need it." Which was untrue as well as obnoxious. *Calm down, Ileni.*

Evin looked over his shoulder. "I wasn't talking to you."

Ileni whirled. Karyn was leaning against the far wall of the cavern, watching them, the light of the glowstones turning the edges of her hair silver.

Ileni turned again, just in time to see Evin saunter out the door.

"This should be interesting," Karyn said. "Are you ready to begin?"

Are you ready to begin? *the Elder had said. His voice was kind, and that was the worst part. In Ileni's other testings—the ones where she had been expected to excel, where failure merely meant she had to push herself harder—the Elders had never been kind. They had been harsh and pitiless.*

They had not been kind until they started expecting her to fail.

Karyn stood with her feet braced far apart, fingers lightly curled. There was nothing kind in *her* face. Clearly, the sorceress was looking forward to this.

I could refuse. But then what? Ileni was here on Karyn's sufferance. And she had to stay here, to discover the truth about the Empire. She needed that truth before she could make her choice.

She had grown up believing that destroying the Empire was her life's goal, the hope of every Renegai. But too many of her childhood beliefs had been shattered in the Assassins' Caves. She needed to see for herself. And if she wanted the chance to do that, she had to go along with Karyn's cruel little game.

Ileni bit her lip. She walked to the raised rock and sat on it.

The rock, it was immediately obvious, was not intended for sitting. It was curved upward and extraordinarily uncomfortable. But Karyn was watching, so Ileni remained seated, trying to appear at ease.

Karyn's lips twitched, but all she said was, "Should we start with basic sparring?"

Ileni wondered again why Karyn hadn't killed her already. Maybe the sorceress just wanted to play with her first.

"No? Something simpler, then." Karyn raised her hand, fist closed, then slowly opened it. A glowing orb hovered in front of her palm, intensely white. Karyn flicked her fingers, and the orb shot through the air.

Ileni had just enough time to block her face. The orb splattered against her bare forearm and vanished. Burning pain tore into Ileni's skin, and she bit down on a scream.

Karyn blinked at her. "What was that?"

Before Ileni could think up an answer, Karyn sent another orb flying at her.

This one was aimed at her shoulder. Ileni managed to avoid it by twisting to the side, but at the cost of her balance. She slid off the rock, flailed, and landed hard on the ground.

Grunting, she got to her feet just in time for the next orb to hit her cheek. This time she did scream, tears stinging her eyes.

None of them had been large or hot enough to seriously injure her. The point of this was not to test Ileni. It was to humiliate her.

Adding an entry to the *Reasons to kill them all* list in her head, Ileni dodged the next orb. It flew clear across the cavern and hit the wall, where it exploded harmlessly, a shower of white sparks against the gray rock.

"Oh, come *on*," Karyn snapped. "You bedded an assassin, and you're still stuck on these stupid scruples?"

Ileni had a swift recollection of Karyn's face bulging, her feet kicking helplessly against white stone, while Sorin's hands tightened inexorably around her neck. Sorin had almost killed Karyn, back in the caves, when he had discovered that she was from the Empire.

It was really Sorin who Karyn wanted to hurt and humiliate. But Sorin wasn't here, and Ileni was.

How would Sorin handle this? Ileni couldn't imagine him ever getting into a situation where he was so helpless.

She had to throw herself to the ground to avoid the next orb. It whizzed so close over her head that her hair sizzled.

"I'll keep throwing them," Karyn warned, "until—"

"Until *what*?" Ileni shouted. But another white light spun toward her, too fast to avoid, and she gave in. She knew what Karyn wanted to see: the terrible truth, the ultimate humiliation. She wanted Ileni to try and fail.

Ileni couldn't help it. As the white ball whizzed toward

her, she called instinctively upon the powers that were lost to her, reaching inside herself for magic.

And found it.

The white orb stopped an inch from her face. Ileni was still cringing away when she realized that her block had worked. She had stopped the orb without touching it. Something so easy, something she had been sure she would never do again.

Time froze. The orb whirled impotently in the air, its brightness blinding her.

Stupid scruples, Karyn had said, and suddenly Ileni understood. It wasn't *her* magic.

Stolen magic. There must be lodestones in the walls around her, magic ripped from murdered souls, their life energies trapped in stone and collected by the Academy. Black magic. Not hers.

But it felt like hers.

Ileni swirled the orb, once, then flung it back at Karyn.

Karyn's eyes widened. She lifted her arms and soared into the air, graceful as a bird, landing lightly on the ground after the orb had passed below her. She jerked her arms together, crossing them over her chest. When she spread them apart, there were a dozen orbs hovering in front of her, so hot they shot off tiny sputtering sparks.

She smiled, a thin unpleasant smile, and the fiery balls spread apart and sped toward Ileni.

There was no way Ileni could dodge, no way she could duck—there were too many of them, taking up too much space, coming too fast. She had no choice. She drew in more power, a rush of magic that went straight through her skin.

Ileni shot upward, and the barrage of glowing balls streamed harmlessly beneath her. As they hurled toward the far wall, she twisted in midair and stopped them with a silent, magic-fueled shout.

Then, with a whisper, she extinguished the fire in the orbs, leaving a dozen clear translucent spheres frozen inches from the stone wall.

She called them to her and gathered them in her arms, sparing a sliver of magic to make sure she didn't drop any. She landed in front of Karyn, opened her arms, and let the orbs drop onto the ground.

They landed in a cacophony of thuds and immediately began rolling in random directions. Karyn flicked a finger, and they all disappeared, but she never took her eyes off Ileni.

Ileni's heart pounded so hard it almost drowned out the

tingling in her hands, where the magic had poured out, where it had responded to her command. She had worked so hard to put this grief away, to not wish for the impossible, that she still couldn't believe it. Doubt wriggled through her, as if the last few seconds might have been a dream.

She lifted her hand and whispered a quick spell. *Call up fire*, Evin had said.

The fire wreathed around her hand, flickering in and out between her fingers. She added a surge of power, and her whole arm was encased by a leaping flame that didn't hurt her and didn't touch her skin, even though its heat warmed her face.

"That's enough," Karyn snapped.

Ileni twisted her arm, murmured a word, and banished the fire. She turned in a slow circle, eyes flickering over the glowstones embedded in the wall. She chose one at random and stared at it, long enough to see the rainbow colors swirling beneath its surface. To understand that it wasn't a glowstone at all.

Hundreds of lodestones, representing hundreds of deaths, hundreds of innocents tortured and murdered. Harvested for their power. She had grown up singing songs of mourning for those victims, swearing vows of vengeance.

In the caves, she had thought she was surrounded by evil. She'd had no idea.

That evil had been nowhere near as seductive as this one.

She met Karyn's dark, speculative eyes. And realized, too late, that it wasn't only her skill that was being tested.

It was how vulnerable she was to temptation.

Karyn's smile was a white slash in her pale face. "The Academy doesn't allow just anyone to access the lodestones. It's a privilege. Remember that."

The underlying threat was clear: *I can take this away.*

Karyn watched Ileni's face carefully—predatorily. "That's all I need to see. You'll be training with the most advanced students." She turned, and Ileni couldn't tell whether she meant it or not when she added, over her shoulder, "Congratulations."

On the way back along the narrow, curving ledge, Ileni tried to feel guilty. The Empire's sorcery was evil. It was wrong to use power that wasn't your own, power that could only be given up at the moment of death. And yet she couldn't feel guilt—or anything, really—through the exaltation bubbling up in her.

And she couldn't stop smiling.

Karyn led her down a long, flower-scented passageway, where they passed a man in a brown cape who handed Karyn a sheaf of papers, two girls in green dresses giggling as they walked, and a very tall man who vanished in a flare of blue light. Finally, Karyn stopped at one of the closed doors. "This will be your room."

Ileni still didn't trust herself to speak. She nodded.

Karyn gave her a dour look that only made Ileni grin wider. The sorceress continued down the passageway, her shoes clicking on the stone. Ileni pulled the door open and stepped inside.

Where Arxis was waiting for her.

CHAPTER 4

The assassin was sitting on the bed by the wall, in the relaxed yet ready pose Ileni knew so well, his arms braced behind him and the balls of his feet resting on the floor.

Good, Ileni thought, and pulled the air around her into a barrier, tough enough to deflect knives. *Magic, magic, magic . . .* it was so easy, and she was finally as powerful as she had spent all those weeks pretending to be. Buzzing with anticipation, she said, "Well?"

Arxis bowed his head, very slightly, the faintest possible gesture of respect. When he raised it, his eyes were cold. "What are you doing here, Teacher?"

The magic sizzling through her made Ileni brazen, dying to take a crazy risk. She shrugged. "I was sent to help you."

"And that . . . demonstration . . . earlier? Was that supposed to *help*? You threatened an identity I've spent weeks building up."

Weeks. So Arxis had been here for most of the time Ileni had been in the caves. Assassins, once sent on their missions, had no contact with the caves until they succeeded. Which meant that not only did he not know she had killed the master, he didn't know about her and Sorin.

He had no reason to kill her. Attacking him had been a colossally stupid move.

"I apologize." Ileni crossed the room and sat on the bed, right next to the assassin. "That was a mistake."

"I would say so." Arxis stood, a smooth, fluid motion that reminded her of Sorin, and strode for the door.

"Wait," Ileni said. "The master didn't tell me who you were sent to kill."

He didn't stop until he was at the door, and then he only half-turned, so she couldn't make out his expression. She had seen Sorin's profile, at that exact frustrating angle, a dozen times. She hadn't realized until now that the pose was something he had been trained in.

"He wanted you to tell me," she added. "So I can help you."

"You're lying."

He said it so flatly she couldn't muster up a denial. Instead she said, "Oh, really? And how do you know that?"

"Because I don't need help." And with that, he was gone.

Assassins, Ileni thought, trying to roll her eyes and not quite managing it. She sat back down. Her hands were shaking.

Why? *She* wasn't his target; she was safe. And it wasn't her responsibility to stop him. The sorcerers were targeting the assassins. She had been in the caves when they attacked. She had almost died. The assassins had a right to strike back.

Sorin's voice, in her mind: *In war people die. You have to accept that, if you're going to fight.*

It took a few moments of steady breathing before she got back to her feet to investigate her new room. It was a small rectangular chamber, with a desk and chair along one wall and a polished wooden wardrobe along the other. With the bed, that made four whole pieces of furniture— grand in comparison to her room in the Assassins' Caves. But this time, there were no wards on her door, reinforced by generations of Renegai. And there was a window at the end of her room, near the wardrobe, which she went to, immediately. Through it she could see a dusky sky streaked blue and pink. Mountains faded into the distance, solid gray behind a veil of white sunlight. To her left, the mountains sloped into a mosaic of red and white. A city.

She backed away from the window. It reminded her of another window carved into a mountainside, of a wiry boy who had crouched on that windowsill and thrown himself into the night. This window was higher. If someone jumped from it, the thud when he landed probably wouldn't be audible.

That boy had jumped at the master's command, proud to die for his cause. The caves were full of young men just like him, waiting for the command to die. And when they did, it would be her turn to attack.

But the sorcerers had thousands of lodestones. The life force of hundreds of assassins—if she agreed to take it, and wield it—couldn't stand against that.

Unless it was a surprise attack. One blow, swift and sudden, struck at the moment of the assassins' deaths.

But aimed at what? What was she supposed to attack?

Not what. Who. She knew how assassins thought. Whatever strike Absalm and the master had planned, it would be aimed at killing as many sorcerers as possible.

But the master was dead. So it would be Absalm and Sorin's plan, now.

Thinking of Sorin physically hurt, a knife slicing at her from the inside. She had been so afraid that he would hate her, once he knew she had killed his master. But he had looked at her exactly the way he had back in the caves. As if what he felt for her mattered more than all the other things he was supposed to feel. As if being with her made him, for those brief stolen moments, less of an assassin.

But he wasn't just any assassin, not anymore. He was their leader. More than ever, he couldn't afford that weakness.

And neither could she.

She turned from the window and went to the bed. It had an ornate iron headboard and colorful bedding and was raised higher than her simple bed in the caves. But furniture or no, the room felt familiar, right up to the sense of rock closing in around her. She would have traded that window in a second for the possibility that Sorin could knock on her door. She wanted desperately to rest her head on his shoulder and cry.

Not that he would have much sympathy for her.

She hadn't thought it would feel like this, after she walked away. She had never been all that comfortable around him anyhow. It didn't make sense that missing him was a constant gnawing ache within her, a thin fog of sadness that colored everything.

And it made even less sense that seeing him today had made it worse instead of better.

How did he know where I was?

But of course he knew. He was the master now.

No. He isn't. She forced her mind steady. He wasn't some cold, all-knowing puppet master. He was the boy who had cradled her in caves beneath the earth, had kissed her fiercely and against his better judgment, had let her walk away when his duty was to stop her. He wasn't the master.

Yet.

And if she did what he wanted, maybe he never would be. Would he still be a killer if this war didn't require it?

She opened her hand. The borrowed magic surged within her, and a magelight floated above her palm. The simplest of magics, a child's trick, that had been impossible for her just this morning. She smiled even as tears burned her cheeks.

She had power, now, too—and even without power, she had outsmarted Sorin before. She would figure out how he had found her, and she would determine what exactly his plan was, and then she—*she*—would decide whether to play her designated part in it.

She kept the magelight afloat as she readied herself for bed, its light warming the insides of her eyelids until the moment she fell asleep.

The next morning, Ileni woke with the dawn, so tense and excited and terrified she didn't even consider going back to sleep. Magic waited for her, and she itched to use it. She sat up, rubbed her crusty eyes, and resisted the urge to vault out of bed. It had been so long since she had been eager to start her day that she didn't trust the feeling.

And she shouldn't. *This is the Empire. I am surrounded by my enemies, and I am a weapon.*

She reached out for the lodestones . . . so close, and brimming with power. Her skin tingled, and she realized that she had drawn some of the magic in without thinking.

It was like being herself again, after she had been someone else—a stranger—for months.

But who was really the stranger? The girl with no power? Or the girl who would use power she knew was evil, just so she could pretend magic was still a part of her?

She squeezed her eyes shut, trying to think past the

shame and the joy twined tightly within her. If she was going to pretend she was a student here, she had to use the magic.

But she couldn't let herself forget that it was evil.

She pushed the blanket off her legs and got to her feet. The wardrobe contained a selection of clothes, none of which fit exactly right. She chose a large plain dress with a belt she could pull tight. There was no mirror in the room—because there didn't have to be: a flicker of magic turned a section of the stone wall reflective, and Ileni gave herself a cursory glance. The dress was far from elegant, but it would do.

She had forgotten how much *easier* magic made everything. The belt tied in back—no problem. The tangles in her hair unknotted at her command. Dirt disappeared from her skin, and the tinges of blood that had been clinging to her for days took only a moment to banish. How had she ever lived without this?

How will I live without it again?

She was in the middle of a spell to make her dress blue when someone knocked. She hesitated, then let the spell go and opened the door.

Evin's eyes swept up and down her dress. "You didn't have to stop on my account. What color were you going for?"

She was startled enough to answer. "Blue."

"Dark or light?"

"Uh—"

"Never mind." He murmured a spell. A surge of power tingled over her, and her dress was midnight blue, close to black. "Dark looks better when you're threatening people with knives, I think."

Ileni gaped at him.

"What?" He held up both hands, his sleeves falling to his elbows. "I can change it back, if you don't like the color, or—"

"*I* can change it back," Ileni snapped.

"Okay." He hesitated. "I'm sorry. Breakfast?"

Ileni blinked hard and forced herself to step back. "I'm sorry. I . . ." She had no idea how to finish that sentence.

It had taken him a *second* to do that spell. She had been working on it for several minutes before he showed up and interrupted her. She had never met anyone that powerful. Even she, back when she had been the most advanced Renegai in her village, couldn't have worked such a complex spell so fast.

"It's all right." Evin gave her a confident, devastatingly beautiful smile. The smile didn't transform his face so much as accentuate it, making her pay attention to his appearance for the first time.

His smile widened indulgently, making it clear what he assumed her silence meant. Before she could think of a way to disillusion him, he started down the hall.

Well, that was for the best. Let him think she was struck dumb by his handsomeness. What better explanation did she have to offer?

I used to be very powerful. And now all I can do is steal magic from stones and be close to people who are very powerful.

Well, actually. Another thing I can do is kill you all.

That made her feel slightly better.

Even with magic to keep her safe, the walk along the ledge made Ileni's stomach turn over. The path curved around the mountainside and became a narrow staircase cut into the rock, descending to yet another path below. The sky was bisected by a second mountain spire, bare gray rock with a flat top, as if it had been sliced by a giant knife. Between the path they stood on and that other spire hung a narrow, graceful bridge, swaying slightly in the wind.

Ileni tried not to gulp with relief when, instead of the staircase or the bridge, Evin slid into a crevice in the rock face, bringing them back inside the mountain. Her muscles unclenched as she strode into the dimness and quiet, the solidity of rock closing snugly around her.

She had only the space of a short passageway to feel safe. Then the scent of cooked eggs hit her, a moment before Evin called ahead, "Prepare your polite faces. Or in Lis's case, your *politest* face. We have a newcomer."

You'll be training with the most advanced students, Karyn had said. Ileni set her jaw and followed Evin into a chamber filled with mouthwatering smells.

She had been expecting a large dining chamber, but it was a small room, with a single wooden table in its center. The only other people at the table were two girls with sleek black hair and identical faces. Their features—and their hair—reminded her of Irun; these girls were from the imperial nobility. Unlike Irun, however, they both had startling blue eyes.

"Lis and Cyn," Evin said, gesturing toward them in turn. Their only distinguishing feature was the cut of their hair. Lis's was long enough to brush her hips, while Cyn's sliced across her cheek as she nodded. Neither smiled.

"Ileni," Evin declared, watching the twins expectantly, "is a new student. She'll be training with us."

Ileni braced herself for their reactions. But Cyn merely rubbed a napkin across her lips, and Lis flicked a black strand of hair over her shoulder and said, "You're late. Again."

"We were about to leave without you," Cyn added.

Evin glanced at Ileni. "We'll catch up. As long as you've left us some food—"

"I don't need to eat," Ileni said. Despite her hunger, she wasn't even sure she could force anything down. Her stomach was tight with anticipation, and it was hard to stand still. In just a few minutes, she would be using magic again.

Cyn swung her legs over the bench and sprang to her feet. "Excellent," she said, speaking directly to Ileni for the first time. "Let's go."

"*I* need to eat," Evin protested. "I'm disappointingly commonplace that way."

"In that case," Cyn said, "may I suggest you wake up earlier?"

"You may," Evin replied graciously. "You may suggest it every morning, if it makes you feel better."

Cyn sighed. Evin sighed back, an exact echo. "I suppose I can skip breakfast for one day. But don't expect me to be up to my usual dazzling standards."

Cyn's lips parted. "I never—"

But he was already heading back out of the room.

This time, their path took them down to the bridge. The staircase barely deserved the name, with steep, slippery steps, but the two black-haired girls raced down as if there were yards of solid ground between them and the precipice. Evin, who was right in front of Ileni, maintained a relatively sane pace, so she didn't have to try and keep up—or be humiliated by the fact that she was afraid to.

At the bottom of the stairs, where the path veered around the rocky mountainside, Cyn looked back and rolled her eyes. Ileni flushed and tried to move faster.

When she and Evin rounded the turn—the path sloping toward the abyss so steeply Ileni had to squeeze her eyes shut—they found Lis and Cyn waiting for them. Lis was leaning against the mountainside, and Cyn was standing next to the bridge, one elbow propped on its rail. Neither position looked particularly comfortable.

Evin eyed them warily. "Sorry to keep you waiting."

"Again," Lis pointed out.

After a moment, Ileni realized that no one was moving. Lis and Cyn were standing back, allowing enough space for her to pass. Cyn put a hand on her hip, cocking her head at Ileni.

All right, then.

Ileni walked past them, tensing as she got closer to the bridge. It was made of broad wooden slats, with enough space between them for her to see the horrifying distance below. She didn't quite have enough willpower to not look down.

At least there were rails, even if they were little more than thick ropes strung alongside the wooden slats. Ileni gripped them with both hands, which turned out to be a mistake. It made the entire bridge sway beneath her feet.

She stepped onto the next slat, not allowing herself to hesitate, glad the imperial sorcerers couldn't see her face. If she just kept moving, they wouldn't know how terrified she was. The bridge stretched ahead of her, terribly long.

She thought of Sorin, of his unflinching black eyes, of the courage she had seen in the depths of the caves. She could do this. She knew courage. She had spent over a month expecting to die every day.

But not expecting to *fall*.

A gust of wind made the bridge swing wildly. She sucked in a breath and took another step.

And then she heard the snickers from above.

Above?

She looked up. All three of her fellow students were hovering in the air, arms spread to the sides. The girls' white dresses fluttered around them.

Lis swooped, grabbed the bridge rail, and gave it a shake. Ileni gripped the ropes tightly and used a nudge of magic to keep her feet on the slats.

"The bridges," Cyn said, "are for students who aren't advanced enough to fly."

"Leave it, Cyn," Evin said. "It's her first day."

Cyn rolled her eyes. "So she needs a strong protector, then, does she?"

Evin preened. "Are you calling me strong?"

"Actually," Ileni said, in her sweetest voice, "I can take care of myself."

Back in the Renegai village, she had flown only a few times. It was difficult magic, draining and tiring, and her people saw it as wasteful. But those few times, it had been easy for her.

Everything had been easy for her.

She lifted into the air without changing position, magic surging through her like a draught of ice-cold water on a hot day. The wind struck at her body, and she used a tendril of magic to hold herself steady, arms close to her sides. She didn't need to spread them—they weren't wings, and she wasn't a bird.

She tilted sideways. A prickle of unease sizzled through

her exhilaration. *This is wrong. It shouldn't feel so good.* She ignored it. She had to pretend she was one of them. That it didn't bother her at all.

She met Cyn's stare head-on.

Cyn and Lis turned in sync and swooped away, arcing under and over the bridge as they made their way toward the plateau.

"It's a show for your benefit," Evin said. He was perched in the air as if on a tree branch, his legs dangling. His voice was sympathetic, but his eyes were laughing. "They actually hate each other. You'll see."

Ileni grinned at him. The vast distance below her was suddenly thrilling rather than terrifying, and she couldn't have cared less about the other girls' posturing. With a swell of magic, she sliced through the air. The distant treetops rushed beneath her, and she pushed harder, white fluttering past the corners of her eyes as she passed the twins.

Then the magic vanished, and she fell.

CHAPTER
5

The bridge and the mountainside rushed past her. The wind seared her face, and her body flailed, graceless and helpless. She screamed, but the wind ripped it away.

The treetops and the ground rushed at her.

And stopped.

Ileni hung suspended in midair, upside down, sobbing. All around her stretched empty air, and she could make out individual treetops far below. She reached for magic to right herself, to keep herself safe, but knew what she would find.

Nothing.

Her power was gone, again. But this time it had happened abruptly and without warning. No slow draining of strength, just there one second and then gone.

Because it wasn't her magic at all. She had borrowed it— no, stolen it. And so of course, it had betrayed her.

A swoop of green to her right, of white to her left, and her fellow students were all around her. Cyn took her wrist and, with a push of magic, righted her.

There was no mockery on Cyn's face. Only sympathy. Which was worse.

"Are you insane?" There was nothing sympathetic in Lis's voice. Her hair blew wildly across her face and around her shoulders. "You didn't say you were powerless. You can't fly without a lodestone! If Evin hadn't moved so fast, you would be dead right now."

"All right, Lis," Cyn snapped. "I think she noticed that."

Lis surged forward so that her face was only inches from Ileni's. "There are only two collections of lodestones students can access. In the testing arena and on the training plateau. If you're very skilled, you might be able to access the testing stones from your bedroom, and you might be able to store enough to keep you going for a while. But you can't *depend* on it. Don't you know anything?"

"Right now," Evin observed, "she knows exactly what your breath smells like. Back *off*, Lis."

Lis snarled at him, but when Evin swooped closer, she floated backward.

Ileni swallowed hard, closed her eyes, and concentrated on not crying. The bickering washed around her, meaningless noise.

Even worse than her almost-plunge—at least, now that it was over—was the emptiness within her, the gaping ache the magic had left. In the caves she had become accustomed to that emptiness, slowly—still always aware of what she was missing, but able to bear it. Now the wound had been gashed open again. Once, she had wanted to die rather than live without magic.

If not for the empty chasm beneath her, the still-fading terror, she might have thought she still wanted to die.

A hand closed around her wrist. She opened her eyes. Evin hovered in front of her, his broad forehead creased. Behind him, the gray mountainside stretched upward, patches of weeds growing from cracks in the rock.

"Are you all right?" he asked.

It was such a stupid question she didn't bother to answer. After a moment, Evin let go and flew upward, his magic pulling her along like useless cargo.

● ● ●

Karyn was waiting for them on the plateau at the other end of the bridge, wearing a flowing white gown, her mouth pressed into a grim line. Her voice snapped across the windy surface of the plateau. "Where have you been?"

The plateau was large and irregularly shaped, about fifteen paces across, with spiky mountains forming a jagged gray line against the sky behind it. Its surface was unnaturally smooth and gleamed in the sunlight. As soon as Ileni's feet touched the ground, she reached for the power, and it rushed back into her. Lodestones were embedded in the plateau's stone floor, in regular intervals around its edges. This time she recognized them instantly.

"Sorry," Lis said. "Lost track of time."

"By which she means," Evin said, "that she and Cyn had a little impromptu flying contest."

Karyn didn't say anything. She didn't have to.

"I tried to stop them," Evin added virtuously.

Cyn rolled her eyes. "Not very hard."

Karyn tapped her foot on the ground, an angry staccato. "This isn't a game. Cyn, I expect better from you."

Cyn flushed—though Lis, Ileni noticed, flushed darker.

"All right." Karyn's voice was cold and clipped. "Let's get

back to the exercises we were practicing last class. Ileni, you can observe, until you become familiar with—"

"No," Ileni said. "I'm ready to start."

Her fellow students all gave her startled looks. Karyn shrugged. "As you wish. Did you learn the invisible knife technique, back where you're from?"

"No," Ileni said. The power was rushing through her and the ground was solid beneath her, and she wanted to wipe that supercilious expression from Karyn's face almost as much as she wanted to wipe the sense of hopelessness from her own chest. "But don't hold back for my sake. I'm sure I'll catch on."

"Are you? Very well. Then we'll move on to sparring."

More startled glances, this time directed at Karyn. Ignoring them, the dark-haired sorceress gestured at the twins. "Cyn and Lis, why don't you begin?"

"Oh, good," Evin murmured. "That's always entertaining."

Cyn swaggered to the center of the plateau. Lis stalked to a spot five yards from her sister, her hair hanging heavily down her back. The two faced each other.

"Forearms," Karyn said, and each girl held up one arm. Their flowing white sleeves fell around their elbows, leaving their forearms bare but for a thick metallic bracelet around Lis's wrist.

Karyn clapped her hands.

Immediately, both girls' lips began moving rapidly. A savage force ripped through the air between them, magic that made Ileni flinch even from yards away.

Cyn gasped in pain. Lis whimpered. Long lines of blood gushed from each of their right arms.

"Typical," Evin said into Ileni's ear. "They haven't spared any spells for defense."

Ileni twisted to stare at him. She couldn't keep the horror off her face, even though she vaguely sensed that it was counteracting whatever credit she had gained with her earlier brashness.

Attack spells. Abhorrent, vicious, and completely forbidden by her people. Not that Renegai novices didn't play with the idea, especially when they were young. Ileni herself had once devised a spell to hang a rival upside down in midair. The other girl had retaliated by slamming Ileni to the floor and rolling her over and over. The Elders had been aghast at such a display of violence.

But they couldn't have been this brutal, even if they had wanted to. They hadn't been taught spells designed solely to cause pain to other people.

A grunt pulled Ileni's attention back to the twins. Their

arms were covered in blood, so much blood Ileni couldn't see where the new cuts were forming. She could tell they *were* forming by the pain that spasmed across the combatants' faces.

And even through her revulsion, she couldn't help admiring the grace and cleanness of their spells, the taut focus of the magic, barely a spark of energy wasted.

Finally, Lis cried out, and Karyn clapped her hands again.

"Enough," she said. "You both made the same mistake. Can you tell me what it was?"

Cyn and Lis kept their eyes locked on each other. Blood dripped from their arms. And everyone else just stood there, watching them as if nothing was wrong.

"Well?" Karyn snapped. "It's not exactly the first time you've made this mistake. What was it?"

"I'd say it was pitting them against each other in the first place," Evin observed.

Karyn looked at him. "You have something to say?"

Her expression could have shriveled grass, but Evin just lifted one shoulder. "Nothing that would do any good, I'm sure."

"Then please don't bother." Karyn looked again at the twins. "Well?"

Lis and Cyn glared at each other stubbornly. The silence was broken only by the sound of blood hitting the stone in a series of uneven splats, until Ileni couldn't take it anymore. She pulled up the power that wasn't hers, curled her fingers into a well-practiced pattern, and muttered a few words.

Lis gasped, but this time it wasn't in pain. She lowered her bloodstained arm and blinked at it. Cyn snapped her head around.

Ileni couldn't help smiling. Not at their shock—she hadn't been at all sure how they would react—but at the ease with which she had wielded those long-ignored skills. It was like stretching a muscle that had been cramped for months.

Even though she knew how wrong and treacherous that magic was. Even though it had almost killed her less than an hour ago.

Karyn stepped toward her. "What did you do?"

"Healed their cuts," Ileni said. "I'm sorry if bleeding to death was supposed to be part of the lesson."

"We weren't in danger of bleeding to death," Lis snapped.

"You're welcome," Ileni said sweetly.

Karyn stalked forward. She passed a hand over Cyn's arm, and a surge of power made the bloodstains vanish. Karyn grabbed Cyn's wrist, yanked it upward, and stared at her smooth, unblemished skin as if she had never seen an arm before.

A chuckle next to her made Ileni glance sideways. Evin was grinning openly. "You *are* full of surprises, aren't you?"

"I'm glad they provide you with so much amusement," Ileni said tightly.

Evin cocked his head to the side. "So am I."

Karyn dropped Cyn's arm and strode over to Ileni. "How did you do that?"

"Um," Ileni said. "There's this thing called magic—"

"Do it again."

"How—"

Twin surges of power from Karyn, and blood welled again from both twins' arms.

"Hey," Cyn snapped, but a glance from Karyn silenced her.

Ileni choked. "What is *wrong* with you?"

"Heal them," Karyn said. "I want to pay closer attention to the spell this time."

The healing spell to knit skin was a relatively simple one; the Renegai used it for everything from paper cuts to difficult childbirths. But it had taken Ileni a year to learn the basics of magical healing, before she had been allowed to start attempting spells. Karyn was an experienced sorceress, but even she wouldn't grasp it from one demonstration. How many times would the twins let their skins be ripped open so Ileni could heal them?

She didn't really wonder. Once she had seen a boy leap from a window to his death, at the command of his master and in service to a greater cause. Why shouldn't the imperial sorcerers have the same dedication, the same blind obedience?

"No," Ileni said.

Karyn's face went very still. "You are not a guest here."

"I thought I was a student," Ileni said. "Not a teacher."

"I didn't realize—"

"That I had anything worth teaching?"

Silence. The loudest sound was the twins' harsh breathing. Karyn's fingers twitched.

"I'll teach you," Ileni said. "But not like this. Step by step, the way I learned."

She felt power coil around Karyn, and knew Karyn could sense the power rising within her. She had no doubt that if it came to a fight, Karyn would win. Ileni didn't know the first thing about combat magic.

The plateau was dead silent. Over Karyn's shoulder, Lis's face was chalk white, her jaw clenched. Cyn leaned back, eyes flickering speculatively between Karyn and Ileni.

"All right," Karyn said finally, and the power within her drained slowly away. "In the mornings, then, before breakfast. Just you and me, to start."

Ileni blinked, so startled she held onto the power for a moment longer—a moment that made Evin draw in his breath audibly—before letting it go.

"Is that acceptable?" Karyn asked acidly.

It was, but it didn't make sense. Karyn had all the control here. She could banish Ileni from the Academy, or order her killed, with a word. Why was she agreeing so easily?

She must really want to learn healing magic.

Or she must really want Ileni at the Academy.

Karyn gestured at Evin without waiting for Ileni's answer, and he walked to the center of the plateau, brow furrowed. Lis, for some reason, smirked as she strolled over to stand next to Ileni.

It was only when Evin and Cyn were halfway through their next sparring match that Ileni wondered: How would her people feel about her teaching Renegai magic to imperial sorcerers?

Well, if her people found out any number of the things she had done since leaving her village to serve as tutor to the assassins, they would exile her forever and speak her name in horrified whispers. Besides, if she decided to be the weapon she had been designed to be—if, in the end, she fulfilled Absalm's plan and became the Renegai who toppled the Empire—it wouldn't matter. Anything else would be not just forgiven, but forgotten.

Evin and Cyn took longer to get through their combat, because each was defending as well as attacking. Evin leaned back slightly, eyes half-lidded, while Cyn stood straight as a rod, face grim, her arm a patchwork of drying blood. After ten minutes, neither had harmed the other, though Ileni could feel the thrusts and parries of power between them, the feints and blocks. This, presumably, was how the exercise was supposed to go.

Lis stood to the side, pressing a cloth against the cut on her arm. Ileni hesitated, then whispered to her, "I can heal—"

"You can get away from me," Lis snapped.

Ileni blinked. Lis lifted her hand and made a gesture that Ileni had never seen before, but that didn't need interpretation.

It would be my pleasure. Too late to say it, though. Apparently, Ileni had gotten so used to being on the receiving end of implacable hatred that she had forgotten how to deal with petty spite.

That probably should have made Lis's scorn sting less.

Cyn grunted, and Ileni returned her attention to the fight. A red line ran up Cyn's arm—barely more than a scratch, a trickle of blood forming a thin dash against the back of her wrist.

"Very good," Karyn said, "Did any of you see how he did that?"

"By being ten times more powerful than Cyn?" Lis suggested.

Cyn narrowed her eyes at her sister. Then she glanced at Karyn and shrugged. "That would be my guess, too."

"But he held back for most of the fight, then brought the double-point spell to bear on a weak spot in Cyn's defense." Karyn put her hands on her hips. "It's not how much power you have. It's how you use it. Remember that."

"Pay attention, Lis," Cyn said. "She's talking to you."

Lis gave her sister a look that, had it been a spell, would have scorched a hole through her chest.

"Next," Karyn said, "Ileni can spar with me."

Danger prickled up Ileni's spine, but the magic surging through her wiped it out. She was fairly sure she could show these sorcerers a trick or two. Rehearsing a spell in her mind, she stepped forward.

"That's all right," Evin said. "It's my turn, according to the rules. I'll spar with you."

Karyn shook her head. "That was a long match. You must be tired."

"And I'll never be tired in battle?" Evin shrugged. "Besides, I hear it's not how much power I have. It's how I use it."

"Let's see if that's true." Lips pressed together, Karyn gestured at Cyn. She stepped away, and Karyn took her spot.

The combat between Evin and Karyn was longer and more complicated than anything that had come before. Nothing visible happened, but Ileni felt spells and counterspells weaving through the air between the combatants. Both muttered fast and furiously, their hands forming intricate patterns in the air. Cyn and Lis stood several yards from Ileni, watching.

The match finally ended with a victory Ileni didn't catch, though she heard Evin's grunt and Karyn's triumphant exhale. The two stepped back from each other and inclined their heads. A strand of Karyn's hair was plastered against her cheek, dark with sweat.

"That's enough for today," Karyn said. "Practice mental pathways in your rooms. Lis, you need to work on your defenses. Cyn, I will show you what you did wrong at the beginning of your match. Evin, I will stop by to make sure you're doing what you're supposed to and to administer punishment when I find out that you're not."

Her gaze moved to Ileni, who stiffened. But Karyn just nodded and vanished.

"Well, well." Evin let out a low whistle. "Congratulations, Ileni. It's not every day we get to see Karyn surprised."

"What is she?" Ileni blurted.

Three surprised pairs of eyes turned on her. Ileni flushed. "I mean—is she the master of the Academy?"

"The emperor is the master of the Academy," Lis said, as if to a child. "Karyn is the head teacher."

"Which is, practically, the same thing," Evin added. "Since the emperor is rather far away and has other things on his mind."

Ileni had always been told that at the time of the Renegai exile, the emperor was merely a figurehead, and the Empire was truly controlled by the Academy. Judging by Cyn's dismissive snort, that was still true four hundred years later.

"But how can Karyn be head teacher," Ileni said,

"when she doesn't even have power of her own?"

Lis's voice was like acid. "We all try to pretend that doesn't matter."

"We have lodestones to spare." Evin's voice was wary, which Ileni could already tell was unusual for him. "It's skill that matters, not power."

"Easy for you to say," Lis said, but suddenly she didn't sound spiteful. She sounded weary. "The head teacher of the Academy never has her own power. This way, she serves at the emperor's sufferance. He gave her the magic, and he can take it away."

A breeze blew across the plateau, cooling Ileni's flushed face and rustling her hair. Cyn lifted her face to it. "In theory," she murmured. "The current emperor would never dare."

"There aren't many people who have enough power to be worth training," Lis added, crossing her arms over her chest. "People with small amounts of power can't do much with it, anyhow. But those of us without any power at all can draw it from a lodestone, as much as we're capable of holding and using."

"Which," Cyn said smugly, "is more for some people than for others."

"But . . ." Ileni couldn't find words for her horror. "Don't you . . . don't you mind?"

Evin's eyes darted to her swiftly, and away, and Ileni wished fervently that she had thought before she spoke. The last thing she wanted was to give away just how much *she* minded. She was done with being pitied.

Cyn laughed. "I can't answer that for you, and neither can Evin. But Lis . . ."

Lis made a rude gesture at her sister.

Cyn blew her a kiss, then turned her attention back to Ileni. "Right now, the only advanced sorcerers with their own power are me and Evin. Is it more common among your people?"

"Is it . . ." Ileni was still struggling to catch up. "Yes. Yes, it is."

Lis snorted. "I guess that's what happens when most of the sorcerers in the Empire go off to the mountains and spend a few hundred years inbreeding."

"There used to be more of us," Cyn said. "But not many. I'm told there are a couple of fourth-levels, and even more second-levels, who might have enough power to be worth training. But most of our sorcerers rely on lodestones. It's more efficient that way, really."

She sounded absolutely sincere, but her words passed through Ileni's mind like a swift breeze, too foreign to leave an impression.

"You obviously don't have your own magic anymore." Cyn said it casually, but Ileni flinched. "It really doesn't matter. You'll see." She flicked a strand of hair away from her face. "But it does mean you had better stay on Karyn's good side—which means doing as you're told. Let's go."

She walked off the end of the plateau and lifted gracefully into the air. Lis watched her sister fly away, then held a hand out to Ileni. Her expression was indecipherable. "You can fly with me."

"How will that—"

Lis turned her arm over. Her forearm was covered with a faint tracing of scars that Ileni hadn't noticed before. Set into the underside of her thick bracelet was a small round globe with colors swirling in its depths.

"Lodestones to spare, remember? I've got my own portable source of magic." Her tone was slightly bitter. "This stone is almost drained, which is why you can't feel it. But get close enough and you should be able to borrow some."

Ileni *could* feel the magic coming from the stone, but only faintly; Lis was soaking it up through her skin, leaving nothing Ileni could have grasped. Even if she wanted to. She bit her lip. "Did you lose your own magic?"

Lis's laugh was more than just slightly bitter. "Cyn and

I are twins, but we aren't very alike. I never had any."

Like Karyn. People who would never have tasted magic on their own, being trained to use power stolen from others.

Ileni pulled her arm back to her side. "Thank you. But I think I'll use the bridge."

Lis pivoted and flung herself upward, a swirl of white cloth and black hair.

"Go," Ileni snapped at Evin. She wanted desperately to be alone. "You don't have to wait for me."

"That's good to know," Evin said, "since I wasn't planning to."

Within seconds, he had caught up to the two girls, looping and curling elaborately through the air. Tears stung the backs of Ileni's eyes, and she turned away, not wanting to admire the grace and joy of his body in flight.

It was just as well that she had fallen. How close she had come to forgetting that this magic wasn't hers. That just because something felt good didn't mean it *was* good.

That she wasn't whole, and never would be again.

The bridge swayed unsteadily as she walked, death yawning below her on both sides. Fragments of mist swirled far beneath her feet, drifting across the distant treetops. Far ahead, she saw two white figures touch down on the mountainside and a third swoop effortlessly around the bridge.

Ileni set her jaw and walked, placing her feet slowly and carefully on the slats and keeping her hands tight around the rails.

When she got to her room, there was something new there. A mirror, large and oval, standing in the corner on an ornate silver base.

Ileni recognized that mirror.

She walked over and touched it, tentatively, as if Sorin was still watching from the smooth glass. But she saw only her own face, wide brown eyes and trembling chin, and the fingertips she touched were her own.

Sorin.

The remnants of the spell he had used to reach her shimmered in the glass. The portal was still there. Given enough power, she could open it again.

And she had all the power she could ever want.

But someone had brought the mirror here. Who, and why? Did someone want her to reopen the portal, to talk to Sorin?

She *could.* It would take just a few minutes, and she would be talking to him, watching his rare, subtle smile warm his face. Reminding her that somewhere, far away from this world of stolen power and lodestones, she was loved. If she opened the portal far enough, she could step right through and touch him. . . .

Her fingers pressed hard on the glass. She curled them into a fist and made her way to the bed. She had nothing to say to the new master of the assassins.

Not yet.

CHAPTER
6

That night, Ileni couldn't sleep. A cold ache spread through her chest, painful and deeply familiar. Even though, a mere half year ago, she'd had no idea that loneliness could actually hurt.

She reached for thoughts of Sorin, but that only made the empty feeling deepen. Even with him, she had felt alone. He had always been half her enemy. But he had eased the loneliness anyhow, if only by distracting her from it.

Odd that the excitement of having magic couldn't do the same.

A sob pushed its way up her throat, and she forced it

down. She sat up abruptly, making the glowstones flicker.

She reached for magic. The power was easy to grasp, to pull in and around herself. The magic swirled through her, making her feel both safe and tainted.

And bringing home the true import of what she had learned that day.

She had told Sorin she was leaving to find out if the imperial sorcerers were evil—and she had hoped, deep down, that they were. That her choice would be clear and simple and totally right.

That she and Sorin would be on the same side.

But back in the caves, she hadn't known that most of the sorcerers weren't true sorcerers at all. That their power came almost entirely from lodestones.

All her life, she had thought the Empire was invincible, a destructive force. And maybe it was. But it was also a tottering edifice, propped up by the lodestones. If she destroyed the lodestones, she could tip over that edifice.

Killing was one thing. She wouldn't—couldn't—do that, not unless she was absolutely sure she had to. But maybe she could bring down the Empire without killing a single person.

She could almost see Sorin's sneer, but she pushed it to

the back of her mind as she got dressed and stepped out into the hall.

A quick spell, a nudge of power, and she could see in the dark. Everything looked hazy and red, as was usual with this spell, but it was more than enough to make her way through the corridors unobserved. She crept through the dark curved passageways, using more power to keep the glowstones from flickering on. Finding her way was no problem. The power from the testing arena was a roaring fire, pulling her toward its warmth and brightness.

The testing arena was empty. Ileni paced slowly around its edges, touching her fingers to the lodestones embedded in the walls. There were hundreds.

Power stolen, power misused, power drawn from pain and death. How many times had she chanted that Renegai children's song? She found herself humming the familiar tune as she paced, as that same power surrounded her and filled her.

She put her hand on one lodestone and tried a spell—a small, simple one, that would have cracked an ordinary piece of glass. She didn't really expect it to work, but it would give her a sense of what she was up against.

The lodestone grabbed the spell and sucked it in, so fiercely Ileni cried out. Her scream echoed in the large cavern.

A sharp pain pierced the center of her chest, as if the spell had gouged out some of her flesh.

She waited, teeth clenched, as the echoes of her scream died. After several moments passed and no one came, she forced herself closer to the stone. Time for a more complex attack. She called up a piece of chalk, drew a swift pattern around her feet, and began a chant. It wasn't one of the silent spells—her words rang musically in the stillness of the cave, echoing back and forth—which meant that if someone did come, she wouldn't be able to hide what she was doing. But it was the most powerful spell she knew for dissolving magical wards and protections. She chanted as fast as she dared, the magic twisting and bending, forming an intricate pattern. Despite the danger, she lost herself in its creation, and regret twinged through her when it was done.

The spell strained within her, beautiful and dangerous. She glanced back at the wooden door—not that it mattered, now, if anyone came—and let it go.

She was prepared, this time, for the lodestone's reaction. She gasped, but didn't scream, when the magic was ripped out of her. She bit her lip hard, tears filling her eyes, and doubled over. But she didn't make a sound, and finally the pain faded.

She had planned to try a third time, but she didn't need to. No matter how much power she threw at them, the lodestones would do exactly what they were made for: pull it in. They were indestructible.

If it had been a ward, or a defense, she could have tried to figure something out. But the Renegai didn't believe in changing the intrinsic nature of things. Nothing she had ever learned could be used to destroy these stones.

Well. So much for that.

"Satisfied?" Karyn inquired archly.

Ileni jumped, but managed not to scream again.

"There are quite a lot of them, aren't there?" Karyn said. The sorceress was leaning against the wall across the cavern.

"Yes," Ileni said. She tried to say it neutrally, but some of her revulsion must have shown, because Karyn stiffened.

"We need every one," the sorceress said. "Without magic, the Empire would disintegrate into a hundred warring nations—the way it was centuries ago. Far more people would die than the number of lodestones in this cavern. And they would die in far more terrible ways."

"But you wouldn't be the one killing them," Ileni said.

"That might make *me* feel better. I suspect, however, it wouldn't help the dead." Karyn straightened. "But let's not pretend you're here to engage in moral debates. If you want a lodestone of your own, I'm the only one who can give that to you."

Ileni concentrated on slowing her breathing. This wasn't as bad as she had feared. If Karyn didn't realize that Ileni was trying to destroy the lodestones—if she thought Ileni just wanted power of her own—she would let Ileni stay.

Ileni rubbed out the chalk pattern with her foot—no point in leaving clues to enlighten the sorceress—then braced her legs apart.

"What do I have to do," she said, "to get one?"

Karyn shook her head, slowly and smugly.

Ileni strove to keep her voice steady. "I told you I'd give you information."

"And that will be a pleasant conversation, I'm sure. But you could be so much more useful if you were working *with* us."

I never will. She managed not to say it, but she couldn't stop her chin from going up. "What do you want me to do?"

"Not yet," Karyn said. "I'll tell you when the time is right."

"When I've been away from the assassins longer," Ileni said, "and am more willing to betray them?"

Karyn's smirk turned into a grin. "Exactly." And at Ileni's suspicious glare, it became a laugh. "I see no reason to lie to you. You must realize I'm not letting you stay here for whatever tidbits of information you learned from your assassin lover. You can be far more valuable than that, once you're willing."

It was stupid to argue—she *wanted* Karyn to let her stay—but Ileni dug her fingernails into her palms. "And you assume I'll be willing because you'll give me power?"

"Yes," Karyn said. "That tends to be effective."

"In the Empire, maybe."

"Oh, right," Karyn said. "I forgot. The assassins murder out of pure idealism. They're not after *power*."

The savagery in her voice shocked Ileni into silence. Karyn kept her smile, but it seemed more like a thin veil for a snarl.

"Oh, yes," she said. "I hate them. Every bit as much as your people hate us. And I'll do whatever is necessary to put an end to them."

Ileni bit her lip. It was like talking to Sorin. . . . or to the master. Was everyone in the world full of passion and certainty except for her?

Once, she had hated the Empire—and everyone in it—

just as much. Things had been a lot simpler then.

"I spent years infiltrating the caves." Karyn rubbed her thumb over her wrist, where her lodestone bracelet would have been. "I gave up more than you can imagine to do it—people in my position don't normally go out on spying expeditions. But Arum and I were the only ones willing. Now, thanks to you, Arum is dead, and the assassins are aware that there's a back way into the caves. I'm sure they're guarding it now, so I'm right back where I started. Unless you can help me."

Arum. The blond man, Karyn's companion, who had died in a spray of red blood on white stone. Ileni found her voice. "I didn't kill him."

"No. You led your assassin friend to him instead. Do you think that makes you innocent?"

"I didn't—I mean, I didn't know—"

"That things would get messy, once you started exposing secrets to killers?" Karyn's laugh, too, sounded like a thinly disguised snarl. "Are all Renegai as deliberately simpleminded as you?"

Rage came to Ileni's aid, wiping away her uncertainty. "If by *simpleminded* you mean *pure*, then yes. We don't need elaborate explanations of whose fault murder is or when it's justified."

Karyn's face went blank, just for a moment. Then her lashes swooped down to shield her eyes. "Well," she said, "I envy you that."

She sounded sincere, which was not what Ileni had expected. Sorin would have responded with scorn.

When Karyn's lashes swept up, though, her expression was speculative. "You should be getting back to bed. I have something to take care of tomorrow, so I won't see you, but you'll still get to play with magic all day. Have fun."

Ileni tried not to react, though she wasn't entirely sure what she was concealing. Guilt? Joy? Anticipation?

Whatever it was, she knew by Karyn's pleased expression that she had not succeeded in hiding it.

CHAPTER
7

In the large, echoing training cavern, dozens of assassins whirled and lunged at each other, wielding swords and garrotes and metal discs. But Irun, as he advanced on Ileni, bore only a knife. It was already dripping with her blood.

Kill him, *Sorin whispered. He stood behind Ileni, hands firm on her waist, lips pressed to the nape of her neck. Ileni leaned back into him, resting against his chest.* Kill him, *and prove that you are one of us.*

Ileni woke with a start. Confusion swirled as she blinked at walls that were not slick black rock but pink-speckled gray stone.

"Sorry," Cyn said from Ileni's chair. "I didn't mean to startle you."

Ileni shrieked and whirled. The blanket tangled around her legs, and she nearly pitched sideways off the bed. She caught herself on the edge of the mattress and struggled to sit straight, kicking the blanket away.

"What are you doing here?" she snapped with all the dignity she could muster. Which wasn't much.

Cyn shrugged, pretending not to notice Ileni's display of grace. She was wearing a shockingly bright red gown. "Karyn couldn't come. I was sent to tell you."

I have something to take care of tomorrow. Ileni tried to sound surprised. "Really? Why can't she come?"

"She had to go deal with the Gaeran rebels."

Ileni had no idea what that meant but couldn't bring herself to ask. She'd had enough of displaying her ignorance the day before.

"Do you know," Cyn said, "what she wants from you?"

"You heard her," Ileni replied as evenly as she could. "She wants to learn healing."

Cyn laughed. "I doubt that. We don't spend much time on healing."

"Among my people," Ileni said, "we believe healing

is the most important use for magic."

"How nice," Cyn said. "But you're here now."

"And so are you, apparently." Ileni swung her legs over the side of her bed. "Why?"

Cyn stood, pushing the chair back. "I was thinking we could spar, before anyone else gets up."

Danger bells went off all over Ileni's mind. "Why?"

"Apparently you're good enough to be placed in our advanced group." Cyn's tone made it clear just how likely she thought *that* was. "I like to check out my competition."

"Competition for what?"

"For being the best," Cyn said with a calm assurance that sent a pang through Ileni. Cyn sounded like Ileni would have, once. When she had been the most powerful of her people, with a future and a destiny and no reason or desire to question either of them.

But the thought that Ileni could be competition—even without her own power—sent a sharp, half-pleasant thrill through her.

"The best? Is that what you are?" Ileni said, and her tone made it clear just how likely *she* thought *that* was.

Cyn leaned back on the polished wood desk. "Oh, yes.

Not that there's much competition. Just Evin and Lis. And now, maybe, you. We'll see."

"So it's really just the four of you?"

"Since the Battle of Rinzo." Cyn lowered her voice, though she didn't entirely lose her grin. "Before that, there were ten."

So much for not displaying her ignorance. "Why?"

"Because the Rinzoans tricked us into an ambush and caused an avalanche." Now the grin was gone. "It was five years ago. Evin, Lis, and I were too young to be there, and Karyn was on one of her missions to the mountains. All the sorcerers there died. We still haven't recovered." Her smile turned hard and brittle. "Of course, the Rinzoans will *never* recover."

Questions beat against each other in Ileni's mind. She went with, "I meant, why so few?"

"I just told you—"

"But even before—there were ten? Out of the whole Empire?"

Cyn's snort was surprisingly loud and indelicate. "How many people do you *think* are talented at magic?"

Among the Renegai, it was generally ten percent of the population—though that was people with skill *and* power.

Then again, the Renegai had started out as a community of exiled sorcerers.

"There are plenty of beginner and intermediate students," Cyn said. "They help with minor skirmishes, and of course they have plenty to do aside from war—communication, mostly. Without magic, it would take several weeks for a message to get from one end of the Empire to another. Some of them will become advanced enough for combat, eventually. But for now, it's just us."

Just us.

And all at once, Ileni knew exactly what Absalm wanted her to do.

This was how assassins worked: targeted strikes aimed precisely where they would do the most damage. Without these four people, the Empire would be weakened enough for the assasssins to go in for the kill.

They would do what assassins did best, spread panic and terror, and the people of the Empire would no longer believe that magic could keep them safe. It would be chaos and destruction.

It would be the end of the Empire.

Cyn stepped forward in a swirl of red fabric, eyes sparkling, and Ileni's stomach twisted. She didn't have to do it. There could still be a better way, even if the lodestones were indestructible. If most of the sorcerers' magic came from lodestones, they must go through thousands and need to replenish them constantly. And *that* was why her people had left: because of those hundreds of thousands of people who were imprisoned and enslaved and tortured until they agreed to give up their lives. Whose power, at the moment of their deaths, was sucked into lodestones and stored there for other people to use.

Maybe there was a way to stop *that*. Free the slaves, cut off the flow of power to the lodestones, without killing anyone.

From his place at the edge of her awareness, Sorin laughed at her.

"How many lodestones do you have?" Ileni asked.

Cyn's smug expression slipped. Was that suspicion on her face, or was Ileni imagining it? Hastily, Ileni added, "It sounds like you must use up a lot of them." A lot of lives.

"Not *us*," Cyn said. "Lower-level magic users need a constant supply. But lodestones last a long time if you have the skill to craft spells with a minimum of power. Karyn's bracelet lasted her seven years before she took it off to go infiltrate the assassins, and she was never exactly a light user of magic."

"She only gets to use one lodestone at a time? Even though she's the head teacher?"

"No one can handle power from more than one lodestone at once."

That's not true. In the Testing Arena, Ileni had already drawn power from more than one, without even needing to. She looked away to hide her expression, not sure what it would be. The Renegai Elders had always claimed they were the masters at magic, more skilled than the imperial sorcerers despite having less power. It was nice to know *something* she had been taught was true.

It also meant she had a better chance of striking at the Academy. If she could draw on a hundred deaths at once, and each imperial sorcerer could only manage the power of one lodestone at a time, it evened the odds. A bit.

Cyn's eyes narrowed, and Ileni realized that she had been silent for too long. She searched her mind for something to deflect Cyn's attention, then had an inspiration. "And Lis? She must not be as skilled as you."

It worked. Cyn's face changed entirely, and when she spoke, her tone was scornful and superior. "Lis goes through a lodestone every two years or so. The lower-level sorcerers do, too. They're not as skilled, so their spells cost them more power."

"Then you must need a constant supply of new lodestones. Where do you get them?"

"That's a question you should ask Lis." Cyn tilted her head to the side, sleek hair falling over one blue eye. "The question that interests me is, what are *you*?"

A weapon. Ileni crossed her arms over her chest. "What do you mean?"

"The Academy trains sorcerers to uphold and expand the Empire. We don't have many applicants from rebellious fringe groups."

Under other circumstances, Ileni might have found this directness charming. At the moment, she did not. But she summoned up her best approximation of a friendly smile and said, "I'm unique."

"If you say so." Cyn leaned forward. "What made you see the error of your people's ways?"

Ileni's breath hissed through her teeth. She was about to say something extremely injudicious when she saw the glint in Cyn's eyes.

"I haven't," she said with her own shrug. It wasn't quite as insouciant as Cyn's, but it was passable. "I don't care about the Empire. I just want to be powerful. I came here to continue my training in magic."

She suspected Cyn would have no trouble believing that.

Cyn paced across the room, and even though she only took three steps, Ileni felt like she was being circled. "So your people don't use lodestones, and your power faded after you were already trained? How often does that happen?"

"Never. Childhood power doesn't always last to adulthood, but we have tests that can determine whose power is permanent." The old fury rose in Ileni. Absalm had faked her test, given her a place in the world, and then ripped it away, on *purpose*. "Usually, only those with lasting power are trained. In my case, someone made a mistake."

Even now, it was hard to say.

"Ah. Too bad." The sympathy in Cyn's voice was equally hard to hear.

"And no, my people don't have lodestones." *Because lodestones are evil.* "So this is the only place where I can still use magic."

Cyn crossed the room and plopped down next to Ileni on the bed. "It will be all right. Wait until you see how much magic you can wield now that you're drawing from lodestones." She leaned back on her elbows. "I'll show you."

"Will you."

"Of course. If you truly are as skilled as Karyn thinks,

you're quite valuable now. Besides, it will be nice to have someone around who's almost as good as I am."

"Almost?"

Cyn laughed and leaped to her feet, somehow managing not to trip on the hem of her gown. "Come on. No one else will be at the training plateau. We can get in some practice before the others manage to drag themselves out of bed."

Ileni stood and had to pause as a wave of dizziness made the room whirl around her. She hadn't eaten since breakfast the day before. But fasting was a regular part of Renegai discipline, and she was sure she could make it until breakfast.

The question was: should she?

Yes. This was an opportunity to find out if Cyn knew anything about how the lodestones were created. An opportunity to prove to the sorcerers that she was who she was pretending to be.

And an opportunity to use the magic thrumming through her.

"All right," she said, and heard the eagerness in her voice. It would have been a good act, if she had been acting. "Let's go."

Ileni had finally beaten Cyn for the first time, using a spell that sliced through Cyn's wards and skin simultaneously, when Evin and Lis swooped from the cloudless blue sky and landed on the plateau. Ileni brushed her sweat-soaked hair away from her face, pretending she didn't care that they had an audience.

Or that they had, apparently, missed breakfast.

"I yield," Cyn said, sounding genuinely pleased. "You are full of surprises, Renegai girl. How do you weave that much power at once?"

They had been sparring for hours, Ileni concentrating on Cyn's spells and doing her best to imitate them. About twenty minutes ago, it had finally clicked, how to hold the magic sharp and use it to *hurt*. A backward shiver ran through her every time, an instinctive recoil against the wrongness of it. But in the intensity of the match, that was easy to ignore.

Cyn held up an arm. Her skin was laced with blood. "I'll figure out your secret, don't worry. In the meantime, care to do that healing thing?"

"Sure." The healing spell felt dull in comparison to the fighting spells, running through well-worn grooves in her mind. But even that, Ileni had to admit, was not as smooth as it should have been; the grooves were rough, neglected. She was going to have to start doing regular exercises again.

"You know," Cyn said thoughtfully, "you should use

healing to fight. It makes you impervious to injury. You could attack when you should be blocking, let my spell get through, and then just heal your injury once you've struck me."

"I suppose so," Ileni said after a moment.

"So why don't you?"

Because she had never thought of healing as a weapon. "It would still *hurt*, you know."

Cyn flicked a finger dismissively. "We learn how to handle pain. If you let it interfere with your magic, you're useless as a battle mage."

Pain is nothing but a distraction. Sorin's voice was so clear in her mind that Ileni almost turned to look for him.

"*We*," she said as haughtily as she could, "learn to avoid it."

Evin's laugh, from the edge of the plateau, was low and smooth. Behind him, the Academy's main mountain peak rose into the sky, a sharp line of dark gray against the brilliant blue. "Is it too late to join your side?"

Ileni tried to match his casual tone, as if they weren't truly on different sides. "Is that allowed?"

"Nope," Evin said cheerfully. He was dressed in threadbare black breeches and a green tunic almost as bright as Cyn's gown. "But since Karyn isn't here to snarl at me about it, I'm not sure it matters."

"Karyn will be gone for a few days," Lis said. She had landed on the opposite side of the plateau from Evin and was standing with her feet braced apart, arms crossed over her chest, the edges of her hair brushing her elbows. Unlike the others, she was wearing drab, functional clothes, in a shade of gray that reminded Ileni of the assassins.

A few days. That would give her time to find out more. Maybe she could discover the source of the lodestones before Karyn came back.

And, while she was doing that, she would also get to use her magic.

Not mine.

"You wouldn't want to join our side," she said to Evin. "We don't have lodestones."

The sentence plunked into the conversation awkwardly, but after a strained moment, Evin gave a friendly shrug and said, "I don't need them. But I can see how that would be a disadvantage."

Ileni strove hard to keep her voice nonchalant. Lis was eyeing her sharply, but Cyn's expression was preoccupied. "I'd heard of them before I came here, but never seen one. Where does their power come from?"

"It's given to us," Cyn said.

Power stolen, power misused, power drawn from pain and death. Every muscle in Ileni's body tensed. "Given to you? What does that—"

But Cyn was still focused on Lis. "Why the delay? It really shouldn't take a few days just to mop up some Gaeran rebels."

"No, it shouldn't," Evin agreed. "I don't even know why Karyn had to go handle it herself. Lis, did Karyn tell you any details?"

Ileni shoved her frustration aside. She couldn't risk pushing for more information, not with the way Lis had looked at her.

Though now Lis was studying the smooth gray ground as if it was more fascinating than any of the people standing on it. Her voice emerged sullenly from behind the dark curtain of her hair. "The governor of the Gaeran territory died after the revolt started. They think it was poison."

"Assassins?" Evin said, with an edge in his voice that made Ileni snap her head around to stare at him.

Casual. Relaxed. She didn't think she was pulling it off. Fortunately, none of them was paying enough attention to notice.

"That's the suspicion," Lis mumbled. "Karyn is trying to find the culprit."

Ileni concentrated on keeping her breathing slow and even, at odds with the racing of her heart. She cleared her throat. "Why would Karyn think she could find an assassin? I thought . . . I mean, I was told . . . even among my people, we heard they were never caught alive."

Evin was holding himself still—something Ileni should have been used to, after weeks among assassins, who never made an unnecessary motion. But on him, it was unnatural. It drew her gaze toward him, even as she focused on Lis.

Lis pushed her hair back, giving a brief glimpse of her set, pale face before the shiny strands fell back into place. "It's true. They aren't." She sounded almost proud of that, as if she was looking forward to Karyn's failure. "Most people would know better than to try."

"The assassins are a threat to the safety of everyone in the Empire," Cyn said. "They need to be eliminated."

"It's more than that, with her," Lis said.

"*What* is it?" Ileni asked, and heard her voice emerge a bit too eager. She hesitated, then pressed on anyhow, heedless of the risk. "Why is she so obsessed with the assassins?"

In the short, awkward silence, a bird called out high

overhead. Cyn said, cautiously, "They killed some of her family."

Cyn was being cautious, and Evin was being somber? Even after one day, Ileni could tell that meant something was wrong. She glanced over at Lis and was almost relieved to see bitter sullenness settled on her face.

Then Evin twitched his shoulders. "We're wasting time. What should we do for the next few days? I have some ideas."

No one answered. Cyn watched Evin with her eyebrows drawn together, while Lis remained stone-faced. Clearly, they all knew something Ileni didn't, and they had no intention of sharing it.

Hunching her shoulders, Ileni turned and stared over the edge of the plateau. Against the bright blue sky, two slate-gray pillars rose into the air, their sides unnaturally smooth and even. They looked like long, narrow stone triangles with their points cut off.

"Dramatic, aren't they?" Evin said, stepping up to her side. Whatever had been on his face earlier was gone; he looked like he hadn't had a serious thought in a decade.

But that exchange had been a good reminder: *Don't underestimate anyone.* He was an imperial sorcerer. He used magic to fight. And he, too, might know the truth about the lodestones.

Evin's eyebrows lifted almost to his unruly hair, and Ileni realized that she was staring at him. She resisted her first impulse and didn't look away. The breeze stirred her hair, so that it tickled her face and floated a few stands in front of her eyes. "What are they?"

Evin grimaced. "Somewhere you never want to be."

"The Judgment Spires," Cyn filled in, somewhat more helpfully, from behind them. "Karyn will stick students up there sometimes, for punishment. When serious punishment is required."

"Fortunately," Evin said, "Karyn has never sent anyone to the spires for slacking off."

"Are we slacking off?" Cyn said.

"Not *yet*," Evin said. "But we're about to."

"We'll be in trouble later," Cyn warned.

"So we will." Evin made a tossing motion with his hand. A ball of colored lights flew up from his palm, spun in the air, and exploded in a shower of rainbow sparks. "But the fun thing about *later* is that it's not *right now*."

Cyn rolled her eyes, a bit too dramatically. "Do whatever you want. Ileni, let's keep going."

Ileni was still trying to think of a way to ask Evin about the lodestones. "I . . . um . . . I need a break."

Cyn wrinkled her nose dismissively, and Ileni tensed. But before she could strike back—or change her mind—Cyn stepped away from the edge in a long swish of skirts. "All right, then. Lis?"

"What, because your preferred partner isn't available?" Lis said.

Ileni turned around, feeling the abyss at her back. She was just in time to catch the poisonous look Lis shot her.

Cyn wielded her words like blades, sharp and deliberate. "Really, Lis, you should get used to being second choice. It's going to happen a lot in your life."

"I volunteer to be third choice," Evin said promptly. He propped one elbow back, resting it on thin air, and tilted his head at Cyn. "In fact, if there's a fourth place available . . ."

Lis ignored him. She glared at her sister. "Someday, you'll realize that not everybody loves you as much as you think they do. I'm looking forward to that moment."

"How nice," Cyn said. "It's not as if you have much to look forward to."

"What about that slacking?" Evin said hastily as Lis stepped forward. "We *all* have that to look forward to. I'm brimming with anticipation."

Lis made a sound that was almost a snarl. Her gaze

snagged on Ileni, and her mouth worked as if she was tasting something sour. "And I'd imagine *you've* never been anyone's first choice in your life."

"You're wrong," Ileni said, but her voice cracked. She had always thought she was first . . . but it had been an illusion. Only her power had mattered. She hadn't even been first to Tellis, not in the end.

And she had never dreamed she might come first to Sorin.

Ileni stood in front of the mirror that night, marveling that she looked the same. Soon after that morning's conversation, the training plateau had been taken over by a dozen younger students, whom Cyn had dismissively referred to as "noble novices." The advanced students had gone to the dining cavern for lunch, and then Ileni had spent the rest of the afternoon training in her room, despite an invitation from Evin and Cyn to join them in some sort of flying game— and despite Lis's clear delight that she had declined.

She stared at her reflection for a long time, feeding herself reasons for not killing the four people who propped up the Empire, reasons more substantial than *I don't want to.*

Or, worse: *I like them. They don't deserve to die.*

Those thoughts were betrayals, signs of weakness, so

she came up with others. Reasons that would make sense to Sorin.

I don't know enough yet.

There might be a better way.

The magic hummed within her, calling her a liar.

She had thought, in the Assassins' Caves, that she was strong. She had wanted Sorin so desperately—she still wanted him—and she had left anyhow. But that had been nothing compared to this.

Sorin was a part of her, a piece of her heart. The constant ache inside her, the pain of ripping out that part, was her price for walking away from him. But magic was *all* of her. She wasn't sure she was strong enough to walk away from it.

Knowing your weakness is itself a strength. The master's words, in Sorin's voice.

Ileni turned her back on the mirror. She could not spend weeks here, as she had at the caves, learning the truth and making up her mind. She couldn't trust her mind. Another few days of using magic and she would be trapped by her own weakness.

She had to find the source of the lodestones' power. Find out if there was another way. If she could stop the flow of power into stones, without killing anyone, she would do it now. Tonight. Rip away her own magic along with the Empire's, before it hurt too badly.

Too late. It *would* hurt, and terribly. But she would do it anyhow.

She pulled her dagger from under her pillow—the dagger Arxis had handed her, as a taunt and a warning. More fool he. A finding spell based merely on touch was immensely difficult—but power filled her, pulled from the testing arena with its hundreds of lodestones, and she knew it wouldn't be difficult at all.

She shouted the words of the spell, and the silence swallowed them. The magic flowed through her, vast and intoxicating, and she couldn't stop herself from smiling. What she could do, with this much power . . .

Knowing your weakness.

She didn't let herself stop to think. When the dagger flared red and violet, when a spark from it hovered in the air, she banished the magic. Then she hastily pulled on a too-loose dress from the wardrobe and followed the spark out into the dark corridor.

By now, Ileni knew better than to surprise an assassin. But she also didn't want to alert anyone else to her presence in Arxis's room. So when her initial soft knock elicited no reaction, she spent a few minutes wrapping a ward around herself, then used a sliver of magic to open the door. She slipped inside and braced herself.

Arxis's first dagger bounced off her chest. His second slid sideways across her throat without leaving a mark and dropped to the floor at her feet. Then he was behind her, a thin wire wrapped around her neck, jerking Ileni's head back even as the wire pressed harmlessly against her warded throat.

"I just want to talk," Ileni croaked.

Arxis's response was to pull the garrote tighter. If Ileni's ward had been less well made, she wouldn't have been able to make a sound. Irun's method for killing sorcerers was, apparently, now common knowledge among the assassins.

But she had been prepared for this, and what would have worked on an imperial sorcerer was less effective against a carefully prepared Renegai ward. Ileni drew in a breath and uttered a spell.

The garrote snapped in half. Arxis rolled and came to his feet in front of her. With a word, Ileni froze him where he stood.

"I'm on your side," she snapped. *Well, sort of.* "Stop trying to kill me."

Arxis didn't bother to strain against her spell. He didn't try a counterspell, either—which was smart; against Ileni, it would have been futile. He pressed his lips together and said nothing.

"I came," Ileni said, "because I need your help to accomplish my own mission."

Still Arxis said nothing. Cautiously, Ileni released him, holding the spell ready just in case. The assassin didn't move.

She took a deep breath. "I am here to stop the flow of power to the lodestones."

Arxis leaned back slightly, and she tensed, but all he did was smile scornfully. "Are you."

"Yes. But in order to do that, I have to know where the source of that power is." Sweat tickled the edge of her brow. She resisted the urge to wipe it away, though she was sure he had already noticed it. "The master told me you would take me there."

Silence.

"He said . . ." A surge of inspiration. "He said you would understand what had to be done."

A muscle twitched in Arxis's jaw.

In her village—and, probably, in the Empire—people

spoke of the assassins as blindly obedient, killing tools with no thoughts of their own. Ileni knew better. The master had always challenged his students to make their own decisions.

"And he said," Ileni added, "that we are both being tested."

Arxis's lips remained curled in a sneer, but his eyes were thoughtful. The master's tests were both legendary and constant within the caves. It was a rare advantage to actually be told one was being tested.

At least, it was an advantage when it wasn't a trick.

Ileni couldn't tell whether Arxis believed her or not. Finally, he jerked his chin and said, "I will show you. But not tonight."

When? and *How?* and *Show me what?* jostled against her teeth. Ileni said, "Why not tonight?"

"Because my own mission takes precedence. I have no excuse for going into the city in the middle of the night. If we're caught, I'll be exposed."

"In the city? That's where they keep them?" Ileni frowned. "Wouldn't it be safer to keep them here?"

Arxis tilted his head to the side. "When you say *them*, Teacher, who exactly do you mean?"

The way he said *Teacher* reminded her of Irun, of his fingers clamped over her mouth. She shivered slightly. "The slaves."

Arxis remained perfectly still for a moment, and then he began to laugh.

A flush crept over Ileni's body. "You know what I mean. The people they breed and keep in cages—" He laughed harder, though no louder, and she ground to a halt.

His laugh shut off as abruptly as her words. "You know, Teacher, I find it hard to believe the master sent you here still believing Renegai children's stories."

The sense of danger overwhelmed Ileni's embarrassment. She tried to fight down her blush, and when that didn't work, she tried to ignore it. "He told me I wouldn't understand the truth until I saw it."

Arxis snorted. "That's probably true. I hope he's right about you understanding it once you *do* see it." He started toward his bed.

"Wait," Ileni said. "When will you show me?"

He spoke without turning. "In two weeks."

"*Two weeks?*" Ileni's chest tightened. "That's too long. What's going to happen in two weeks?"

"I've made arrangements to go to the city then. Find a reason to come with me."

"But—"

Arxis sighed and looked at her over his shoulder. "Do you think you can manage that?"

Ileni ground her teeth together. "I'll do my best," she said as haughtily as she could.

"Excellent."

He waited, watching her, his body relaxed and predatory at once. After a moment, Ileni let herself out.

Arxis's laughter rang in her ears as she headed down the corridors toward her room. Her skin tingled with embarassment. Was *nothing* she knew about the world true? And if so, how could she—ignorant, naive, wrong about everything—possibly make a decision that would affect the world so drastically?

But beneath her despair ran a tingle of hope. If her whole past was a lie, it changed the possibilities for her future. Maybe the Empire wasn't evil. Maybe using the magic wasn't so wrong.

And if so, maybe she wouldn't have to give it up after all.

CHAPTER 8

"Blue really isn't your color." Cyn's cool voice interrupted Ileni's spell, making her jump. Strands of magic scattered through the room. "With your complexion, I would try orange. Or maybe dark green."

Ileni unclenched her muscles, one by one, and pulled the magic back in. She had been planning to use it to lengthen her dress, but instead she took the time to turn the dress even bluer—until it was the shade of the sky through her small window—before she turned around, as slowly as she could manage.

Cyn was leaning in the doorway, wearing black leggings

and a black tunic with a single red stripe across its front. She tilted her head back against the wall. "Just some friendly advice."

You know, Ileni thought sourly, *when I lived with assassins, my door was warded.* What she said, as she smoothed down the front of her dress, was, "What are you doing here? Did you forget to show me a really, *really* nasty way to kill people?"

"Several," Cyn said. She wasn't joking.

Ileni rolled her eyes. "I can't wait."

Cyn shrugged. "Sorry for the intrusion, but you're the first worthy sparring partner I've had in years. Lis is barely worth spending magic on, and Evin is too lazy to be interesting. Want to get in some practice before breakfast?"

Ileni hesitated, so she could tell herself she had, before she pulled in more magic and strode toward the door. "Sure."

Ileni and Cyn strolled into breakfast together, late and sweat soaked. Evin looked from one of them to the other, then tilted his head back and studied the stone ceiling. "I think we're all in trouble."

"Where's Lis?" Ileni asked.

"She had somewhere she had to be." Cyn said it smugly, for some reason, as she slid onto the bench. Breakfast today consisted of some sort of strongly scented thin noodles, already heaped into ceramic bowls. Next to each bowl lay three oddly shaped sticks. Ileni eyed both the noodles and the sticks doubtfully. "Don't worry, Evin. Apply yourself at practice today and you just might catch up to us."

"Tempting." Evin twirled noodles onto the sticks with practiced ease. Ileni tried to pay attention to how he did it. "But I'm going to be practicing with Arxis today."

Ileni's gaze shot from Evin's hands to his face. Cyn scowled. "Arxis is barely a second-level."

"At magic." Evin slid some noodles into his mouth and spoke around them. "But at kobi, he's a master."

Before Ileni could say, *What is kobi?*, Cyn said, "Karyn *will* get back eventually, you know."

"And then I will be very, very contrite." Evin's grin included Ileni. "You could both come. We'll play with only three dice, for low stakes, to ease Ileni into it. And apparently you've had all the combat practice you need today."

"Say that when you're facing an assassin." Cyn flicked a strand of hair away from her eyes. "Besides, not all of us get the benefits of being the headmistress's nephew."

"More to the point," Evin said, "not all of us know how to act contrite."

There were so many things Ileni should ask. But when she opened her mouth, what came out was, "You shouldn't spend so much time with Arxis."

Cyn picked up her own sticks, all three in one hand, and said, mildly, "I think he's probably harmless if you don't fall in love with him."

Ileni snapped her jaw shut. "I didn't—"

"Attack him when you first met? With a *dagger*? We all heard about it." Cyn sounded amused, but it was Evin she was watching, not Ileni. Ileni braced herself for one of Evin's quips, but he was suddenly quite focused on his noodles.

She bent her head over her food. Let them believe it. It wasn't as if she had a better explanation.

Or as if Evin would believe her warning, anyhow.

Besides, what did she care? She wasn't one of them. She was on a mission, too. The real question might be whether Arxis killed Evin before she did.

When they stepped out onto the mountain ledge after breakfast, cold droplets pelted Ileni's face. A gray-white sky spread across the mountains, spitting rain, and fog wreathed around the craggy peaks, softening their harsh edges.

A jolt of homesickness took Ileni by surprise. She hadn't

even *wanted* to go home, back when she'd thought she had to. But in the Renegai village, rain was a nearly everyday occurrence, though it was usually swept swiftly away by the mountain winds. With a day of training ahead of her, with magic flowing through her and the rain forming a cool mist against her face, she could almost have been home.

Almost. With just a few slight differences. The loneliness reared up within her, threatening to overwhelm her, and she shoved it down fiercely. She didn't have time for that.

On a ledge on one of the farther peaks, a line of people walked slowly alongside the mountain, holding rain shields in tight formation. Someone else—an instructor, probably— flew next to them, directing the raindrops in torrents against the shield. A training exercise.

"Well," Evin said, "you know what I call this? Napping weather."

"You would," Cyn said, with the same disdain Ileni felt.

Evin laughed again. Even after only two days, his laugh was starting to grate on Ileni, like a wrongly accented spell. He seemed incapable of taking anything seriously. She waited for Cyn to put him in his place.

But Cyn just sighed, and a moment later Evin soared away, a speeding black line against the roiling gray clouds.

Cyn held a hand out to Ileni. "Want to fly?"

Ileni hesitated. But it was too damp and too early for noble gestures. She took Cyn's hand.

Her shoulder was nearly jerked out of its socket as Cyn leaped upward, pulling her along so fast the wind split in front of them. After the first moment of terror, Ileni used a touch of magic to hold herself streamlined, the wind beating at her face and whipping her hair back. The distant treetops sped beneath them, and Cyn laughed, wild and exhilarated.

They slowed down at the last moment and landed gently on the plateau. Ileni let go of Cyn's hand and swayed unsteadily. She was breathing hard, even though she hadn't been the one doing the work, and a laugh bubbled out of her.

Cyn's expression was sheer joy, and Ileni's laugh died. Her own exhilaration was tainted by envy, deep in the pit of her stomach.

"What does someone have to do," she said, "to get one of those lodestone bracelets?"

As soon as the question was out of her mouth, she was struck with horror at herself. But Cyn, of course, found it perfectly natural. She ran her fingers through her hair and shook it out. "First you have to test for eighth-level, of course, and do the containment training."

It was not, Ileni had realized by now, that Cyn was trying to make her feel stupid. She truly didn't grasp how ignorant Ileni was of things she took for granted. Usually Ileni let it pass—she didn't particularly want Cyn to see her as ignorant—but this time she gritted her teeth and said, "What does that mean?"

Cyn blinked. "You don't know . . . well, I guess you wouldn't. It would take a long time to explain. But I'm not sure how much it matters for you. Even after the required trainings, it's still up to Karyn. And she doesn't seem to trust you." She grimaced. "Can you think of a way to win her over?"

By turning traitor. Though of course, Cyn wouldn't see it that way.

Cyn summoned up a globe of pink light and began twirling it slowly through the air—warming up. "Don't think having Evin on your side will help, either. He might be Karyn's nephew, but he doesn't exactly go out of his way to curry favor with her."

"I noticed." Ileni hesitated. "He's her nephew? Where are his parents?"

"His parents are dead." The pink globe stilled. "His mother was a battle commander, and his father was high sorcerer. That family has always had incredible amounts of power."

Ileni blinked. "The high sorcerer who—"

"Was murdered by assassins." Cyn muttered a word, and the globe began to spin, faster and faster. "The first high sorcerer to ever fall to a mundane blade. His mother wasn't a sorceress, but she was murdered by assassins, too."

It's so easy, Irun had said, *once you're not afraid*. Evin's father might have been the first, but he wouldn't be the last.

Was Evin intended to be the second? It made perfect sense, if you thought like an assassin. It would be a deadly warning, a double strike, spreading fear exponentially. A clear message: *We can kill any of you whenever we want.*

The only question was why Arxis hadn't done it yet.

A thud behind her signaled Lis's arrival on the plateau. A moment later, Lis stormed past Ileni toward Cyn, hair swinging violently back and forth. She stopped in front of her sister, her shoulders so tense they shook.

"That," Lis spat, "was quite the mess you left."

Cyn's exuberance sharpened into an edged smile. "I hope it wasn't too much trouble. If you're feeling faint, perhaps you should lie down."

Lis aimed a crude spell at the pink globe. It popped and

vanished. "If you're feeling proud of what you did, perhaps you should jump off the edge of the mountain."

Cyn patted her sister on the cheek, making Lis pull back with a hiss. Cyn glanced at Ileni. "Ignore her. Lis is always in a bad mood when she comes back from a battlefield."

"Battlefield?" Now Ileni noticed that Lis, too, was wearing a black tunic with a red stripe across its front.

"Just a minor skirmish in the mountains," Cyn said. "One of the battle commanders asked for my help just before dawn. It took less than an hour. Bracing start to the morning, in fact."

She was talking to Ileni, but her words were clearly aimed at her sister. Lis's lips whitened.

"In the mountains?" Ileni's heart thumped sickeningly. "Against the Renegai?"

Cyn gave her a blank, confused look. Ileni swallowed. No, of course not. But if not the Renegai . . . "Against the assassins?"

Lis's head snapped up. Cyn laughed. "There's no such thing as a *minor* skirmish against the assassins."

"You're thinking of the wrong mountains," Lis cut in. "This battle was in the south. Today we brought the might of the Empire—"

"Meaning me." Cyn curtsied.

"—against some fishermen with swords. My sister really outdid herself. It was very brave."

"These things flare up from time to time," Cyn explained to Ileni. "Something sets off a segment of the local populace, and they try to start a rebellion. It's kindest to crush it as soon as possible, before too many people get involved. This time it was about some imperial soldier taking a piss in a holy lake."

"And Cyn was so *terribly* kind," Lis said.

Cyn's hands flexed. For a moment, Ileni was afraid for Lis.

"So many dead," Lis went on. "And so *creatively* dead, too. You must have really enjoyed yourself."

"Would you rather it be our own soldiers who died?" Cyn snapped. "Or that we let the Empire fall to pieces?"

"Wouldn't *you* rather it was our soldiers?" Lis said, poisonous and sweet. "For the good of the Empire. Think how many lodestones would be in the training arena now."

What did that mean? But Ileni didn't dare ask a question; she barely dared breathe.

"That part," Cyn snarled, "is not on *my* conscience." Lis flinched, and Cyn laughed, low and vicious. "What, do you see yourself as innocent?"

"No," Lis said. Her face was twisted so savagely it no longer resembled her sister's. "None of us are innocent. It's just that some of us know it, and some of us don't. Tell Ileni why we always rush into battle so fast. Is it because we're *kind*?"

"Shut up, Lis," Cyn said.

"The real reason," Lis said, "is because we win either way. Tell her, Cyn."

"We fight because we have to," Cyn snapped. "I'm not happy about the rebels' deaths. I just prefer them to *our* deaths. Terribly selfish of me, I know. Lis, if you're not going to be useful, why don't you go sleep your mood off?"

"I'm sure it would be that easy," Lis said, "for you. You're so good at not thinking about things that might make you uncomfortable."

"One of the advantages," Cyn said, "of having things that are actually important to think about."

Lis slapped her sister across the face.

Cyn stepped back, her cheek mottled red. She spat out a series of vicious spell words, then raised her hand, fist clenched, and spread her fingers. A black fog rolled from her hand, slowly, almost lazily—until it reached Lis. Then, swift as a striking snake, it shot into Lis's nose and throat.

Lis opened her mouth to scream. Black smoke came out, but no sound.

Tiny tendrils of smoke began leaking out of her skin—slowly, slowly, through her pores, then wreathing gracefully around her body. Lis's eyes widened, and smoke poured out of them, too. Translucent black vines wrapped around her head, twining through her hair.

"Stop it," Ileni said. Cyn was smiling, a tight, vengeful smile. Ileni darted forward and grabbed Cyn's hand. *"Stop it!"*

Cyn tried to slap her away, but Ileni had learned enough in the Assassins' Caves to outfight one distracted sorceress. She blocked the blow and yanked Cyn sideways. Cyn swore, then turned the curse into a snarled phrase that ended the spell.

Lis collapsed on the plateau. She lay huddled for a moment on the ground, a series of tremors rippling up and down her body. Then she pressed her forehead to the ground and vanished, leaving a small damp patch of tears on the gray stone.

Ileni let go of Cyn's arm, shaking all over. Disappointment clogged her throat—but why? Because Cyn had been friendly? Because they'd been having *fun*? Cyn was an imperial sorceress, with everything that implied. Trained in pain, thriving on conflict.

What was wrong with her, that she could so easily forget what people truly were? First Sorin, now Cyn.

Cyn rolled her eyes. "Calm down. I didn't really hurt her." She sauntered to the center of the plateau, avoiding Ileni's eyes, and summoned up a piece of chalk with a snap of her fingers. "I just scared her."

Ileni swallowed, and what went down tasted thick and bitter.

Cyn dropped to her knees and began drawing a pattern, the scratching of chalk almost frenzied against the stone ground. The pattern was like nothing Ileni had ever seen before, everything about it off-center and unbalanced. When Cyn stood, the chalk snapped in two in her hand.

"My sister likes self-righteousness almost as much as she likes self-pity," she said. "But she's wrong. I do terrible things, but only because I have to."

I've heard that before. Ileni didn't dare say it.

"This is what I did," Cyn said. "This is how I won the battle without a single imperial soldier lost. I fashioned the spell myself."

Ileni tried to make sense of the elements of the pattern. "It's for . . . breaking something?"

"Not some*thing*."

A chill crept under Ileni's skin. "You used this against *people?*"

"Froze their bodies and shattered them into a million tiny pieces," Cyn said. "It tends to have a devastating effect on their fellow rebels, too, especially those who get hit by pieces of their dead friends."

"That's how you won the battle?" Ileni's voice cracked.

"Evin and I are the only ones who can do it," Cyn said. There was pride—*pride*—in her voice.

The pause seemed to demand a response. Ileni came up with, "Oh."

Cyn flung both pieces of chalk behind her. "Do you think *you* could?"

"*No,*" Ileni said, and realized it wasn't true as she said it. The spell was intricate and tricky, but well within her skill. And Cyn knew it.

"I'll teach you," Cyn said, her voice suddenly silken. "We can practice on rocks."

Ileni resisted the urge to back away. Using a spell like this, letting her mind coil around such destructive magic, would be a betrayal of everything she was.

Then again, so was everything she had done lately. This would be no different from learning to fight with Sorin, throwing knives into people-shaped targets, over and over until her muscles ached.

"I don't want to do it," she said. "Let's work on something else."

"No." Cyn's eyes narrowed until they were slits in her face. "Let's work on *this*."

She should have been more careful. Should have remembered that these were imperial sorcerers. Why should *anything* they did horrify her?

"Watch closely," Cyn said, and stepped carefully onto one of the thick white lines. Magic shimmered through the pattern, a long, delicious shiver. "You'll try next. Trust me, Ileni. You won't know what you're capable of until you do it."

I can't, Ileni thought, and a memory struck her: pushing the dagger through Irun's skin, blood flowing over her hand. The savage joy that ran through her as she wrenched the blade out. Perhaps it was time to stop pretending she was better than the sorcerers, or the assassins, or anyone at all.

"All right," she said. Her voice trembled, but she swallowed hard and added, "Go ahead. I'm watching."

That night, Ileni traced a finger along the mirror's smooth surface, forming the pattern that—if written with chalk on stone, joined with the right words, fueled by enough power—could shatter not just a person, but a mountain. Gray stone, crumbling down and around them, the might of the Empire buried beneath it.

She had managed to keep herself from thinking, until this moment, of the use she could put today's lesson to. Of what Cyn had foolishly taught her to do.

The lodestones couldn't be destroyed. But they could be buried, along with every person in this Academy. *That* would put an end to the Empire's power, more dramatically than even the assassins had hoped.

Cyn had no idea what Ileni was capable of.

Her finger left no trace on the mirror's surface. She pressed her fingertip against it, so hard her nail turned white. Another pattern, a much shorter, simpler one, and she could tell Sorin what she knew.

He would want to use it immediately.

She imagined telling him that she wanted to find another way—that she wanted to put an end to the lodestones without killing anyone—and it was all too easy to envision his expression.

She felt again the surge of power going through her, the shattering of rock spraying in a million different directions.

She had met Cyn's smile through a cascade of pebbles and dust.

She hadn't realized until that moment that she had been smiling, too.

Oh, yes. She could do it.

But she didn't want to.

I'll find another way. The hope felt threadbare and forlorn. She didn't even need Sorin to tell her she was being weak.

She stepped back from the mirror, not much liking what she saw in it.

The next four days sped by like a dream, the type of dream that might at any moment twist into a nightmare. Ileni practiced magic all day with Cyn—and, sometimes, with Evin and Lis—and got used to the odd concoctions the imperial sorcerers called food, many of which she had already tasted in the caves. She passed other sorcerers-in-training, on the ledges and in the passageways, and saw them practicing from afar. They never spoke to her, and she—perhaps influenced by Cyn's aloofness—never spoke to them. It occurred to her, sometimes, that she might be making a mistake. But she was too busy to dwell on it.

She tried to ask about the lodestones, but it was a slippery subject. She couldn't even tell whether Cyn was avoiding the topic—it seemed, rather, that there was always something more interesting to talk about—but after four days, she still had no idea where the magic filling the lodestones came from. It was with vague, guilty relief that she eventually gave up. Arxis had promised her the truth. All she had to do was wait. There were eleven days left—and then ten—and then nine—and then just eight.

It was only at night, in the few minutes before sleep, that despair came creeping in. And even then, it wasn't over magic, and it wasn't over the lodestones. It was thoughts of Sorin that slid between Ileni and sleep, a sore spot in her heart that she couldn't stop poking. Over and over, she went through their last encounter, when he had told her he would wait for her.

Over and over, she reminded herself that he was a killer.

The mirror in the corner was a constant taunt, an itch she didn't dare scratch. It was a trap, somehow—it had to be—though she couldn't fathom its purpose. More than once, she stood in front of it for minutes she didn't count. It would be so easy to open the portal again, to see Sorin's eyes in the glass instead of her own.

Usually, she turned away before her thoughts could

lead her down that path. Sometimes, she didn't turn away until she noticed how wet her eyes were.

And for all the very good reasons she had to turn away, the one that finally spurred her to do it, on those nights, was a simple and stupid one: she didn't want Sorin to see her cry.

CHAPTER 9

Ileni woke suddenly from a dreamless sleep, not certain where she was. The glowstones flickered dimly, revealing smooth gray stone and dark polished wood in a foreign, too-large room.

Then the glowstones' light vanished, the room went black and featureless, and someone yanked her blanket off her body.

"Get up," Karyn said, and all the glowstones turned bright at once. The sorceress stood over Ileni's bed, dressed in a lacy black tunic and purple leggings. "I have some questions."

Ileni was already upright in bed, heart pounding, mind forming the pattern of an attack spell. The bolt of fire shot straight toward Karyn's face, but Karyn blocked it with an impatient wave of her hand. The backlash of repelled magic hit Ileni like a punch.

"You need to calm down," Karyn said. She lowered her hand, and her flowing sleeve fell over her wrist, but not before Ileni saw the metallic bracelet clamped around it. "You're not among assassins anymore. No one *here* is trying to kill you."

Ileni wasn't even sure how that was ironic, but she knew it was. She pulled the blanket back over her bare legs. "It's a bit early."

"This is when I have time. Get dressed."

As slowly as she dared, Ileni got out of bed and walked to the wardrobe. When she had fastened a long gray skirt over her sleeping tunic and slipped on shoes, Karyn said, "Sit down."

Ileni glanced at the chair, then whispered a quick spell under her breath. She drew her legs up and crossed them beneath her, sitting calmly on empty air, floating several feet above the ground.

Karyn rolled her eyes. Then she muttered a spell. A gash

tore down the skin of her own forearm and immediately filled with blood.

Ileni flinched. Karyn held out her arm. "Teach me how to heal it."

Ileni had managed not to think about this: how she had promised to betray not just herself, not just the assassins, but her own people. As she watched the blood spill onto Karyn's skin, her fear and longing and confusion struck against something deep within her, something rock solid. No. She wasn't going to do *this*. Not for any reason.

She laughed.

A muscle twitched in Karyn's sharp chin. "Is something amusing?"

"Many things," Ileni said. "But at the moment, mostly your arrogance."

"Indeed."

"It took me years to get to the point where I could heal myself." Ileni leaned back, extending her spell so her hands, too, could support her on thin air. Blood spread over Karyn's arm, but the sorceress didn't even glance at it. "You're not going to learn it in a morning. First you have to master the basic patterns of healing spells—they're very different from other spells—and then you need to understand what's inside a person's body, and *then*—"

"Understood," Karyn snapped. "Unfortunately, I have no interest in devoting my life to becoming a Renegai healer. I have a war to win."

"Unfortunately for who?" Ileni said coolly.

"For you." Karyn stretched both hands high above her head, fingertips pointing up. Blood curved down her left arm. Ileni felt the magic coiling in Karyn's hands and pulled in as much magic as she could from the lodestones, but then didn't know what to do with it. She didn't recognize Karyn's spell.

Karyn's eyes glinted. She brought her arms down sharply, all her fingertips pointed at Ileni.

Ileni threw her power into a ward. It was unplanned and messy—her Renegai teachers would have been appalled—and Karyn batted it aside with a flippant hand gesture. Then she whispered a word and released her spell.

A wave of dizziness, tinged with nausea, ran through Ileni. With a suddenness that made her scream, she fell several feet to the ground.

The impact thudded all the way up her spine. But the collision didn't hurt as much as the sudden absence within her. She reached desperately for the lodestones, knowing what she would find.

Nothing. She couldn't draw on the magic anymore. It was gone.

As she had always known, deep down, it would be.

That pain should have been familiar to her by now, but it still felt like someone had scooped out a part of her soul. She didn't even try to get to her feet. Instead, she heard herself say, "I could help you defeat the assassins."

Karyn looked both interested and unsurprised. "Could you indeed?"

"I—" What was she saying? What was she *thinking*? "I mean—I don't—"

"Because if you could," Karyn purred, "that would be reason to allow you to stay."

Ileni was so hot with shame it was hard to think. *Betrayer.* Just a week ago, she had sworn she would never do this.

She could only be glad that no one but an imperial sorceress was here to see how loathsome she was. How weak.

Karyn murmured a word, and a white cloth appeared in her right hand. She pressed it to her arm, and it turned swiftly crimson as blood soaked it. "But if you can't, I'm afraid it's not just a question of letting you leave. It's a question of letting you live."

Ileni couldn't even manage to be afraid. "If you kill me,"

she said, "the assassins will stop at nothing until you're dead."

"Oh, indeed? Are they stopping at something now?" Karyn snorted. "I wonder if I was this stupid when I was young, or if it's only assassins who turn girls' heads around. Are you implying that the blond killer you were so dove-eyed with in the caves would change his strategy because of *you*?"

"Yes," Ileni said. The thought of Sorin steadied her, and she tried to think of what he would do, if he were here. He would never dream of accepting Karyn's offer. . . .

Except he would. Of course he would. As a ruse.

The fog of shame lifted, leaving her head a bit clearer. It *could* be a ruse. She knew an assassin who had lived at the emperor's court for forty years, then accomplished his mission and walked away. He hadn't been seduced from his cause. Surely she could manage that kind of steadfastness for a few weeks.

Surely. Except her heart was already pounding, fast and eager, at the thought of getting the magic back.

Karyn's face pulled into a sneer. "Really? Even after you've polluted yourself with imperial magic? He must truly love you."

"He does," Ileni said, without hesitation.

"So he wouldn't betray you?"

"Oh, no," Ileni said. "He would."

Karyn blinked. Then she leaned forward. "So I suppose it's only fair that you would betray him as well."

Ileni paused for only a moment before she nodded.

Karyn lifted the blood-soaked cloth from her arm. "You will tell me all about their magical training, what spells they know, what defenses they have. And about the wards around the caves." She crumpled the cloth into a ball. "To start with."

It won't matter, Ileni thought. Once she put an end to the Empire, it wouldn't matter what Karyn knew.

"All right," she said. "I'll tell you. But first, give me my magic back."

The sky outside her window was faintly pink when Ileni left her room, tingling all over with magic, aching with guilt. Karyn, though clearly not finished, had left for "a meeting with the skyriders' battle commander." "But this is most useful," she had added. "I hadn't realized their fire spells were still so primitive. I will be back for another talk soon."

"What are the skyriders?" Ileni had asked. But Karyn had simply vanished.

The assassins' fire spells were, in fact, far from primitive. Ileni had done her best to mix falsehoods with truths, supplying as much misinformation as she thought Karyn would believe. Which wasn't much, but was better than nothing. It seemed she had gotten away with it. Next time, when she wasn't caught off guard, she could probably get away with more. . . .

Next time. The contents of her stomach surged upward, making her clamp her mouth shut. How many mornings could she play the betrayer—*be* the betrayer—with an imperial sorceress, spilling secrets the assassins had kept for centuries?

Why not end it now? Sorin whispered in her mind, and she had no coherent answer. But she never had, in the face of his certainty.

She reached for magic—finally, even though she didn't deserve to—and called up a magelight. Power rushed through her like cool water, a thread of joy even in her turmoil.

Maybe she could get in some early practice today.

By now she knew her way through the corridors, so she kept the magelight dim, just enough of a glow to prevent her from walking into a wall. She didn't want to attract attention—not because she was afraid, but because she was in no mood to talk to anyone. When she heard a door creak, she stopped and snuffed the magelight out, standing cloaked in darkness until whoever it was could pass and leave her alone.

A new magelight flickered on—also softly, but bright enough to illuminate the face of the person closing the door.

Arxis.

And judging by the rumpled state of his clothes, the room he was coming out of wasn't his own.

Ileni froze, and Arxis looked straight at her despite the darkness. Then he continued down the hall and disappeared around a curve.

Ileni stood with her back pressed against the wall, heart pounding. She wasn't sure why this bothered her so much. Something about his expression . . . as if he was saying, *I fooled you.* Perhaps she should wonder if someone was dead in that room, but . . .

Assassins were not discouraged from assignations outside the caves, and their appeal to women was legendary. What would it have been like to meet Sorin on a mission, to sense the undercurrent of danger in him without knowing its source? She would have been drawn to him even more strongly, surely, if she hadn't known he was a murderer.

She felt a stab of sympathy for whoever was in that room, followed swiftly by wariness.

Seduction was a perk, but it was also a tool. Her attraction to Sorin had been part of the master's plan. This assignation might be part of a plan, too.

Which meant Ileni had to know who that room belonged to. Ignoring a squeamish reluctance, she whispered a spell, silent and invisible, to tell her who was still in the room Arxis had left.

She cast the spell, not sure she would recognize whoever it was. But she did, instantly, and heard her own gasp tear through the darkness.

So much for silence.

Fortunately, there was no one to hear. Arxis was long gone. And the spell showed Lis fast asleep in her room, hair lying in tangled black strands over her face.

This might mean nothing. It could be that Arxis was dallying with Lis just for fun. But if so . . . why Lis and not Cyn? Cyn was the prettier twin—which sounded ridiculous, but was true nonetheless. Ileni had no doubt, either, that Arxis could have found his way into Cyn's room if he had wanted to.

Was Lis a way to Arxis's target? The duke of Famis

had been killed when his wife's assassin lover coated her skin with poison. But Evin and Lis barely spoke, so that didn't make sense . . . unless Evin wasn't Arxis's target after all. Ileni's mind whirled, her suspicions tilting on their axis.

Why should it matter to me?

She scowled and continued to the bridge. She didn't want to think about any of this, not now, not when her mind was already cluttered with shame and confusion. All she wanted was to use her magic, and do it alone, in silence.

So of course, when she got to the plateau, Evin was already there.

The sky was lighter by then, the hazy beginnings of sunrise pouring over the tops of the mountains, gathering strength to break through the dusky gray sky. Evin sat on the plateau with his back to the bridge. The air around him shimmered with color, as if he was in the center of a rainbow bubble. The spell he was using—multiple spells, she realized, all working simultaneously—were immensely powerful, and he played with them as lightly as if they were magelights or umbrella shields.

A hard, hot knot coalesced deep in Ileni's gut. Evin glanced over his shoulder at her, and she snapped, "Can you take up a little less space with your pretty colors? I need to practice."

Evin leaped to his feet in a graceful arc, using a hint of power to propel himself. He braced his legs apart and murmured swiftly and musically under his breath. The colors swirled and gathered in toward him, then exploded above his head, a burst of lights and colors shooting upward into the sky.

They lasted only a moment before fading into sparkles, and then into nothing. The plateau seemed empty and dull, the only colors the stark contrast of gray stone and paler gray sky.

"All yours," Evin said, with a sweeping bow.

A shard of guilt pricked Ileni. "I didn't say you had to get rid of it. You could have just made it smaller."

Evin sat on the ground with a thud and leaned back on his elbows. "I *could* have, but it would have been greatly taxing."

That was a lie—Evin had enough skill to contain a spell without even noticing. The knot in Ileni's gut tightened. She strode to the other end of the plateau and focused on the latest thing Cyn had taught her—a complicated spell to call up and focus rain. Water, it turned out, could be an extremely effective weapon.

With her back to the bridge, Ileni found herself facing a range of mountains so high that the clouds floated beneath their snow-splattered peaks. They reared toward the horizon in a way that made the sky look low, rather than the mountains high. Above and between them, a formation of black figures circled against the gray sky; it took Ileni a moment to realize they weren't birds, but people. *Skyriders*, presumably. She could feel, even from this far away, the massive amounts of magic surrounding them.

Behind her, Evin was silent—which was, for him, a small miracle—but she could feel him watching her, and it made her shoulders tighten. She waited until the skyriders had disappeared into the gray horizon, then tried to loosen her muscles as she waved her arms through the preparatory exercise and began the chant. His presence sliced through her concentration, like a strain of discordant music. She got an accent wrong and stumbled to a stop.

"You don't have to, you know," Evin said.

Ileni lowered her arms and spun around. He wasn't watching her after all; he was lying flat on his back, hands laced together behind his head, studying the hazy sky. "Excuse me?"

"You're not a citizen of the Empire. You don't have to

devote your life to combat, just because you have the skill. Not if you don't want to."

Her jaw tightened. "Why wouldn't I want to?"

Evin laughed. There was something odd in it—almost bitter, and very unlike him. But his voice was lazy and relaxed. "Well, you might die. That bothers some people."

"I'm sure it does." The scorn in her own voice surprised Ileni. She sounded, just then, like Sorin. "Shouldn't you be glad to die for the Empire?"

"Whatever gave you that idea?" Evin rolled onto his stomach and clambered to his feet. "Why would anyone be glad to die?"

Ileni opened her mouth, then closed it.

"Don't pay too much attention to Cyn." Evin spread his hands apart, making twines of colored light dance between them. "She likes fighting, and she doesn't mind killing as much as she should, but even *she* would prefer to avoid dying."

Ileni didn't doubt it. Cyn was fierce and violent, and cruel in her anger, but she was no assassin.

Evin studied her face, his broad brow creased. "I don't know if you realized what you were getting into when you came here. I can help you."

"I don't need your help," Ileni said.

In the silence, she heard the echoes of her nastiness and winced. She tried to think up an apology, hoping she could manage to get it out once she did. But Evin didn't look hurt or angry. He frowned at her, and all he said was, "Are you going to tell me why you're always angry at me?"

It sounded so reasonable. But what could she say? *If I were you, I would do so much more with what you have.*

She couldn't say that, and she couldn't bear the patient, open expression on Evin's face. She whirled on her heel without a word and walked across the plateau and over the bridge.

As she reached the middle, the sky above her erupted in streaks of fiery green light. They danced in the sky, shifting and wavering, widening and narrowing, eerie ghosts that turned the entire sky unearthly.

Ileni didn't stop. Whatever Evin was trying to say, however beautifully he was saying it, she didn't care. It was nothing but an illusion, and she wasn't in the mood for illusions.

She had been living with them long enough—since she was old enough to be told them. But she knew better now. She had no power and no destiny, and she didn't even have anything to believe in. There was nothing worth fighting for, nothing good and pure, no path that didn't end in pain.

It was her illusions that had brought her to this point. And she was going to need more than illusions to get past it.

Ileni learned fast that the casual nonchalance of the first few days had been an anomaly. With Karyn back, the training was more intense than anything she had experienced among her own people. Ileni threw herself eagerly into the mental focus, the grim dedication, the constant tension. It kept her too occupied to think.

At least, when she was sparring with Cyn. Which was most of the time.

Lis was sometimes intense, too, but spent most of her time deep in a sulk that nobody seemed inclined to rouse her from. Evin was, even in Karyn's presence, a slacker: refusing to take anything seriously, so powerful it didn't matter. Sometimes Ileni admired him for his self-confidence, the ease with which he ignored Karyn's anger and Cyn's contempt. Other times, she hated him so much she could barely breathe.

But that wasn't his fault, not really. So two days later, when she found herself alone on the training plateau with him, she said, "I'm sorry."

Evin glanced at her over his shoulder. They were supposed to be practicing a ward Karyn had taught them that morning, but he was twirling a cloud of colorful sparkles around his hand, stretching and closing his fingers, playing with the ephemeral colors as if they were putty. "About what?"

"The day before yesterday, when you were doing that thing with the colors. I shouldn't have snapped at you." He regarded her through long-lashed dark eyes, and for some reason she felt compelled to add, "I'd just come from talking to Karyn. I was in a bad mood."

He snapped his fingers, and the colors twirled. "Well, that would do it."

Ileni hesitated. But he seemed genuinely unresentful. "Cyn said . . . is Karyn your aunt?"

Something dangerous dropped over his carefree features, then was gone almost before she had noticed it. "Yes. My mother's sister."

Every social grace Ileni possessed was screaming at her to drop this topic. But she was not here to be liked. And she didn't care what Evin thought of her. "I've never seen your mother here."

"No, I would imagine you haven't." He closed his hand,

and the colors coalesced into a tight, swirling ball. "Why does it matter?"

Ileni didn't know why it mattered, but she suspected it did. The assassins were known to kill people as punishment—or warning—for their relatives' actions. And Karyn had infiltrated and attacked the Assassins' Caves.

Evin opened his hands wide, turning the sparkles into many-hued streams. He traced them lazily through the air, forming a series of shimmering curlicues. "It doesn't give me any sort of extra privileges, if that's what you think. Karyn finds me quite a disappointment." He twirled his finger, tightening the colors into a long spiral. "Of course, you agree with her."

"No," Ileni said, utterly unconvincingly. "Where are your parents, then?"

"Dead," Evin said.

He said it lightly, easily, the way he said everything. The colors continued spinning fanciful designs, bright and airy. It had to be a pretense, didn't it? It wasn't possible that even he truly didn't care. Not about this.

But his carefree mask made it easier to push him. "I'm sorry. How did they die?"

Evin dropped his hand, leaving his designs to fade in the

air. His tone remained mild. "This is an odd follow-up to an apology."

Ileni turned briefly to examine the vista of gray stone and blue sky, afraid her face would flush. Impoliteness was surprisingly difficult, even when directed at someone who didn't deserve her respect. "You don't seem very grief-stricken, which among my people would mean—" She couldn't figure out any sensible end to that sentence. "Never mind."

Evin jerked his shoulders, a motion that seemed to have been intended as a shrug. "They chose to put themselves in the path of death, and they didn't care much about me when they made that decision. So it seems only fair for me not to care about them in return. I'm sure you would be above such emotions, since you're in general so much better than everyone here."

"I—" *Hadn't realized I was being obvious about it.* "I don't think I'm better than everyone," she finished weakly.

To her surprise, Evin burst out laughing. "Only than me?"

"I—"

"Oh, come. You might despise me a little more than you do Cyn, but you look down on all of us."

"If you say so." Ileni summoned up a piece of chalk. "I'll be getting back to wards now."

"An excellent idea," Evin said. "Me, too."

His mildness was a goad—a deliberate one. Ileni knew she shouldn't rise to it.

"And what were *you* doing?" she snapped. "Practicing a light show?"

Evin bit his lower lip. Before Ileni could say anything, he nodded slightly and said, "Why don't I show you how else you could use magic?"

"I don't think—"

But he was already kneeling on the stone ground, drawing a series of complex patterns with a piece of chalk he hadn't been holding a second ago. He drew swiftly, with assured, well-practiced strokes, his concentration wholly on the pattern. When he was done, he leaped to his feet and let out a string of syllables, a spell Ileni had never heard before. The words spilled through the air like gurgling water.

For a moment after Evin finished, nothing happened. Then shards of color shot up from the lines he had drawn, bursts of pale green and blue, pink and violet. They scattered into sparks and pale halos, then faded into each other, an intricate design of color and light.

Something inside Ileni rose and fell and shifted with the lights. Despite the complete silence on the plateau, she could almost hear the music the colors were dancing to as they melded and faded and changed.

She couldn't have said how long it went on, the dance becoming faster and faster, the twirls and twines ever more intricate, before the colors burst. A shower of lines and sparkles crisscrossed the air, a million tiny lights making the plateau a mosaic of moving colors.

Even after the final color vanished, Ileni remained frozen, staring at the space where they had been. What robbed her of speech was not so much the display itself—though she had never seen anything so beautiful in her life—but the effort and practice that must have gone into crafting it. Evin's face was flushed and shining, his head tipped back toward the sky.

She had been wrong about him. He wasn't lazy.

He was just uninterested in power.

When Evin caught her looking at him, she didn't look away. Easy strength lay in every line of his body, in the tilt of his chin, in the arch of his eyebrows as he raised them. He had no idea what it meant to be weak, or he wouldn't waste his power on pretty displays.

She hated him, in that moment, more than she ever had.

Evin's eyes shone, but his shoulders went back a bit. His voice was hesitant beneath its typical nonchalance. "What did you think?"

"It was beautiful," Ileni said, and heard the wonder in her voice. She cleared her throat, feeling oddly as if she had lost a sparring match. "And useless."

Evin's broad grin didn't falter. "Exactly the effect I was aiming for."

Ileni crossed her arms over her chest, hoping he couldn't see the awe shivering through her. Her own people didn't waste magic on displays, except during important ceremonies. And there was, of course, no time for pretty pictures in the Assassins' Caves. "A self-portrait, then?"

Evin roared with laughter, spontaneous and unfeigned. He cocked his head to the side. "You're interesting."

The way he said it, she couldn't tell if it was a compliment or an insult. Fortunately, she didn't care.

Interesting. Sorin had thought so, too. But she didn't want to be interesting. Interesting meant that she was different, that she didn't fit anywhere, that she couldn't be part of anything. That there were parts of her that didn't fit together, that rubbed against each other jaggedly, that *hurt.*

She wanted to be like everyone else. For a moment she

didn't even care which *everyone*. Whether in the Academy or the caves, or even back among her own people, she wanted to be whole again, to be moving in the same direction as the people around her, filled with certainty and surrounded by agreement. To be part of a tide, instead of a sinking straggler who had no idea which way she wanted to go, much less how to get there.

CHAPTER 10

The walls of the small cavern were black, but the surface of the mirror was blacker—a darkness so intense it sucked the light out of the small room, making the glowstones flicker and the moon outside the window seem dim as starlight. The two men standing before the mirror did not falter. Neither was afraid of darkness.

"I don't think I have to tell you," Absalm said, "why this is a mistake."

"No," Sorin said curtly. "You do not. Nor do I have to explain to you why you are wrong."

Their eyes met. The chalk pattern on the black floor glowed, subtly but unmistakably.

A muscle jumped beneath Absalm's eye. He drew his lips back, uttered a short phrase, and unleashed magic on the mirror.

The glass surface exploded with color. Absalm closed his eyes, deep lines creasing his brow. Sorin considered taking the opportunity to let out a breath, but chose the safer path. He stood perfectly still while the sorcerer wrestled with the spell.

But for all Sorin's control, when the colors vanished, he leaned forward.

On the other side of the mirror was a colorfully decorated bedroom. There was a window, a wardrobe, and a desk. Otherwise, the room was empty.

Sorin did not straighten. That would have been a bigger mistake than leaning forward in the first place. He examined the room carefully, noting every detail.

"Whose room is it?" Absalm asked. The sorcerer's forehead had smoothed, though it was still beaded with sweat.

"Ileni's," Sorin said shortly.

"How can you be sure?"

Sorin poured scorn into his voice. "We are trained to observe."

And he had been observing Ileni for weeks. A dozen

subtle signs told him it was her room: The blanket shoved carelessly against the wall toward the foot of the bed. The tunic folded carefully but unevenly on the chair. The faint dust that covered both the top of the wardrobe and the dark corners of the floor, but not the wide windowsill.

"It doesn't look like a prison room," Absalm observed.

"No." Sorin's voice was steady. "It does not."

"So she could have contacted you by now. She chose not to. What does that mean?"

Sorin didn't know. For all his scrutiny of Ileni, he had never been able to fully predict what she would do.

A failure in his training, perhaps.

Or perhaps not. The master's voice whispered in his memory: *Never be confident in your knowledge of your enemy. No one, no matter how predictable, can be fully understood.*

Except—the clear implication—by the master himself. Who understood everyone.

Sometimes, Sorin wondered if the master had foreseen his own death. If they were all, still, enmeshed in his plans. It wasn't hard to believe.

Especially since, if it was true, Sorin had no reason to hate Ileni for killing him.

Despite all his training, keeping still was impossible. Sorin spun on his heel and stalked across the room. He wanted to hit the black wall. Ever since the master had died—ever since Ileni had left—the wildness in him had simmered close to the surface, urging him toward unplanned violence.

He could not afford to give in.

He stood for several seconds facing the black rock, fists clenched at his sides. Absalm's gaze jabbed at him, two hot pinpricks beneath his shoulder blades. When Sorin turned, he kept his face impassive.

"Someone needs to go after her," he said.

Absalm drew in a breath. Sorin watched him in complete silence for two, three, four seconds.

"To do what?" Absalm said finally. "Murder is a blunt tool. I can't see what it would accomplish here."

It was meant as a challenge, but fell flat. The balance of power between them shifted subtly but unmistakably in Sorin's favor.

Sorin knelt and, very deliberately, rubbed out a corner of the chalk pattern. Absalm gasped, a small, pained sound. The image of the room in the mirror vanished, and the mirror's surface roiled with dense gray fog.

Sorin straightened, daring the sorcerer to say something. Outside the window, the wind howled and then went still.

"I'm not going to kill anyone. Yet." Sorin walked to the window. Far below, the narrow path curved between the mountains, winding away from the caves. "There are things in the Empire Ileni should know about. Things she should see. And I intend to make sure she sees them."

CHAPTER
II

"Tell me," Karyn said, "about the Renegai."

Ileni sat up slowly in bed. She was almost used to these morning appearances, always before dawn—not just because Karyn was busy, she had realized, but because that was when Ileni was off-guard.

Ileni had a defense against that. Usually she pretended to wake slowly, giving her mind a chance to clear before the interrogation began.

But this morning, she didn't need the extra time. "No."

Karyn lifted her eyebrows, surprise and threat compressed into a single gesture. She leaned back in Ileni's chair and crossed her legs at the ankles. "I beg your pardon?"

"The Renegai are no threat to you." Ileni's fingers dug into her blanket, drawing it up in front of her. "They haven't made a move against you since our exile, and they have too little power and too many scruples to threaten you now. Leave them alone."

"I know they're no threat," Karyn said, and her casual contempt made Ileni curl her fingers tighter. "I was thinking, however, that they might be an ally."

The blanket dropped back over Ileni's legs with a tiny swoosh.

Karyn tapped a finger against the armrest. "You must have realized, by now, that the Empire has changed since the time when we drove your people into exile. Perhaps it's time for a reconciliation."

Her calm assurance made it hard for Ileni to find words. Finally she sputtered, "Why would they *want* a reconciliation?"

Karyn's eyebrows, which had never come down, arched even higher. Her feet thudded on the floor as she leaned forward. "Why wouldn't they?"

Growing up, Ileni and her friends had told tales of sacrifice and heroism under the Empire's evil reign, spat when they spoke of the Imperial Academy of Sorcery, fantasized about ways to destroy it. It was oddly disheartening to realize the imperial sorcerers had no idea how much they were hated.

"They're fine as they are," Ileni said finally. And it was true; in exile, her people could stay true to their ideals, far from the messy complexities of the world they had left. As she had been when she lived in the Renegai compound, surrounded by people who thought exactly like her, knowing she was on the right side of . . . of everything, really. Sometimes, she had guiltily suspected their cause might be hopeless. But she had never doubted it was just.

She missed being that person. She missed living a life where everything was simple and clear. Even if that simplicity had been a lie—and she wasn't entirely convinced it had been—it was a lie she missed living in.

Ileni had grown up wanting the exile to end, for the Empire to be defeated. And wishing for it had been far, far better than getting the chance to do it.

"Leave them alone," she said again. "They have nothing to do with any of this."

Karyn's shoulder lifted, an airy shrug that reminded Ileni of Evin. "So you're willing to betray the new master of the assassins, but not the people who abandoned you and sent you to your death? Interesting."

Ileni shoved the blanket to the wall and swung her legs over the side of the bed.

"How," she said, "did you know there was a new master of the assassins?"

Karyn froze for a fraction of a second. Then she straightened in the chair, resting both hands carefully on the armrests. "I know you're trying to be careful, but you're an amateur. You've betrayed more than you thought."

"No," Ileni said firmly. Of this she was sure: she remembered every single word she had said to Karyn about Sorin. "No, I didn't. So how did you know?"

"I'll tell you," Karyn said, "when you're on our side."

She was so smug, so sure, that Ileni's mouth opened to protest. Silence felt like acquiescence, like the first step toward defeat. If she didn't deny it out loud, Karyn's certainty would seep into her mind and settle there. Ileni's eventual betrayal would start seeming inevitable, even to her.

But it was only Karyn's certainty—her arrogant, superior assumptions—that was allowing Ileni to remain in the Academy. So Ileni kept her mouth shut, biting the insides of her lips, until Karyn said, "Now. I have some more questions about the wards. . . ."

◉ ◉ ◉

Are you willing to betray the new master of the assassins? Sorin asked.

He stood behind her, one hand sliding along her waist, the other resting on her wrist. She held a throwing dagger in her hand.

I love you, Ileni whispered. Her heart pounded, and she couldn't tell if it was because he was about to kiss her, or because he was about to wrest the dagger from her and lay it against her throat.

I love you, too. His fingers slid along her wrist, and then the dagger was in his hand, so fast she didn't have a chance to tighten her grip. He whirled her around to face him, and as his mouth came down on hers, she heard the thunk of the dagger hitting the cloth target behind her.

When he pushed her away, she clung to him blindly. It didn't matter, of course, not against his strength. He held her in front of him, eyes black and blazing.

Betray me, he whispered, before pulling her in and kissing her again, or don't. But make a decision before it's too late.

Ileni woke with her heart pounding, her stomach clenched tight. She doubled over in her bed, not sure whether she was going to cry or puke or both.

She waited for several minutes before she realized that she was going to do neither. Instead, she threw her blanket against the wall and pulled the wardrobe doors open with a surge of angry power. They flew apart with a clash, and she yanked out the first dress she saw. It snagged on the edge of a door and ripped, a jagged tear across the seam of its neckline.

Calm down. She managed to get the next dress across the room intact but didn't bother with changing its size. It shifted loosely across her shoulders as she hurried out of her room.

The halls were unusually busy—she had overslept—but Ileni had to ask four students before she found one who knew Arxis. The student, a plump girl with mint-green hair, nodded. "Arxis? He's in the beginner's class."

"Right. Can you take me there?"

The girl gave her one of those looks Ileni was becoming used to. She had asked something stupid, missed something obvious. Revealed yet again how vastly ignorant she was.

"All right," the girl said finally. "This way."

She led Ileni through a curving corridor to the top of a spiral staircase, then gestured curtly at the stairs and walked away.

The stairs wound their way down a narrow column inside the mountain and ended in a large cavern, walls studded with a mix of glowstones. A dozen students stood in the center of the cavern, in a circle around a tall man holding up a lodestone while demonstrating a spell. Arxis looked exactly like the other students, right down to his rigid posture and the attentive angle of his jaw.

Ileni settled on the base of the bottom step, jiggling her foot against the stone floor. The instructor was running through a fairly simple sound-enhancing spell, one every Renegai sorcerer perfected by the age of five. Ileni had figured it out at the age of two and a half. It had been the earliest sign of her great potential.

When it was the students' turn to attempt the spell, half of them fumbled it, and one managed to make herself deaf—Ileni felt that spell going wrong and winced, but remained where she was, hidden in the dimness of the stairwell. Arxis was one of the students who failed, but as the spell fizzled out around him, he looked over his shoulder directly at Ileni.

She should have realized he would know she was there. Giving in to her escalating impatience, Ileni got to her feet and walked into the cavern.

The instructor held up a hand to silence the students. He had a gaunt, dark face, with white markings coiling up his right cheek.

"I need to speak to Arxis," Ileni said.

She had no idea how he would react—among the

Renegai, interrupting a lesson would have earned her at least an evening of kitchen duty, and in the caves it might have gotten her killed. But the instructor just nodded. "Take it outside."

They walked in silence until almost the top of the spiral staircase, where Arxis stopped. The threat in his stance made Ileni pull her power in tighter, readying it for a spell.

Arxis's voice was flat. "Coming here wasn't particularly discreet. You're an advanced student. You're supposed to ignore me."

"Like Evin does?" *Like Lis does?* she almost added, but didn't quite dare.

"Everyone knows Evin doesn't care about his status. That doesn't mean I can rub shoulders with all of you. I am trying *not* to stand out, you know."

"Your secrets are not my concern," Ileni retorted, keeping her voice low. Even with the sound-enhancing spells, the students in the cavern below shouldn't be able to hear them, but there was no point in taking chances. Well. Unnecessary chances. "I need you to take me to the source of the lodestones. Now."

Arxis stepped up one stair. "I thought we discussed this. You have four days left."

She had to crane her neck to look up at him, which she didn't like; but he was standing in the middle of the stair, so she couldn't step up without pushing him out of the way. Or *trying* to push him out of the way.

"Take me," she said, "or I'll expose you."

"Will you, indeed?"

"Yes."

Arxis leaned against the wall. "And yet I could keep you from exposing me—or annoying me—in just a second, couldn't I? I could make it look like a fall. Or an accident. I could be far away by the time they found you. Do you believe me?"

She did. Ileni stepped up next to him on the stairs. "Then why are you talking about it, instead of doing it?"

Back when she had entered the Assassins' Caves, she had managed to say things like that without the slightest tremor. But somewhere in the interim, she had started to care again whether she lived.

That was going to be very inconvenient.

Arxis's lip curled. "I'm still making up my mind."

His eyes were cold and ruthless and familiar. She had been surrounded by eyes like that not so long ago. A primal fear rose in her: *Irun's hand pressing her face against the blanket. The gag in her mouth. The blade against her throat.* She reached for the magic within herself, pulling it all recklessly into a ward, but it wouldn't be enough. The assassins knew how to kill sorcerers now.

Her voice still emerged cool. Later, she would be impressed with herself. "The master will be quite unhappy with you if you do."

Because she was used to assassins, she saw the tiny tic in his cheek. "I don't believe you."

"Why not? I am also part of the master's plan. You're an assassin on a mission—nothing unusual about you. *I* am far more important than that."

Arxis grabbed her arm, so fast she didn't have time to block him with a spell. His breath was hot and sour on her face. "Why would the master send you without telling you about the assets we already have here?"

His fingers squeezed painfully against the bones of her wrist. She lifted her chin. "Who knows why the master does anything?"

He laughed, short and harsh, and released her. Ileni pitched backward—she had been pulling back without realizing it—and slammed her arm against the stone wall to steady herself.

"True enough," Arxis said. "Maybe he was testing you. And maybe you failed."

Maybe I killed him. "All interesting possibilities. Here's another: maybe you're the one failing, right now. *A plan you won't change is a plan that will get you killed.*"

It was one of the master's sayings—one she had heard from Sorin—and she heard her voice drop into the rhythmic, reverent tone he always used when quoting the master. Arxis heard it, too. He regarded her intently.

"All right," he said finally. "Tomorrow morning. I'll arrange to go into the city with Evin. Get yourself invited along. After that, you *stop interfering* with me. Because if you prevent me from fulfilling my mission, I truly will kill you."

He strode down the stairs, brushing hard against her—deliberately, she was sure; in all her time in the caves, she had never seen an assassin make a clumsy move. She couldn't help shrinking away, even though she knew it was what he wanted. He could kill her as easily as he breathed.

But he probably wouldn't. Not as long as he thought they were on the same side.

Which, she reminded herself, they very well might be.

CHAPTER 12

The next morning at breakfast, Ileni tried to figure out how to get Evin to invite her to the city. This endeavor was complicated by two factors: one, that Evin wasn't saying anything about going to the city, and two, that he wasn't saying anything to *her*. His remarks, which were solely about the food, were directed at Lis. Lis was in one of her rare good moods, which seemed to often follow close on the heels of her truly horrible ones (or upon Arxis's visits to her room? Ileni tried not to think about that). Evin was teasing her because she was already on her third bowl of spiced lentils.

"Don't look so intense," Cyn said, and Ileni blinked at

her. "I'm going to be your only sparring partner today, and I find it intimidating."

Ileni tried not to appear pleased. It had been a long time since anyone had been intimidated by her. And here was her opportunity, practically dropped into her lap. *Thank you,* she thought at Cyn, before saying, as casually as she could, "Why will I be your only partner?"

"And now you're overwhelming me with your enthusiasm." Cyn propped one leg up on the bench. "Lis is . . . busy. And Evin's going into the city with Arxis."

Ileni looked at Evin—*calm, mild interest,* she coached herself—who shrugged. "Arxis has business in the Merchants' Triangle. He needs someone to show him around."

"Can I come with you?" Ileni said.

Everyone stopped in mid-motion and stared at her.

"I've never seen a city," Ileni added, and watched Cyn's suspicion fade into superiority. "I was thinking I'd like to."

"Sure." Evin shrugged and took another bite of fruit. "Cyn, you get the fun task of explaining to Karyn why we're not at practice."

"Don't expect me to try too hard," Cyn said. She pushed her bowl away. "By which I mean, at all."

"Why don't you talk to Karyn before you go?" Lis said.

There was something smug and knowing in her expression; even when she was in a good mood, Lis always managed to be irritating. "I'm sure she'll permit it. And then *you* get the job of keeping Ileni and Arxis from killing each other on the way down."

"I am," Evin said, "almost sure I am up to the task."

Ileni fought to keep her face calm. Everyone was still convinced that she and Arxis had been in a torrid, dramatic relationship. Ileni wondered if Lis thought so, too, if she saw Ileni as some sort of rival for Arxis's affections.

It would have been funny, if its conclusion hadn't been so inevitably tragic. Eventually, everyone would know Arxis's true, terrible purpose here. And then they would realize that Ileni had known it all along and kept it hidden.

Lis laughed, softly, as if she was the only one in the room who understood the joke. "If Karyn is letting *you* go, Evin, she'll let anyone go."

"I didn't say she *let* me go, precisely." Evin swung his legs over the bench. "But I bet she will. She's probably in the Mirror Chamber now."

"Wait—" Ileni began. But Evin was already halfway to the door, and she wasn't sure what she had been going to say anyhow.

Arxis was waiting for them outside, standing close to the outer edge of the path, with the same careless lack of concern the advanced sorcerers showed—even though he, surely, didn't have enough skill to fly. But a trained assassin would never fall. He glanced at Ileni with cool disinterest.

"Slight detour," Evin said. "Ileni wants to come, so we have to check with Karyn."

Arxis blinked. "I thought the idea was to avoid Karyn."

A faint pink touched Evin's cheekbones. Ileni hadn't realized he was changing his plan so she could come, and judging by the irritated look he shot Arxis, he would have preferred that she didn't know. "Ileni's a bit new to be breaking rules the way I do. But I'm sure Karyn will say yes."

"Are you?" Arxis stared hard at Ileni, then stretched his arms over his head, a sinuous, almost feline movement. "Let's go, then."

The two young men strode along the ledge. Ileni followed at her own cautious pace. When she finally caught up to them, they were waiting for her at a stone door in the interior of the mountain—Arxis with exaggerated patience, and Evin, as usual, looking like he had nothing better to do.

Ileni felt the by-now familiar shrinking in her stomach.

Once she had been in the lead, not the one holding everyone back.

"Ready?" Arxis drawled, and pushed the door open.

The cavern inside was a perfect octagon, each side covered by a large mirror—but the mirrors didn't reflect Karyn, who was turning in a slow circle in the center of the room. In one, a bald woman wearing blue robes sat with her hands folded in front of her. In another, a city was in flames, red fire and black smoke bursting within the glass. In a third, a mob rampaged through a marble building, mouths open in screams that couldn't be heard through the glass. In the other mirrors, a pair of riders raced across a desert on black horses, a family of giant serpents curled around each other on a large gray rock, and a ship sailed peacefully on a surface of vast blue water flecked with white.

Karyn glared at them over her shoulder, and Evin and Ileni stopped in mid-step, simultaneously and automatically. Arxis took one step forward and stopped a fraction before he entered the room, with precise, almost unnatural control. The move would have given his identity away to anyone who had spent time among assassins. Ileni glanced quickly at Karyn, but the sorceress didn't seem to have noticed.

Karyn turned her back on them, focusing on the

blue-robed woman. "Send the fifth section of fourth-levels to Siandar," she said crisply. "The serpents will have to wait, for now, and I will send Cyn to Askarli to quell the riot."

The woman in the blue robe nodded. "Will you send someone to court?"

Karyn swiveled and focused on one of the mirrors near the door. "No. I can't spare anyone. Once a new high sorcerer is appointed, I'll send a delegation."

The blue-robed woman nodded, bowed her head, and disappeared. Her image was replaced by the view of a snow-speckled forest.

Evin stepped calmly into the room, and Ileni followed. From inside, she could see the mirrors nearest the door. One showed what must have been a battlefield, round tents stretched across a grassy plain. The other revealed a vast throne room, where hundreds of men and women in elaborately layered robes milled about in front of a throne. On the throne sat a tall, black-haired man, wearing a crown and a bored expression.

The emperor. He had been a figure in songs for so long it was difficult, even staring right at him, to think of him as a real person. He was more imposing than she would have thought. Since long before the exile, the emperor had been ruler in name only, dependent upon the Academy and its sorcerers for his pretense of power.

Evin cleared his throat. "Excuse me. Ileni requests permission to go to the city with us."

Everyone seemed to want to stare menacingly at Ileni today. She met Karyn's glare with the same unmoved calm she had used on Arxis. Finally the sorceress shrugged one shoulder and said, "You have my permission."

Too easy, that familiar voice warned. Ileni nodded. "Thank you."

But Karyn had already dismissed her and was focused on Evin. Ileni wasn't sure whether she was trying to intimidate *him,* too, or whether that was just leftover menace. "And you?"

Evin bent his head humbly. "May I please have permission, too, Gracious One?"

Karyn folded her arms over her chest. "Will you see your brother?"

"Yes," Evin said, keeping his head bowed.

"Why don't you bring him back with you for a visit? It's past time—"

"Of course," Evin said, lifting his head.

Karyn narrowed her eyes. "Good. Bring him to me when you get back."

Once they were back on the ledge outside the mountain, the sky vast and blue above them, Arxis asked, "Did you mean it? Girad will be coming back with us?"

"No," Evin said flatly. "But whatever excuses I would have made now will be far more effective later, when it's too late for her to argue."

"She's going to be furious," Arxis said.

"My, you are a bearer of great wisdom. Tell me, which way *is* the city? Up or—"

Arxis shoved him—a little too forcefully, a little too close to the edge—and every muscle in Ileni's body tensed. But Evin just laughed and shoved back.

You're walking with two people who might kill you, Ileni thought at him.

He glanced back at her, as if feeling the force of her gaze, and she looked quickly away. She wasn't sure what he might read on her face.

CHAPTER
13

The city started before the mountain ended, wooden huts and streets clinging to the slopes, harried-looking men carrying gigantic packs up narrow stairways. Within two minutes, Ileni had seen more people—and more different types of people—than in her entire seventeen years of life. She did her best not to gawk, aware that both Evin and Arxis were watching her.

But when they finally got to level land, she couldn't help herself. The city stretched ahead of them, a warren of streets and alleyways, weathered stone and iron rails, and *people*. Most of them were walking calmly down the streets, turning into the narrow alleyways, hair streaming behind them in the breeze, or cropped short, or wrapped in colorful kerchiefs. All around her conversation hummed, and it took her a moment to realize, through the cacophony, that much of it was in a language—or languages—she didn't understand.

A man ran in front of her pushing a large wheeled crate, shouting at the top of his lungs, as if the noise itself would blast any obstacles out of his way. Ileni stopped short.

The vastness of the city spilled over her, making her feel small. It made everything she had ever known feel small. How tiny and insignificant her people really were, and how peculiar her life would seem to these masses. Even if she had fulfilled her destiny and become the greatest leader the Renegai had ever known, she still would have been nothing and no one to any of the hundreds of people milling in the streets in front of her.

Evin cleared his throat. Ileni glanced at him sideways and saw that he was watching her. Arxis was watching her, too, and a shiver ran through her. The assassins were even fewer in number than the Renegai, yet probably every person in this city had heard of *them*.

"Impressive, isn't it?" Evin said.

Ileni tried to compose her face, aware that she was failing miserably. But he didn't look smug. He looked . . . proud. Like it meant something to him that she was impressed. Like the Empire was a work of art for him to show off.

"Yes," she managed, and his cheeks creased sharply as he grinned at her.

"It's not even the biggest city in the Empire," Arxis added. *He* was definitely smug.

Ileni pulled her gaze from Evin's, reminding herself that the Empire was held together by the Academy, and the Academy's fate lay in her hands. It helped. She straightened and said, "How far is the Merchants' Triangle?"

"Not far," Evin said, which was a singularly unhelpful answer. "But let's go to the Black Sisters first."

They walked through the crowded streets, passing so many people that Ileni couldn't focus on any of them. A few caught her attention briefly—a woman taller than she had realized people could be, a nearly naked man with elaborate blue tattoos wreathing over his body, a child with his ears stretched long by dangling coils of gold. Small, bright green birds whizzed occasionally through the street, veering around unconcerned people, leaking magic from every feather. Neither Evin nor Arxis seemed to find any of this unusual, and every time Ileni opened her mouth to ask a question, a combination of shame and despair made her shut it again.

They turned a corner, and Evin swerved to lead them around a group of ragged children. One, a boy no older than eight, watched them with surly fury. But his anger shone only out of one eye; beneath a dirty lock of ragged hair, his other eye was sealed shut, covered with red and brown pus.

"Keep walking," Evin said, not lowering his voice. "Give them half a chance and they'll rob you blind."

The boy made a rude gesture at them, somewhat hindered by the fact that he had only one hand. His left arm ended in a stump, the skin smooth and round.

Sorin's voice in her mind. She could still remember his exact words, his flat, emotionless tone—back then, she still hadn't been able to read his expressions. *That's the punishment for theft all through the Empire, no matter the age of the thief.*

She almost stopped. Instead she quickened her pace, so that she was right beside Evin.

"Who are they?" she asked.

Her voice was tight with anger, but Evin didn't slow down. "Abandoned children, probably. Or runaways."

He said it the way he would have answered a question

about what was for dinner. And he hadn't spared the children a second glance.

Sorin had been a boy like that once. Ileni dug her fingers into the side of her leg. "Shouldn't someone help them?"

Arxis snorted. "Feel free to be that someone."

"These children are all over the city," Evin said. "There's nothing to be done."

Ileni sucked in her breath. "It must make life easier," she said bitingly, "when you just *accept* everything in it."

"It does." Evin gave her a sideways nod, as if pleased that she'd understood.

A week ago, she might have dropped it, with perhaps a snort at his perpetual laziness. She clenched her hands until they hurt. "There must be something to be done. You— *you*—could make a difference, if you really wanted to. But you'd rather play with lights and colors. I understand."

Evin smiled, but there was something hard in it. "No, Ileni. I don't think you do."

Evin was dangerous, of course—he must be, with the amount of power he possessed—yet she had never, until this moment, thought of him that way. It was an oddly disconcerting realization, even though she was thoroughly accustomed to dangerous people by now. Ileni covered her confusion with a sneer. "What, do you have hidden depths and secret plans?"

He laughed aloud, and the edge vanished, replaced by his perpetual amusement. "If it comforts you to think so, far be it from me to deny it. I have great and noble ambitions. I want to save the world."

And for a moment, she felt as he did: that it was a ridiculous thing to want.

Her breath rasped painfully through her chest. She faced forward and strode ahead.

After some indeterminate amount of time—long enough for Ileni's calves to start aching—the streets widened again, and the press of people thinned out. Another sound became audible through the buzz of conversation and footsteps: a rushing, rhythmic murmur. It sounded like a waterfall, but controlled and regular, almost musical.

Ileni struggled with herself for a moment—she was so tired of the condescending looks her questions always elicited—but curiosity won out. "What's that?"

The corners of Evin's lips curled up. "You'll see."

"Or you could just—" Ileni began, then stopped. Behind Evin, a wiry figure darted between two buildings and out of sight.

She stood frozen, staring at the space between the buildings. An ornate, heavily warded carriage pulled in front of the spot where the figure had disappeared, then rolled on. The space was dark and still. If someone was lurking within it, she couldn't tell.

"I know you're not familiar with our customs," Arxis said. "But if you want to stop and stare at nothing, the middle of the street is not the best place to do it."

Ileni tried to breathe. There were plenty of thin young men in the capital. There might be some who moved with that sinuous grace. She had only seen that sort of swift, flowing movement among the assassins; but obviously, she hadn't seen much in her life.

And she had been daydreaming about Sorin so often, it was no wonder she was imagining glimpses of him.

Arxis was leaning back, watching the street. If he had seen anything, he was hiding it well. Of course, if he had seen anything, he *would* be hiding it well.

"Sorry," Ileni muttered, and started walking again. She looked around carefully as they made their way down the street, less overwhelmed by the sheer number of people now that she was looking for a single one. But she saw no hint of that familiar form, that swift liquid movement.

When Evin stopped in front of a high black wall surrounding some sort of compound, she forced herself to stop looking. It probably hadn't been Sorin at all. And she should be glad it wasn't—it would mean nothing good if Sorin was here.

She wanted to see him so badly she didn't care.

Evin put one hand on the black wall and murmured a short spell. A surge of power almost knocked Ileni over, and then the wall shimmered and vanished, and she could see right through it to the source of the rushing sound.

All thoughts of Sorin fled her mind as she gaped. Arcs of white spray rose from a flat pool of black water, twisting back and forth in sync with each other, swaying and rising and falling. White mist rose to fill the spaces between the columns of water, and then vanished, in perfect harmony.

"Beautiful, isn't it?" Evin said.

"Yes," Ileni breathed. "How—"

"It was made back in the days of conquest, when we took power from captured enemies. They say the high sorceress killed ten thousand enemy soldiers to create these fountains."

She blinked at him, then at the water, so clear and elegant. And still so beautiful.

She remembered the cavern of stone pillars in the

Assassins' Caves, and the Elders' warning: *Parts of the caves are very beautiful, but don't let that distract you from the evil within them.*

"Back in the days?" she said finally. "So you don't do it anymore?"

Evin gave her a horrified look, which made her bristle. "It wasn't our proudest moment. That particular high sorceress was somewhat . . . excessive."

"And also," Arxis said, "they ran out of captured enemies. One of the downsides of having conquered almost everything in sight."

Ileni glanced at him, startled; that seemed like an unwise thing to say. But Evin, of course, just laughed. As Arxis must have known he would.

"What is this place?" Ileni said.

"A home for orphans." Evin gestured at the bland, dust-colored stone building behind the dancing fountains. "The Sisters of the Black God run it."

How many colors of gods were there? Once again, Ileni was overwhelmed by how much she didn't know. The compound was large, but at least half of it was taken up by the fountains. That building couldn't possibly hold all the orphans in the city. How did they decide who got to live in it and who ended up starving on the street?

"All right," Evin said. "If you want, I can meet you—"

A wordless shriek pierced the fountain's music, and a tiny form barreled past the water and threw itself at Evin.

Ileni flung out an instinctive shield, using much of the magic she had pulled in before they left. The shield shot across the space between her and Evin, shimmering white, and enveloped a . . . child. A small, broad-cheeked, brown-haired boy, who struggled for a moment, with his arms and legs thrashing, then shouted an insult and repelled the spell back at her.

The backlash sent Ileni staggering into the street. She collided with a large man, who swore in a language she didn't recognize and shoved her. Still dizzy, Ileni pitched onto the cobblestones, landing on her hands and knees.

Arxis laughed, longer and harder than was really necessary. So did a couple of passersby. Suddenly, being an unknown didn't seem like quite such a terrible fate. Ileni scrambled to her feet, cheeks burning.

The boy who had undone her spell was on his feet, glaring at her. He looked almost exactly like Evin: deep brown eyes, jutting chin, unruly tufts of hair, all in a rounder, softer, smaller version of Evin's face. The main difference was the complete seriousness with which he stared her down.

Ileni tried to think of something to say and came up with nothing better than, "I'm sorry."

The boy glared at her. He couldn't have been older than five or six. "You're not supposed to use magic on people for no reason."

"I thought you were . . . uh . . . attacking Evin."

She braced herself for a *why?* that she would have no answer for. Instead the boy tilted his head to the side and said, "I wasn't. *This* time."

"Er—" Ileni said.

"He didn't hurt me, so I won't hurt him."

"Don't be so sure you *could* hurt me," Evin said, grinning. "Training matters more than raw power, Girad."

"Got it," Arxis said. "You can hurt him more than he can hurt you. Probably. Now, if we can move past this tender brotherly moment—"

Evin's hand closed around Girad's, and the little boy screwed up his face. "Is *she* coming with us?"

"I expect not," Evin said. "I think you scared her off."

Girad threw his head back and laughed. It was so like Evin that Ileni blinked, but there was something different in the pure delight that pealed from him, in the unself-conscious glee on his face. She had thought Evin was completely carefree, but she had been wrong. *This* was what carefree looked like.

Girad's laugh trailed off into a series of uncontrollable giggles. Evin tousled his hair.

Ileni transferred her gaze to Arxis, who was watching Evin and Girad with patient boredom. When he caught her stare, he returned it blankly, as if he had no idea what she wanted from him.

Irritation prickled Ileni. But he had promised to show her the lodestones' source, not to be nice about it. "I'd like to see the Merchants' Triangle," she said. "Will you take me?"

"No," Arxis said.

"What?"

"Find your own way. Just head straight into the city, away from the mountains. You can't miss it."

Ileni stared at him incredulously. Evin cleared his throat. "She's never been here before, Arxis. Maybe you should—"

"She's meeting someone at the Triangle," Arxis said.

"What?" Ileni said again.

"An old friend. I saw him earlier, and I suspect he might be interested in seeing you." His eyes bored into hers.

The lithe, graceful figure disappearing behind a building. *If you need me, I will come.* Ileni drew in her breath.

Reluctantly, Evin said, "I suppose I can take you—"

"No," Ileni said. "I can find my way."

Evin frowned. "I don't want you to get lost. Parts of the city are dangerous."

"*I'm* dangerous," Ileni said. "And I won't get lost. I'll be fine."

The gleam in Evin's eyes reminded her of Sorin, when she had surprised and impressed him. The difference was that she didn't care what Evin thought.

But she wanted to see that expression on Sorin's face again.

"If you're sure . . ." Evin looked back at his brother.

"I am," Ileni said firmly, but she had the distinct sense that he was no longer listening.

Arxis, Evin, and Girad strolled away, around the dancing fountains and toward the stone building. Only then did it occur to Ileni that if this *was* a trap, it might not be for her.

But Arxis and Evin did things together all the time. If Evin was Arxis's target, there was no reason to think today was the day he would die.

Or if it was, that there was anything she could do to stop it.

Ileni turned on her heel and strode down the street.

When she glanced back, neither Evin nor Arxis was anywhere in sight, and the black walls were back in place.

Heading "straight into the city" turned out to be less simple than it sounded. The city was a maze of streets, and not one of them was straight. Ileni walked somewhat randomly, counting on Sorin to find her, keeping track of her twists and turns so at least she would be able to find her way back. She had once done the same in the labyrinthine Assassins' Caves, in dark, narrow passageways far more convoluted than these crowded streets. She had done it alone and she had done it with Sorin at her side, his hand barely brushing hers, his feet soft and silent on the rock.

When she came across a small garden, flowering bushes spilling over colorful rocks, it seemed as good a place as any to be found. She took a seat on the single narrow bench, closed her eyes, and began practicing the lead-up to one of the spells Cyn had shown her last week.

She didn't hear him coming, but the bench shifted slightly as he settled beside her. She forced herself to finish the mental exercise, layering its even, flowing rhythm over her racing pulse, and then she opened her eyes and said, "Don't think I'm not happy to see you. But you shouldn't be here."

The young man on the bench smiled at her, the expression making his round cheeks puff out, his face flushing to match his auburn hair.

"There is no place an assassin shouldn't be," Bazel said. "You of all people should know that by now."

CHAPTER 14

Ileni's heart froze, then went on beating, loud and slow. She could hear it, an echo in her head, overwhelming the silence on the bench.

It was a moment before she recovered her voice enough to say . . . what? She had to speak, to cover up the disappointment that must be burned into her face, to say anything other than, *I thought you were Sorin.*

What an idiot she was.

"I could tell people what you are," she managed finally, in an almost steady voice. "I could scream *assassin* right now."

"You could. I don't think you will."

"Are you sure?" Ileni said. "Don't forget, you tried to *kill* me."

"It was necessary at the time. But I'm not trying to kill you anymore."

"I'm so glad." Her disappointment ebbed slowly away, and rage rushed in to replace it. She remembered lying trapped on the bed, her finger broken, choking on the thick gag. "I can't say the same."

Bazel shrugged. "When it comes to killing, you're an amateur. I'm not surprised you would take it personally."

She remembered driving the knife into Irun's back. The moment she had realized how easy it was to take someone's life, and how little separated her from the killers around her.

Bazel was one of those killers. Yet here he was, trading barbs with her on a park bench. Bazel might be the least competent of the assassins, but he still knew a dozen ways to murder her before she could move. And all the assassins now knew it was possible to kill a sorceress. Someone must have ordered him not to.

It wasn't hard to guess who. *Sorin.*

"Of course," Bazel added, "if you *do* reveal my identity, I'll have to tell your new sorcerer friends all about it. About the time you spent in our caves helping us learn to kill them.

About your skulking in dark corners with our new leader."

Ileni flushed. "Why are you here, Bazel? Who are you on a mission to kill, since it's obviously not me?"

Bazel got to his feet, like a snake uncoiling. "Surprised, are you? I'm sure you thought I would never leave the caves."

She had, and for good reason. The thread of pride in his voice made her stomach twist, and the way he loomed over her made her intensely aware of his physical presence and strength. Once again she felt Irun's hand on the back of her head, the sudden pain and the gush of blood. . . .

She closed her eyes as the garden whirled around her. It had been Bazel's fault, but he hadn't been the one to slash her throat. That had been Irun, and she had killed Irun, with far less magic than she had right now.

"Nobody thought you would leave the caves." She said it scornfully, to remind herself that she didn't have to be afraid. She opened her eyes in time to see fury flare on Bazel's face. Oddly, that made her braver. "And frankly, I didn't think Sorin would ever let you leave alive."

"Our new master—" said with a tinge of bitterness—"is not about to waste an assassin for the sake of an infatuation. We are too valuable for that. Even I am."

Infatuation was his way of striking back. Ileni dug her

fingernails into the bottom of the bench. "But if this involves me, it's a rather important mission. Why would Sorin choose *you*?"

His jaw pulsed—a movement so slight that no one but she, who had spent weeks among assassins, would have noticed it. He said tightly, "Sorin designed the mission. Absalm is the one who chose to send me."

"Was he trying to get you out of the caves before Sorin killed you?"

Bazel leaned over, placing both hands on the back of the bench, on either side of her. Ileni cringed away from him despite herself. "You *killed* the *master*. Do you think Sorin could get away with punishing me for trying to kill *you*? The last thing he can afford is to reveal how much his obsession with you is skewing his judgment."

Despite the fear roiling through her, Ileni couldn't help a surge of satisfaction. So much for *infatuation*. "He's just biding his time, then, before he makes you pay."

Bazel leaned closer. She turned her head to the side, and his breath wafted hot against her cheek, stirring stray strands of hair. "Don't count on him. He might be the new master in name, but he's made mistakes. He's not powerful enough to pursue vengeance."

Ileni pressed against the bench so hard that tiny splinters dug into her back. She shifted sideways, then lifted her chin and looked Bazel straight in the eye. "Yet."

Bazel's jaw clenched. He straightened. "I'm here to show you something. Come with me."

Ileni remained seated. "Come with you where?"

"My mission is to show you, not tell you. Come."

Ileni bit her lip. But if he wanted to kill her, he would have done it before she had time to get suspicious. Besides, Sorin would not have ordered him to do anything that could cause her harm.

She was almost completely certain of that. Which was certain enough to get her off the bench when Bazel walked away.

"How did Arxis know you would find me?" she said as he led her down a long, slanted street and through a crowded market.

Bazel didn't react.

"Now that Sorin is your leader," Ileni said pointedly, "you might want to start being a little nicer to me."

He turned fully to face her, stopping in the middle of the street. "Why? It's not exactly your *opinion* he values."

Ileni's skin shrank inward at the scorn in his voice.

She couldn't even deny it. Her opinions had never had the slightest impact on Sorin's firm, clear faith.

"He'll kill you if I ask him to," she said finally.

"Are you going to ask him to?"

He waited until it was clear she had nothing to say, then strode forward.

At the end of the street, Bazel turned down a wide set of stairs that descended to an alley below. Paper and debris littered the steps, and signs inked with symbols Ileni didn't recognize hung crookedly on the stone walls. By then, Ileni had thought things through, and she hesitated before following. Bazel must know he would never be safe from Sorin . . . assassins could be very patient, but they never gave up. Which meant Bazel's loyalty—to the extent he had any—was to Absalm, not Sorin.

But Absalm didn't want Ileni dead, either. Not when he had been molding her for more than a decade. She was too valuable.

She hurried to catch up. They crossed the alley at the bottom of the stairs and continued down yet another stairway to the next street, and then the next. A line of guards wearing lodestone bracelets crossed in front of them, and Bazel paused, waiting for them to pass with apparent unconcern.

Four streets later, Ileni's knees hurt, and the stairways had grown noticeably rougher, with cracks and loose stones that forced her to pay close attention to her footing. Halfway down the fifth flight of stairs, a large crate leaned against a wall, cutting the width of the steps in half. An old man huddled against the crate, wrapped in a bundle of foul-smelling rags. He watched them pass with pus-filled eyes.

How much longer? would sound like an admission of weakness. But maybe *Is this where we're going* . . . yes, she could say that. Ileni cleared her throat, but just then Bazel stopped short. He gestured at a narrow brown door in the stone building on their right.

"Side entrance," he explained.

Well, that cleared everything right up. Still determined to show no hesitation, Ileni placed the flat of one hand on the door and pushed. The door didn't budge.

She reached for magic, then stopped herself. This far from the Academy, there were no lodestones she could use to replenish her power. Impressing Bazel was not worth the risk of being left defenseless.

"After you," she said.

Bazel reached under his tunic and pulled out a thin metal wire. After a few seconds of swift, silent work, the door swung open, revealing yet more stairs, narrow and dim.

"Not that I haven't enjoyed all the mystery and drama," Ileni said, "but I'm not following you down there until you tell me where we're going."

"Death's Door," Bazel said.

"Excuse me?"

"Don't blame me; that's what they call it. It is over-dramatic, I agree." He stepped through the door. "It's a sickhouse."

"Then why—"

But he was already halfway down the stairs, moving without making a sound.

Ileni hesitated. The wise move would be to turn around and make her way back to the upper part of the city. She had followed Bazel through unknown passageways before, and that had not ended well.

She started down the stairs.

He was waiting for her at the bottom. By then her eyes had adjusted to the near darkness, so she saw at once he had been telling the truth: this *was* a sickhouse. A large square room stretched in front of her, lined with cots and filled with a thick, sour smell. Most of the figures in the cots were unmoving, lumps under blankets, but a few tossed and turned, and enough of them were moaning to make the air quaver discordantly.

Ileni's stomach twisted, shaming her. She had never been drawn to healing, the most important magic of all. Sick people made her feel slightly ill herself. And she had never seen this many sick people in one place before.

She glanced sideways at Bazel, and caught his expression a moment before it slid off his face—a faint grimace that matched her own unease. Bazel, too, was uncomfortable around this much illness. This much *weakness*.

She squared her shoulders. "What's important about—"

Bazel put a finger to her lips. Ileni jerked away from his touch and rubbed the back of her hand against her mouth. Bazel smirked.

Somehow, that smirk—its assurance, its superiority— was the last straw. He was acting like she was still powerless, like she was someone to be toyed with. He didn't know what she had learned over the past two weeks.

Ileni coiled her power within her, flicking her fingers in the beginning patterns of a spell—a combat spell. One that would take only a minimal amount of power, but would hurt nonetheless. Bazel's smirk faltered and vanished.

Then a familiar, high-pitched voice cut through the

room: "He said it was urgent. He's usually right."

Ileni almost let go of the spell—but Karyn would have felt the magic being released. Instead, she pulled it tight within herself as Bazel grabbed her hand and yanked her beneath the stairs. The empty space under the staircase was filled with boxes, but the two of them squeezed in.

Footsteps clattered down the wooden steps above them. Ileni's head hurt. Holding magic in was a basic Renegai exercise, once practiced daily. But that had been months ago, and the combat spell she was holding was sharper and more slippery than any spell she had held as a Renegai, like gripping a tangle of fragmented glass shards.

Somewhere in the room, a blanket rustled, and a quavering voice said, "Leave me alone."

"I don't think that's what you want," Karyn said.

Ileni leaned out, just far enough to see the room. Karyn was sitting on a low stool beside one of the beds. In the bed, a bald man lay propped up on pillows.

Behind Karyn, arms crossed over her chest, stood Lis.

Karyn took the old man's hands in hers—he allowed it without looking at her—and spoke to him in low, earnest tones. Ileni could make out a word or two—"*Empire*," "*right time*," "*sacrifice*"—but most of what Karyn said was too low to hear. When the old man responded, his voice weak and faltering, Ileni couldn't make out even a few words.

Karyn's tone turned sharp, which made it more audible. "It is very selfish of you. It is not a worthy end to your life."

The old man shook his head.

"Lis," Karyn said.

Lis's still face went even stiller.

"*Lis*," Karyn snapped.

Lis walked forward and put one hand on the old man's forehead. His whole body twitched, a long shudder.

He screamed.

Lis stepped back abruptly, releasing the spell. It rushed away from the old man's body, tight and ugly.

Ileni recognized that spell. She had felt it before, in a sparkling white cavern far beneath the earth. Then, it had been Karyn wielding the spell, and Sorin had been the one screaming. It was a spell like the one she still held coiled within her: designed purely to cause pain.

Karyn and Lis were torturing the man.

The old man's shriek ended in a gulp. He was trembling so hard that even the loose skin on his face shook.

"That won't be enough," Karyn said calmly.

Lis did not reply. She took another step away from the bed—this one slow and deliberate. Her hair, tied in a long ponytail, slapped against her back.

"You disappoint me," Karyn said. Her voice was still cool, but the menace in it made Lis flinch. Karyn got to her feet abruptly, making the iron bedframe shake. "You'll get only one more chance."

It wasn't clear who she was talking to, but both Lis and the old man hunched their shoulders. Karyn stalked away, across the room, and disappeared through a door in the far wall.

Lis reached back and pulled her ponytail over her shoulder. She stood for a moment gripping her own hair, and she looked so lost—so hopeless—that Ileni felt a twinge of sympathy for her. Then Lis dropped her hand and followed Karyn.

Ileni waited until the door slammed shut behind Lis before letting her own combat spell go. She sighed with relief as magic rushed harmlessly out of her, not even caring about the waste. "That's what Sorin wanted me to see?"

Bazel's scowl was as thunderous as Karyn's had been. "No. It wasn't."

"Then why did you bring me here?"

"Because there's more to see. But not now," Bazel said, biting off each word. "We have to leave before your new friends come back."

Ileni wrapped her arms around herself. Bazel's clear fury frightened her—had she already grown unaccustomed to people who wanted her dead? But she peeked out and watched the old man slowly sink against his pillow, while in the bed next to his, a woman let out a sob in her sleep.

She reached out and confirmed what she had already guessed: every person in this room had power. Not a great amount, most of them . . . not enough to be worth training, probably, though they would have been competent mid-level sorcerers had they been Renegai.

There were a few with vast amounts, though. Maybe the Academy had another way of deciding who was worth training and who was just worth . . . harvesting.

This was what she had been searching for. This was where the lodestones' power came from.

But if it was, how could Karyn and Lis have walked away?

"I know some healing magic," she said. "I could help some of these people."

"Yes," Bazel said, through gritted teeth. "Maybe later."

"It will just take a minute—"

"A minute in which you'll be seen. Do you want to explain what you're doing here?"

When Bazel started up the stairs, Ileni followed.

It was a relief to emerge into clean, cool sunlight and then climb up the stairs onto a street filled with noise and movement. Ileni let a deep shudder go through her before she turned to Bazel. "That's how they fill the lodestones, isn't it? Every sick person in there has power, and they're just waiting for it to be tortured out of . . ."

The space beside her was empty. Bazel was gone.

Ileni swore. The street was narrow and dilapidated, filled with people whose gazes shifted away from her. She guessed she had to go *up*—that was easy enough, with the mountain rearing against the sky to her left, but she had no idea which street was best to take. If she set out on her own, she would probably run right into a dead end.

She should ask someone, but all the people passing by seemed so . . . disreputable. She turned in the direction of the next staircase going up.

And found her way blocked.

By Karyn.

The sorceress had her arms crossed over her chest, lips

pressed into a flat line. There was no sign of Lis.

"What," Karyn said, each word an arrow shot. "Are. You. Doing. Here."

"I, um," Ileni said. "I got lost."

It didn't sound convincing, even to her.

CHAPTER
15

They brought him in with his head covered by a burlap bag, his hands bound behind him. They thrust him to his knees so hard he lost his balance and, after a brief, humiliating struggle, fell over sideways.

"Gently," Sorin said from his chair at the end of the room. "There is no need for excess."

The two assassins straightened, but a flash of . . . something . . . preceded their obedience. Sorin wasn't sure what it was, but he knew it was something the master had never seen when he ruled these caves.

That was a problem for later. He turned his attention

to the man flailing on the floor. "Help him up and remove the bag."

The assassins obeyed, but they were not gentle. Their captive gasped with pain as the bag scraped over his face. It was a face raw with bruises, bloodstains over purple welts, one eye swollen black. A gag was stuffed deep into his mouth and tied behind his neck. His one good blue eye glared defiance, and his mouth worked at the gag, but no sound emerged.

Sorin nodded at the two assassins. "You have done well," he said.

They bowed and withdrew. The captive drew his lips back, as far as the gag would allow, and managed a muffled snarl.

"Welcome to my caves, Tellis," Sorin said. "I have a proposal to discuss with you."

The Renegai man couldn't spit, because of the gag, but he jerked his head in a spitting motion anyhow.

Sorin got off the seat, calm and unhurried, and crossed the room. "If I remove the gag, I assume you'll try to kill me with magic? Oh, I forgot. Renegai don't kill. Ileni told me that, once."

Tellis went very still.

"Yes," Sorin said. "She's still alive."

Tellis closed his eyes, just for a second, relief and joy

unmistakable on his face. Since his captive's eyes were closed, Sorin allowed himself a scowl but kept his voice smooth. "I need your help to keep her that way."

Tellis snapped his eyes open and glared at him with an absolute hatred that reminded Sorin of Ileni.

"We need her," Sorin said, "and we need her alive. That's why you're here. To help her."

He drew a dagger, reached behind Tellis's head, and cut the gag. It fell to the floor, stained with blood and spittle. Tellis's mouth opened.

"Kill me," Sorin said, "and you fail her. Though I believe it wouldn't be the first time."

"You're lying," Tellis said. He was astonishingly handsome beneath his injuries—blond hair, blue eyes, chiseled face. Once he used magic to heal himself, he would be even more so. Not that it mattered.

"No," Sorin said, allowing nothing to show in his voice. "Nothing I'm about to tell you is a lie. In fact, all I'm going to do is tell you the truth. Then you can decide what to do with it."

Tellis drew in a breath. "Where is she?"

Sorin inclined his head.

"Sit down," he said. It wasn't a suggestion. "This might take a while."

CHAPTER 16

By the time they reached the base of the mountain, up at least five staircases and four steep streets, Ileni's calves were cramping painfully, and her upper arm burned where Karyn's fingers were clenched around it.

They were halfway up the mountain, on a path littered with white and purple wildflowers, when Karyn finally broke the silence. "It's difficult to get lost if you're headed for the Academy. You just go *up*."

Ileni gritted her teeth against the soreness in her legs. She didn't want to waste the little power she had left, but as soon as she got close enough to draw on the lodestones, she could get rid of the pain . . . no. No, she couldn't use the lodestones anymore. Could she?

She had to. Even knowing where the power came from, even with the old man's scream burned into her mind. She had to keep pretending. She had to pretend harder than ever, now that she knew what she was fighting against.

"Thank you," she said. "I'll keep that in mind for next time."

"There won't be a next time." Karyn's fingernails gouged Ileni's arm. Ileni hissed through her teeth and muttered the words of a spell, recently learned, that would send pain sizzling through Karyn's hand. Karyn brushed the spell away with contemptuous ease and sent an arc of agony through Ileni's body.

Ileni cried out despite herself. Then she gritted her teeth and reached for more power. But she had almost none left, and the lodestones were still out of reach.

"Be careful, Ileni," Karyn said softly. "Do you want to go back to what you were? I can take the magic away in a second if I want to."

You should. Shame swept through Ileni. She knew now, without the possibility of doubt, where the magic came from. She had seen the people whose lives would be ripped away to fill the lodestones with power.

And she still wanted it.

"I'm not sure why you're angry," she said, through her teeth. "You gave me permission."

"To accompany Evin. Not to wander alone in the city." Karyn gave Ileni's arm a shake. "What exactly were you looking for?"

Careful. Karyn was only tolerating Ileni because she thought Ileni might be won over to the Empire's side.

But Ileni had to say something, and she didn't think she could keep her revulsion out of her voice. Besides, she wanted to hear Karyn's answer. Wanted to hear that this was, somehow, different from what it looked like. "I'll tell you what I found: the people you steal your magic from."

Karyn stopped short, swinging Ileni around to face her. "We don't steal it. It's given freely." Her lips were white, her eyes dark with fury and something else. Guilt? Fear?

"Freely?" Ileni tried to laugh, but what emerged was a sob. "I *saw* you torture that man."

"He was already there," Karyn snapped. "We don't force anyone to enter Death's Door, but if they do, they are agreeing to give us their power when they die. He made a promise, and he was refusing to keep it."

"Agreed? In exchange for what?"

"Any number of things that people are willing to die for. Gold, sometimes, for people they love. More often, protection for their families, or a place for their children at the Sisters of the Black God. It's worth it to them, and it's their own choice."

It was time to start pretending to be convinced. Instead, Ileni said, "So that's the basis of all your power. Helpless people whose lives you steal when they are too sick to resist and have nowhere else to turn. You could help them, but instead you offer them your *choice.*" *Power stolen, power misused, power drawn from pain and death.* "You think forcing them to kill themselves is somehow nobler than straight-out murdering them? Just because they're old and sick and weak?"

Karyn snapped her mouth shut. She blinked, and Ileni had the now-familiar sense that she had missed something, revealed her ignorance once again.

"Most of them would die anyhow," Karyn said finally. "While they live, they are weak and useless. We are giving them a way to be valuable, to serve the Empire."

"By harvesting their lives to add to your power!"

"You can blame your assassin friends for that," Karyn said. "We need more power for the coming war."

For the coming . . . Ileni drew in her breath.

Wouldn't you rather it was our soldiers? Think how many lodestones would be in the training arena now.

"You get power from war, too," Ileni said. "Don't you? From dying soldiers. *They* can be a source, too."

Karyn pressed her lips together. "Yes. We don't waste lives."

"And because of that, their deaths don't matter to you." Lis had told her the truth, but she hadn't understood: *We win either way.*

It didn't matter, to the Empire, if they won or lost a battle. If they won, their enemies died. And if they lost, *they* died, and their power was gathered into the lodestones. Dead soldiers became power sources for sorcerer-soldiers. Even defeats added to the Empire's strength. No wonder it was unstoppable.

"Why bother going through the motions of a fight?" Ileni snapped. "Why not just order them to kill themselves and give you their power?"

Karyn stared at her. "Who would obey that order?"

Ileni knew several hundred people who would obey. But this was, clearly, not the time to bring that up. She had to back down before it was too late.

Except she suspected it was already too late.

Karyn's eyes narrowed. "I think your viewpoint has been a little skewed by your time in the caves. We don't murder people for no reason. We don't send soldiers into battle to die. We prefer to win. But if we lose, we see no reason to waste their deaths."

Start acting convinced. But Ileni couldn't think of how to do it—how to pretend she thought the murder of innocents could be justified. That the Empire could value life so little, and then hide behind speeches about necessity.

"I . . ." she began, choking before she even knew what to say. And then, just in time, realized that she was going about this all wrong.

Karyn didn't expect Ileni to be convinced. She expected her to be *tempted.*

"I could heal some of those people," she said. "If I . . . if I had a lodestone bracelet of my own."

Karyn let out a tiny victorious snort. "Could you, indeed?"

"Yes." Deep breath. "If what you're saying is true, if you would prefer that people *not* die, then give me a bracelet and let me serve as their healer."

"How noble of you." Karyn let go of Ileni's wrist, and Ileni forced herself not to rub the indentations left by the sorceress's fingers. "I'll consider it. Although you do realize that the lodestone on your bracelet will have cost a life. You'll just be trading one life for another."

So Karyn, too, didn't know how to stop arguing just because she had what she wanted. Ileni shrugged. "Renegai healing spells have been honed for centuries to require as little power as possible. Unless someone is actually dying, it shouldn't drain a lodestone to cure them. I could cure dozens of people with the power of a single stone."

"I see," Karyn said. "I'll consider it."

And now they both had what they wanted. Ileni's mouth tasted sour.

Karyn let out a breath. "Well. Much as I would love to continue this discussion, I don't have the time. The Oksain River is flooding again, and I need a dozen mid-level sorcerers to help me contain it." She stepped back. "By keeping the river in its banks, we'll save hundreds of lives and prevent a famine. But don't let that interfere with your self-righteous horror."

Killing people to save other people's lives. Ileni had heard that before. She bit her lip, hard enough to hurt, and said nothing.

Karyn vanished. But right before she did, she gave Ileni a

look of such triumph, such certainty, that Ileni's entire body clenched.

She ran the rest of the way up the mountain, racing past clustered spikes of grass and thorny bushes clinging to the rock. She pulled in power as soon as she was in range of the lodestones, healing muscles recklessly so she could keep up a breakneck pace. She slammed the door to her room, yanked open two of her desk drawers, and grabbed what she needed: a piece of a chalk and a stone paperweight in the shape of a tiny mountain. She didn't bother to close the drawers. She dropped to her hands and knees and began to draw, so hard and fast that chalk dust sputtered up from the rock.

It was a complicated pattern to work so quickly, and that helped; she had to focus on it entirely, her mind clear and cold, distractions like life and death and betrayal becoming misty and distant. When she was done, she sat cross-legged on the floor with a thump. Then, with slow deliberateness, she placed her fingers on the right places on the paperweight.

She knew how to do this spell. She had run it through her mind a dozen times. And this time, she had to see him. Had to tell him that he was right, that she was ready to come back. . . .

Her fingers froze.

Was she ready?

This wasn't about running away. She was a weapon. If she opened the portal, he would think it meant she was ready to be used.

Was she?

Was she ready to set the assassins loose on the Empire, just because people were dying a few days earlier than they would have died anyhow?

The thought felt slick and ugly in her mind. No Renegai would ever think that way. All lives were worth saving. It was why healing was so central, the most important use of magic. Why they had left the Empire to begin with.

But Ileni hadn't been thinking like a Renegai for a long time now. The Renegai were a tiny group of outcasts, clinging to centuries-old ideals while hiding away in the mountains, where those ideals were never confronted with reality. Nobody else in the entire world saw life as anything more than a bag of coins, to be counted and valued and, ultimately, traded in.

She wished she still thought like a Renegai, confident in what was pure and good. Now she knew that nothing—nothing—was pure and good.

Including her.

Once, she had believed that she was a good person, that she would always choose right. That she would know what *right* meant. Now she was so tainted, so muddled, that she couldn't even make a choice at all.

She heard a sound, an ugly, gulping sob, and clamped her lips together before she could let out another one. Slowly, carefully, she began the finger patterns again, this time doing them backward. Unwinding the spell.

When she was done, she rubbed the floor with her hands until there wasn't a visible trace of chalk left, then kept scrubbing until no more tears fell onto the gray stone.

Arxis was at breakfast the next morning, sitting next to Evin, the two of them laughing and jostling each other. Judging by Cyn's irritated expression, Arxis's presence was a breach of protocol; and judging by Evin's insouciant grin, it was one he didn't care about. But when Ileni walked into the room, his brow furrowed.

Arxis glanced at Ileni, too. Even the way he turned his head was taut and disciplined, and his eyes were opaque. She wondered how none of the others could see him for what he was. A hunter. A killer.

Of course, they were all killers, here.

That morning, Ileni had gotten ready without magic, so it had taken her twice as long as usual. She was only halfway through her breakfast when Cyn pushed away from the table and said, "Let's go."

Fortunately, Ileni hadn't had much appetite anyhow.

When they stepped outside, the sky was so gray it melted into the mountain peaks, and mist drifted across Ileni's skin. She trudged across the bridge while the others soared overhead, Evin towing Arxis along. Apparently they had cemented their friendship while she was watching a man be tortured.

What should I do? She had her answer now, the truth she had come to find: The Empire deserved to end, and she was the only one who could end it. It drew its magic from murder. Torturing the helpless until they surrendered their lives, and their power. . . .

Except the old man at Death's Door hadn't surrendered anything. He was still alive, and Lis had walked away.

But he wouldn't be alive for long. *You'll get only one more chance,* Karyn had threatened. That was, clearly, an isolated act of disobedience, and one that would soon be reversed. Did it really matter that Lis felt bad about what she was doing? She was doing it anyhow.

When Ileni stepped onto the plateau, Evin and Cyn were already sparring, flinging balls of colored light at each other. Cyn's balls were pure white, her strikes direct and dizzyingly fast. Evin's were swirls of translucent color, more beautiful than dangerous. Even so, Evin was clearly winning. His movements were relaxed, almost lazy, while Cyn's breath came in short, ragged bursts. On the other side of the plateau, Lis and Arxis were standing with their heads close together, sleek black and unruly red.

Evin snapped his head around when Ileni's foot touched the plateau. He raised a hand, and a burst of power stopped all the glowing orbs in midair. The vast expenditure of magic almost knocked Ileni back over the edge. She swayed slightly.

"Match over," Evin said cheerfully. "Well, Ileni? Want to give it a try?"

Ileni did want to, and the longing made her feel tight, about to explode.

"No," she said. "I don't."

She said it without thinking, and didn't hear the haughtiness in her voice until it was too late.

Evin shrugged, but Cyn stiffened. "I thought," she said, "that you'd given up the whole shocked-and-superior act. It's getting boring."

"I'll spar with you again—" Evin cut in.

"No. I think I'd like Ileni to have a turn." Cyn ran her fingers through her short hair. "She's proven that she's quite capable of being a challenge, when she can bring herself to forget that she's a—what are your villagers called again?"

"Renegai," Ileni snapped. "And I don't want to forget."

"Clearly. You have my deepest sympathies for that."

Her tone cut deep. The contempt was not just for Ileni, but for Ileni's people, everything the Renegai had achieved and everything they had sacrificed.

Cyn smiled—an ugly smile, the sort she usually aimed at Lis. "Angry now, Renegai girl? Does that mean you're allowed to fight?" She flung out a hand, and a column of sand rose before her and whirled across the plateau at Ileni.

Ileni drew in power from the lodestones and blasted the column apart. Then she raised a hand, and Cyn flew backward across the plateau, slamming into one of Evin's frozen lights. It exploded in a graceful spray of color. Cyn, less gracefully, dropped to the ground and lay still.

The plateau was suddenly, resoundingly silent. Ileni's heart pounded in her chest, and air streamed into her throat, cold and sharp.

Cyn lifted her head and whispered a word.

Pain tore through Ileni's body. She screamed once, a short burst of agony, then sent a pain-numbing spell into her bones. She wrenched in a breath—and magic surged from Cyn again, turning Ileni's body into her enemy, pain searing along her bones and her blood.

She managed not to scream this time, but she wasn't sure how. Another healing spell dulled the pain enough to let her feel the magic Cyn was pouring into the attack. She tried to raise a defense, and a sideways surge of power slapped her attempt aside.

Cyn wasn't even using the full strength of the spell. This was just a taste. If Cyn wanted, she could kill Ileni in a split second of agony. Or she could keep her alive and make her beg for death. *This* was what imperial magic was, what the Academy strove for and the Renegai had rejected. Magic designed to do nothing but cause pain, to hurt a human being beyond endurance.

Ileni crumpled to the floor, fighting the pain, keeping it almost—*almost*—at bay. She wouldn't scream and she wouldn't beg. Not . . . not yet.

"Yield," Cyn said. She was standing over Ileni. Ileni hadn't seen her move.

Ileni spat at her feet.

Cyn's murmured a word, and pain sliced along Ileni's cheek. Blood trickled down her face.

"*Cyn*," Evin said.

"It's our match," Cyn said coolly. "Don't interfere. I'm not causing any permanent damage. She can use one of her cute little healing spells, and she won't even have to waste a bandage." She closed her fist, and Ileni couldn't breathe. Air scraped painfully at her throat, and she gasped and floundered. Panic flooded through her, worse than pain.

"No permanant damage *yet*," Cyn added. "All you have to do is yield."

Ileni was slowly strangling, and she couldn't quite manage defiance, but she squeezed her eyes shut and managed silence.

"Stop it," Evin snapped, and suddenly it was gone— the constriction in her throat, the agony, the terror. Ileni uncurled herself slowly, her muscles strange and loose with the absence of pain. The sharp thrust of Cyn's spell was muted by the power of Evin's blocking spell, a spell that made Ileni's attempt at defense laughable by comparison.

"Really, Evin," Cyn said. She rolled her eyes and sauntered back to the other side of the plateau. "You are such an annoyance. No one asked you to get involved."

"Call it a whim," Evin said. His eyes were on Ileni.

"I call everything you do a whim."

"This shouldn't be too difficult for you, then."

Ileni's body finally believed it could move. A quick, easy spell healed the cut on her cheek, just as Cyn had predicted. She got to her feet and faced the other girl. Cyn propped one hand on her hip.

"I could destroy you," Ileni said. Her voice shook. "I could destroy *all* of you. And I think I will."

Cyn laughed and flicked an errant strand of hair away from her face.

"Well, Evin," she said, "I guess that's your cue to say, *You're welcome.*"

Ileni's throat tightened. She shouldn't have said it. But she also knew there was no risk in saying it. No one here thought she could possibly be a threat.

She turned her back on Cyn's smirk and Evin's frown, soared into the air, and fled.

She didn't soar very far. She kept close to the bridge, and, as soon as she was far enough from Cyn to feel safe, floated down and landed on it, gripping the rail with trembling hands. She was halfway across, close enough to the main peak to see a group of novices in green tunics filing along one of the lower ledges. She probably could have made it farther, but that would have meant using more stolen magic.

She had barely stepped off the bridge when someone swooped in front of her. Ileni tensed, but it wasn't Cyn. It was Evin, and one look at her expression made him switch directions and soar upward instead.

"I'm sorry that happened," he said. He braced himself against the mountainside, his magic holding him to the cliff face, and looked down. "It didn't mean anything. You caught Cyn in a bad mood."

"Sure," Ileni said. "Among my people, we also respond to bad moods by torturing our friends."

His brow furrowed. "We don't all respond that way."

"But you think it's normal. She isn't going to be punished, is she? Nobody's going to treat her like the monster she is. Because you're used to it. Because everything you do is about causing pain."

Evin blinked, and Ileni braced herself for a scathing retort she would very much deserve. She was no better, after all—lashing out at Evin because she was angry at Cyn. And at herself.

But what Evin said was, "She will be punished, if you

go to Karyn. That was unacceptable. She could have really hurt you."

"What will she get?" Ileni asked. "A stern lecture?" Not that any of the asssassins would have gotten even that much. They were too honest to pretend brutality was beneath them. "You're all so important, aren't you? The sorcerers who hold the Empire together. You're untouchable, and you know it."

"We do get away with a lot," Evin admitted. "In my case, that's absolutely justified, but in Cyn's, it's more of an . . . unfortunate necessity."

"Why?" Ileni said. "Why is it necessary? Why can't you just *stop*? You don't need this much power—"

"We do, actually," Evin said. "We have powerful enemies."

"You could leave the assassins alone, find a compromise—"

Evin's laugh was the harshest sound she had ever heard emerge from his mouth. "The assassins want us dead. What sort of compromise do you suggest? Shall we die just a little bit?"

She had managed to forget, for a moment, what the assassins had done to him. Ileni drew in a breath.

Evin looked down at her from his spiderlike perch against the gray rock. "There is no compromise possible. They have made themselves into an enemy that must be destroyed."

She had never heard him sound so fierce. Apparently there was one thing he did care about.

Ileni tilted her head back to meet his eyes. "They can't be destroyed. Haven't you figured that out? Everyone knows the caves are impregnable. No army could ever get in, and the wards are unbreachable. . . ."

Her voice died.

There was a breach. There was a mirror in her room, and the portal still attached to it could reach the Assassins' Caves despite all the wards between them.

It was as if Sorin was there, watching her. She saw herself through his eyes, holding her stolen magic tight, in earnest conversation with an imperial sorcerer. Like it mattered what excuses Evin made.

Evin didn't seem to notice her silence. He slid down the wall until his feet touched the ledge. "I never told you how my parents died."

She found her voice, though it was weak and hoarse. "Cyn told me."

"Did she tell you why they were murdered?"

Ileni shook her head.

"My mother discovered that a city on the southern coast had been taken over by supporters of the assassins. She infiltrated their movement, then organized a raid. She killed them all. Three hundred, officially, though that's probably a bit exaggerated."

A bit exaggerated. "So how many *did* she kill? Merely two hundred?"

Evin's jaw pulsed. "There are *millions* who live under the Empire's protection. The assassins threaten all of them."

A familiar argument. "Then why," Ileni said, "are you so angry at her?"

"My mother was warned." Evin's voice was wound tight, as if the slightest waver might break it. "They sent her a message: if she continued going after the assassins, she would die. I was only ten years old. Girad was an infant. We needed her, and she didn't care."

Ileni hesitated. The pain in his voice seemed to preclude argument. His mother was a murderer. And yet . . . "How could she make a decision based on two people, when it affected the fate of so many others?"

Evin gave her a look of searing contempt, and Ileni's spine snapped so straight she felt a crack.

"*I* never would," she said, and for that moment she was sure of it. "I would never do the wrong thing for the sake of any one person. No matter how much I loved him."

"I'm sure you wouldn't." Evin's expression was every bit as scornful as his voice. "You'll forgive me if I'm not overwhelmed by your nobility of purpose. By your willingness to sacrifice someone you love."

Her heart was pounding too hard for a theoretical conversation. "For the good of—"

"I don't want to hear it." He stepped closer. His eyes were flat and remote, as if he was a different person. "Heap your scorn on me all you want, but don't expect me to care. Because I, Ileni, would sacrifice millions of people I don't know for the sake of one person I love."

No. This wasn't a theoretical conversation, not to either of them. "You're talking about Girad."

Evin's mouth twisted. "He's more powerful than even I am. The Empire needs *him*, too. But they won't have him. I'll be their soldier, but Girad is going to have a different sort of life. No matter what I have to do to protect him."

Ileni swallowed hard. "Shouldn't it be his choice?"

Evin gave her a withering look. "Who gets to make their own choices?"

None of us, Ileni thought. Every one of them had been raised to be a weapon.

But she had refused. She was here, among people who

would all be dead if she agreed to be what Absalm had designed her to be. Despite what she had seen at Death's Door, she could still choose *not* to be a weapon.

Which didn't change the fact that Evin was right. It was too late to choose to be anything else.

The last thing Ileni wanted to do, after Evin flew away, was return to the plateau. But she did it anyhow, one laborious step after another. If she was to have any chance at all of being a weapon of her own choosing, she still needed more answers.

She was in luck; Cyn and Lis were engaged in battle, magic flying fast and furious between them. Neither glanced at Ileni as she crossed the plateau to where Arxis sat, cross-legged and straight backed, watching them. By now, the sky was roiling with dark gray clouds, and a few damp drops dotted the top of the plateau.

"I found Bazel," Ileni said, sitting beside Arxis with a thump. "In the city."

He didn't react—though that meant nothing; he was an assassin. Ileni gambled. "How did you know Bazel would be there to meet me?"

Lis cried out, and Arxis returned his attention to the

fight. "I didn't know. My guess is, he's been in the city for a while, watching for you. As soon as we entered the city, he signaled me that you were to come with him."

"Signaled you how?"

Arxis laughed. "You don't really expect me to tell you that, do you? As teacher, you had access to a few of our secrets. Don't imagine you know them all."

A wind whistled across the plateau, scattering stray droplets on Ileni's face. Cyn adjusted her spell swiftly to compensate, but Lis's next strike went wide. "Right. Well, Bazel and I were interrupted. I don't think I saw everything I was supposed to see."

A volley of green light flashed between the sisters. "Yield," Cyn called, and Arxis got smoothly to his feet, as if Ileni had ceased to exist.

"Wait," Ileni said. "The master—"

He looked down at her, eyes hooded. "The master, apparently, sent Bazel to show you what you need to see. Go pester *him*."

"Yield!" Cyn said again, and Lis gritted her teeth and shook her head. The droplets were now a steady drizzle, hitting Ileni's hair and face.

"Great," Arxis said. "This match will end well."

"Our conversation isn't over," Ileni snapped. "This is Bazel we're talking about. You want me to rely on *him?*"

Lis glanced over at them, and Arxis's face immediately dropped into an expression of concern, focused on her. His voice, though, was cool. "It doesn't matter what I think. The master sent him. That's all I need to know."

The master is dead. I killed him. She had to bite her lip, hard, to keep from saying it. Rain slid across her face and under the neck of her dress.

Magic twisted through the air, and Lis screamed and dropped to her knees. Arxis kept his anxious expression, but his voice was a sneer. "You've been here too long, Teacher, and forgotten how assassins treat our leaders. We don't criticize and lounge about and disobey."

Ileni scrambled to her feet. "You don't understand—"

"I understand," Arxis said, "that we had an agreement. You'll get no more help from me."

"If you'll just listen—"

But Arxis was already rushing toward Lis. He dropped beside her, putting his arms around her. Lis buried her face in his shoulder, and he whispered something into her ear, his lips brushing the side of her face.

Ileni looked quickly away, heat rising to her cheeks. This

was what she and Sorin must have looked like, from the outside. Sordid, and stupid, and predictable.

But this was different. Ileni had known exactly how stupid she was being, falling in love with a killer. Lis had no idea what Arxis was.

Cyn watched the pair, ignoring the rain that slicked her hair to her face. Her lips were pressed together, her eyebrows drawn sharply with concern. For *Lis*?

The rain was pelting Ileni now, pressing her clothes to her skin. No one was paying attention to her, which made it easy to flee yet again.

The mirror seemed misty that night, her reflection indistinct, as if something too faint to see was rippling through the glass. Was Sorin on the other side, trying to reach her? Or was she just imagining it because she wanted to see him so badly?

Or did she? If she really wanted to see him, she could. She could open the portal easily, from this side.

She couldn't imagine what she would say to him once she did.

Ileni touched the mirror's surface. She would get only one chance. Karyn would feel the portal open, and then she would repair the breach in the wards, and Ileni's connection to Sorin would be gone.

This wasn't the time to use it. She didn't need Sorin, not now.

She needed to know what else she had been meant to see at Death's Door.

But who could she ask? Arxis wasn't going to tell her. Evin . . . Evin probably didn't know anything he didn't care to know.

Cyn? Cyn might feel guilty about what she had done on the plateau that day—she seemed good at feeling guilty once it was too late to change anything. Ileni could use that. She could go to Cyn right now, offering forgiveness. She would ask her why she had been so angry, steer that into a discussion about the lodestones. . . .

Ileni let her hand slide away from the mirror. It wouldn't work. Cyn was a true believer, a soldier of the Empire. She might question the tactics, but she would never question the goal.

Ileni had been just like her once.

She tried to despise Cyn for her blindness, but gave up when the effort was only half-born. Cyn knew her place, knew it was important, knew she was striving for something worthwhile. Something great. She knew she was on the right side. And even though she was wrong, that knowledge made her strong.

While Ileni knew—deep in her bones, bound in her heart—the unhappiness that came from suspecting you were on the wrong side.

And so she knew exactly who could provide her with answers.

CHAPTER
17

Outside Lis's door, in a dim hallway lit only by her magelight, Ileni hesitated yet again. What if Lis was asleep? Worse, what if she wasn't alone? An image flashed through her mind: Arxis leaning toward Lis—he, a remorseless predator; she, hypnotized prey.

Just do it. Ileni rapped hard on the wooden door.

Long moments passed in echoing silence. Knock again? Or leave? Ileni lifted her hand, lowered it, and was just stepping back when the door opened.

Lis was, to Ileni's relief, fully dressed. But when she saw Ileni, her smile turned into a blank, disappointed stare.

Seconds later, it was a scowl. "What are you doing here?"

"Where," Ileni said, "does the lodestones' power come from?"

Lis went still for a moment. Then her lip curled. "I think you already know the answer to that. If you're too stupid to figure it out, that's your own problem." She stepped back and started to close the door.

Ileni used a burst of magic to push it back open—perhaps a bit more magic than was, strictly speaking, necessary. Lis staggered back a few steps. Ileni stepped into the doorway. "Do you want to tell me why you hate me?"

"No," Lis said, without blinking. "Not really."

"Fine," Ileni said. "I just want to ask you some questions."

"How fascinating." Lis grabbed the door handle, obviously about to slam the door.

Ileni grabbed the edge of the door. "If you answer them, I won't tell Karyn about you and Arxis."

Lis laughed in her face. "Go right ahead."

So much for that. Ileni tried to think of another threat, and came up empty.

Lis lifted an eyebrow. "Why would she care? Come to think of it, why do *you* care?"

The answer to that should have been obvious, given Ileni

and Arxis's supposed past. Ileni blinked, focusing on Lis. Not a hint of jealousy fueled the other girl's anger. Somehow, she knew that story wasn't true.

What else does she know? Slowly, Ileni said, "I have information about Arxis. You want to hear it."

Lis rolled her eyes. "Do I? Or do you just want to say it?"

"You have to stay away from him. I know him."

Lis leaned back. "I know exactly who Arxis is. Far better than you do."

"I doubt that."

Lis's lip curled. "You don't know *anything*. Haven't you realized that by now?"

"Yes," Ileni said softly. "I have. That's why I'm here. To ask you for help."

It hurt, almost physically—exposing her soft side to an enemy. And it didn't even work. Lis said, "Well, I'm sorry you wasted your time," and used a pulse of magic to slam the door shut.

Ileni snatched her hand back and met Lis's magic with her own—*no, not my own.* They were both drawing on the lodestones, but Ileni was pulling in more magic than Lis, and using it far more skillfully. While holding the door open, she gathered power into a tight pattern, and—with a final, short word—shattered the other girl's spell.

"I know you're not like the others," Ileni hissed. "You know what you're doing is wrong. So prove it. *Tell* me."

Lis's face was flushed red, but she stood her ground. "Why bother? There's nothing you can do about it. No one person can change anything, especially not one with all your interesting . . . scruples. If you knew the truth, you would go back to your village and hide there for the rest of your life. This place ruins everything it touches."

"In that case," Ileni said softly, "you have nothing to lose."

"That's always been true." Lis turned away, and Ileni thought she wasn't going to say anything more. Instead, she snapped, "I know you were at Death's Door."

"What?"

"I saw you. I hope you enjoyed the show." Lis lifted her chin. "You didn't see the whole thing, though, did you? You didn't go down a level?"

"I have no idea what you're talking about," Ileni said.

"I've noticed." Lis put one hand on the door handle. "Do you honestly think it's only the old and sick? That we're willing to steal two days of life—or a week—or a month . . . Where exactly do you think the limit is, Ileni?"

Ileni stepped back.

Lis sneered. "Go deeper, if you want the whole truth. Or don't. Because once you know it, you'll have to live with it."

This time, when Lis slammed the door shut, Ileni didn't fight her. She stood for several seconds staring at the dark, opaque wood.

If you want the whole truth. She did. Which meant she had to go back to Death's Door.

If she left the Academy again, if she snuck down to the city in the middle of the night . . . and if she got caught . . . Karyn would take away her magic. And then she truly would be helpless to find out anything more.

Ileni bit her lip. Her chest was tight. *Go back to what you were,* Karyn had warned. How had she known exactly what Ileni was most afraid of?

Ileni turned on her heel and walked away from Lis's closed door.

The path down the mountain was twisty and treacherous in the darkness. The rain had stopped by now, and the moon slid in and out of fragmented clouds, providing a drifting, inconsistent light. Ileni paused before she left the Academy and soaked up all the magic she could, then used a sliver of it to make her shoes glow. The light was just bright enough to let her see where she was stepping, but—she hoped—not bright enough to catch anyone's attention.

She didn't know how to go directly to Death's Door, so she had to retrace the path to the Black Sisters—which was even darker and more imposing at night, the murmur of the fountains soft and menacing—and then through the narrow streets and crumbling stairways, which now included sudden dark puddles. After she stepped into the first one—and used up some of her magic to get the water out of her shoes— she watched for them carefully, paying equal attention to the ground and to her surroundings. The shops were closed and dark, and men lurked in shadows on the stairs. They would have been frightening if not for the magic that filled her, but she strode past without slowing down. After days of sparring with Cyn, she knew she could hurt anyone who even thought about threatening her.

But nobody did. Perhaps her confident stride warned them, marking her as an imperial sorceress, not to be trifled with.

A vague sense of disappointment pricked her, and she squashed it swiftly. Was this what she had become—someone who *wanted* to use combat magic, just because she practiced it every day? If the Elders could see her now, they would be horrified.

If Sorin could see her, he would be proud.

The memory of his glittering eyes was still in her mind when, with a flicker of power, she unlocked the narrow door on the stairway. Darkness and silence wrapped around her as she crept down the stairs. But in the large fetid room, labored breaths and groans filled the stillness, and a few glowstones in the walls were alight, casting a dim grayness that illuminated rows of narrow beds.

Ileni bit her lip. It seemed wrong to intrude upon all these suffering people. But Lis's challenge rang in her ears, mingled with the image of Sorin's face. She had to know the truth. She could change everything—make things better for all these people. *Maybe*. But first she had to understand what was going on.

She crept silently between the rows of beds, trying not to look too hard at the figures in them. A man tangled in a blanket, moaning in his sleep; a woman, still as stone, hair sweat slicked over her forehead; a curled-up bundle of blankets with only a wizened hand sticking out. She glanced at the bed where the old man had been tortured, but he was gone. There was a younger man there now. She wondered if the old man had given in, in the end, or if he had died naturally.

Or if he had been thrown out into the street for refusing.

At the end of the room was a shut door. Ileni pulled together magic for an unlocking spell, but the door opened without any need for it. Another staircase descended on the other side, steeper and narrower than the first.

Go deeper. Ileni licked dry lips and descended the stairs.

At first glance, the room at the bottom was identical to the one above. Rows of beds, the stink of sweat and pus, the occasional moan. Glowstones flickered sporadically on the walls, casting a dim shifting light, and in it, Ileni saw the difference.

This room was filled with children.

Like the people upstairs, they all had power. But they weren't all sick.

One boy, sitting up in bed, cradled a twisted arm but otherwise looked healthy. Another, a girl, had a cleft lip, a gaping empty space connecting her mouth to her nose. In the corner, a boy of about twelve stared at the ceiling with his tongue lolling out, emitting the occasional giggle.

In the bed nearest to the stairs, a girl who looked just a few years younger than Ileni sat with her back propped up against her pillow, ash blond hair falling to her waist. She was staring straight at Ileni, blue eyes unnervingly direct in a face so pale it was nearly translucent.

Ileni froze. But when the girl's voice emerged, it was a whisper. She shivered as she spoke, a series of tremors from head to toe. "Are you here for me?"

Ileni shook her head.

"Please." The girl's teeth chattered. "I'm ready."

Ileni braced herself and stepped forward, next to the bed. The girl was so hot Ileni could feel it without touching her, and she reeked of sweat.

"Why—" Ileni had to stop and clear her throat. "Why are you here?"

The girl's eyes dropped, and her cheeks reddened. "My baby. I got sick right after she was born, and I can't . . ." She had to stop to catch her breath. "I want the Black Sisters to take her. You can have my life if you promise me that."

"Um," Ileni said, and shifted her weight to back away.

The girl grabbed Ileni's wrist. Her grasp was so feeble Ileni could have shaken it off without trying. "Please. I would wait for a Gatherer, but I don't know if I'll last that long. *Please.*"

The last word was a sob, and the girl had to stop so she

could keep breathing, fast and shallow. Ileni did shake off her grasp, and grabbed *her* wrist instead.

"You're not going to die," she said.

The girl flinched at the fury in her voice, and Ileni probably should have explained that it wasn't aimed at *her*. But she was busy calling up her magic as she focused on the girl, confirming her guess.

Childbed fever. It was common, and the Renegai had half a dozen spells to counteract it. None of them were simple or easy, but Ileni had healed this malady dozens of times in training. She could do it again.

She also thought she remembered being told that if childbed fever wasn't healed swiftly, it would be too late, and the attempt would only hasten the inevitable death. Who had told her that? Tellis? Or maybe he had been talking about some other illness. . . .

She couldn't remember. And anyhow, she couldn't tell whether it was too late for this girl.

Ileni gathered up her power and placed her hands on the girl's stomach. The power spread, pulsing, to her fingers. The girl jerked, but didn't protest. Ileni closed her eyes and felt the girl's swollen womb, the wrongness within it.

The infection was widespread and strong. Most fevers

could be cured with a simple, easy spell, but this would take every bit of power Ileni still had stored within her. She took a deep, hopeful breath and whispered the spell.

The magic shot from her fingertips into the girl's body, a series of painful surges. Finally, when she had given all she had, Ileni let go and stepped back. Emptiness clawed at her from the inside. The girl blinked at her, confused, and her hand dropped limply to the bed. She looked even weaker than before. Possibly she didn't even realize what Ileni had done.

"My daughter," the blond girl managed.

"You'll take care of her yourself," Ileni promised. "You'll be all right now. So will she."

The girl looked at her blankly, eyes glazed with pain, and doubt stabbed Ileni. But healing was often painful and disorienting. She still had vivid memories of having a fever healed when she was seven years old, of how confused and frantic her thoughts had been afterward. So maybe this was normal. Maybe she had succeeded.

The girl sagged back against the pillow, eyes fluttering closed. Ileni hesitated. But if the girl was dying, there was nothing else she could do. She straightened and looked at the boy with the broken arm.

"Why are *you* here?" she said.

The boy's eyes were wide and bright. "It set wrong. Can you heal me, too?"

The lack of magic yawned inside Ileni. The room was filled with at least fifty children, and she felt like they were all watching her. "I . . . not now. But I can come back."

The brightness left the boy's eyes. "It will be too late."

"Come with me, then," Ileni said. "You shouldn't be here. You won't die of a broken arm."

"I can't live with it, either," the boy said. "Can't take care of my brother. But the Black Sisters will."

"No," Ileni said. "You don't have to—"

The girl with the cleft lip spoke in a garbled voice. "Don't be stupid."

Ileni looked from her, to the boy with the broken arm, then around the room again. She took a step back, then another.

The blond girl's eyes popped open. "Don't go!"

"It's all right," Ileni said, though it wasn't.

"No! Take it." The girl's voice rose, shrill and piercing. "I don't have long. I can't wait."

A door slammed. All the glowstones went on, blindingly bright, and across the room, a boy sat up in his bed and screamed.

Ileni spun and ran for the stairs. Behind her, the blond girl shouted, "Stop!" and the boy's scream went on and on. Another child began wailing.

Light flooded the stairway. A bearded man stormed down the steps, holding a long, curved knife that gleamed in the sudden brightness.

If she'd had any magic left, Ileni wouldn't have given the knife a second thought. The man advanced, and fear shot through her. In the beds all around her, children stirred and moaned.

"I'm sorry," she said to the man with the knife, as coolly as she could manage. She had to raise her voice to be heard over the screaming. "I—I didn't mean to—" To *what*? "To, uh, disturb. You. Or anyone."

The man's eyes flickered over her. "You're from the Academy?"

"Yes."

He came closer, and now she was within easy reach of his blade. She forced herself to remain still, tried not to even look at the knife, as if it was of no relevance to her. "We weren't told to expect anyone."

"Um," Ileni said. "I—uh—we—"

"She's here for me," the blond girl said. "I'm ready."

The bearded man slipped past Ileni, nodded quickly—approvingly?—and slid something small and sharp into the blond girl's hand.

"Wait," Ileni said.

The blond girl met her eyes. Her chin trembled. "Take care of my baby. *Promise.*"

And then, without hesitating, she lifted the blade to her throat and slashed it across her smooth skin.

Ileni had seen people die before, and that was the only thing that kept her from screaming. The blond girl gasped, and her mouth opened, as if in protest. The knife dropped to the bed, and blood flowed through her now-limp fingers, soaking the thin blanket.

Power rushed from her into Ileni.

Ileni gasped, first with shock and then with joy. The flood of power was so bright and brilliant it lit her up from the inside. She was too dazzled to see.

With the power came knowledge: the bright glow of the girl's life, the confusion and dizziness of her fever, the pain and terror and despair as blood flowed out of her body. Ileni could feel the frantic beat of her heart, her blood struggling to circulate. It was an echo of a pain she recognized.

She knew how much it hurt to die.

But that pain was hers for only a second before the power rushed over it, overwhelmed it, drowned it. And after that, she felt nothing but joy.

By the time she blinked back to reality, the girl was dead. Her slim body was slumped against the pillow, blue eyes closed, blood soaking into her shirt and blanket. A stillness subtly but dreadfully different from sleep.

Alive just a moment ago, and now irretrievably gone. Ileni began to shake. Did that part ever get easier to understand?

The bearded man scowled at her. "Where's the lodestone? What kind of game are you playing?"

"I—" It was too much. She couldn't think. "Karyn—I have to go—"

He shook his head. "I don't know what you think you're doing, but you're not going anywhere until I find out."

With the magic flowing through her, Ileni was able to ignore that. He couldn't make her do anything. She could throw him across the room with a thought, if she wanted to.

And she wanted to.

But she controlled herself, and merely said, "Get out of my way."

He started to say something, took another look at her face, and changed his mind. Grudgingly, he moved to the foot of the bed. Ileni strode past him up the stairs.

She had just reached the top step when a surge of magic eddied around her, almost knocking her off-balance. She forced herself forward, through the narrow doorway, into the upper room of Death's Door.

Where Karyn was waiting for her.

CHAPTER 18

Ileni flung up a defensive spell, using the power she had taken from the blond girl. It was too late. Pain surged through her body, and violet light wrapped around her and squeezed. All at once she was fighting to breathe, much less utter the words of a spell.

"Mistress Karyn," the bearded man said, "this student took a girl's magic for herself."

Ileni tried to whirl on him and discovered that she couldn't move.

The man brushed past her and bowed briefly. "I had not heard from you, and it seemed irregular—"

"It certainly was." Karyn's fury was so palpable that only the violet light kept Ileni from flinching. "You were right to summon me."

Ileni discovered that even though she couldn't move, she could suck in enough air to speak. "You're too late. I know now."

"Know what?" Karyn's voice was a savage hiss. "You don't know anything you didn't know before."

"I didn't know you were killing children!"

"We're not killing anyone!" Karyn snapped. "They're giving their lives freely."

"Because you've left them no choice!" Ileni stopped and gasped for breath before she could continue. "You're not even trying to save them. Because their deaths are worth more to you than their lives. They're useless unless they fill your lodestones, aren't they?"

"Enough," Karyn snapped.

"No, it's not enough! I—"

The violet light around Ileni flashed, blinding her. A sizzle of power went right through her bones and turned her stomach upside down. She tried to throw up a ward, then a counterspell—panicked attempts that drained all the power she had just stolen—but she might as well have been trying to punch a mountain. Her insides twisted painfully.

She had felt this once before—and it had been Karyn then, too, on the road to her village, with the black mountains rising behind her. Ileni recognized the translocation spell a moment before the ground disappeared from beneath her feet and she was flung into nothingness, Karyn's taut face replaced by swirling darkness.

The violet light turned white, and then black, and then there was nothing at all.

When the world came back, Ileni was falling—a short, sharp drop that ended in an abrupt thud. She screamed once before her mind caught up with the fact that she was on solid ground. Or at least, her chest was. Her hands and feet were dangling over the edge of . . . something.

A wave of dizziness made her clutch the edge of the *something*. Her fingers pressed against sun-warmed rock and she knew, with sickening certainty, where she was. She forced her eyes open.

She was lying on a narrow, too-small base of solid rock, and all around her was a precipitous drop, leagues of empty space ending in blurred green far below.

From atop its peak, the Judgment Spire was even more

terrifying than from afar. The rock was sloped and bumpy, just enough so that a moment of inattention would send her slipping sideways and down.

And down. And down. And down. She could already hear herself screaming as she plummeted.

She didn't even have to check—though she did—to know that she had no power left. She could see the training plateau, flat and brown against a bruised lavender sky, but its lodestones were too far away to access.

Ileni would have shuddered if she had dared move that much. She curled up tighter on the slick bumpy stone, closing her eyes to shut out the sight of the space around her.

All she had to do was wait. If Karyn wanted to kill her, she could have done it at Death's Door. Which meant Karyn still thought she could use Ileni. If neither persuasion nor bribery worked, an imperial sorceress would inevitably turn to fear and pain.

The sorceress was probably watching Ileni now, wrapped in invisibility, waiting for her to show signs of despair. Ileni opened her eyes. Across from her, the other Judgment Spire ended in an empty knobby point. She imagined she heard a snicker, and dug her fingers into the rock. A tiny whimper escaped her.

If she were Sorin, she would call Karyn's bluff. She would jump.

Her stomach almost rose through her throat. She drew her knees tighter against her chest. She was not Sorin.

How long would Karyn leave her here?

Waiting for your enemy's move is a sign of weakness, Sorin had told her once. She thought of his face, his knife-sharp cheekbones and coal-black eyes, as if he was watching her now, as if she could impress him with her actions. It helped her fight down the simmering panic.

She would not leave the decision up to Karyn. There had to be another way to call Karyn's bluff.

And if it wasn't a bluff . . . well, at least coming up with a plan would give her something to think about other than falling.

Ileni considered her options—which didn't take long— then looked again at the green expanse beneath her. This time she managed to keep her eyes open, though her fingers pressed against the rock so hard they hurt. The sides of the spire were completely smooth, no handhold or foothold she could even think about grasping. The other spire was too far to imagine jumping for.

So she didn't have to imagine it. Good.

She reached for her magic again and felt the familiar painful shock when she came up empty. Even if she survived this, there was no way Karyn would allow her to continue using the lodestones' magic. Not that Ileni *would* use it, ever again, after what she had seen last night.

Something to worry about later. If there was a later.

Still, the old familiar despair made her reckless. She tilted her head back into the sunlight and said, "I found what we were looking for. Listen quickly. You were right. The sorcerers are—"

A blunt force propelled her sideways off the spire, and she fell.

The wind ripped the scream from her throat. Her flailing hands slammed futilely against the spire's stone sides. She plummeted downward, tears ripping from her face.

Then she jerked to a stop, halfway down the spire, the mountains and treetops spread like a tiny painting below her.

She kept screaming for a full minute before she managed to stop. Her eyes stung, and drool hung from the corner of her lip. Slowly, she curled herself upward and turned in the air, not bothering to wipe away the wetness streaked across her face.

"Who were you talking to?" Karyn inquired.

She sat cross-legged in midair several feet from Ileni, leaning back on both hands, as if supported by a pane of glass.

It was a moment before Ileni could make her throat work. "Isn't it obvious? And they can still hear us, in case you were wondering."

Karyn narrowed her eyes. "I don't sense any spell."

"No," Ileni said. "You wouldn't. The spell is in the ear of the person I was speaking to."

Karyn's mouth went as narrow as her eyes, skepticism engraved in her face. But her hands clenched. By now, Karyn was well aware that she didn't know everything the Renegai were capable of.

"Be careful," Karyn said softly. "I don't have much reason to keep you alive any more. Given your self-righteous horror at Death's Door, I can't imagine you're still considering joining our side."

She paused, clearly waiting for Ileni to contradict her. And though it would have been the smart thing to do, Ileni couldn't find the words.

Karyn's mouth twisted. "Right. It was worth a try, but you've been indoctrinated too thoroughly. So tell me why I shouldn't kill you now."

Ileni's voice came out far less bold than she had intended.

"Since you haven't yet, you obviously have a reason. Why don't you tell me what *that* is?"

The world dropped away again, just long enough to rip another scream from her, then jerked to a stop. Karyn floated lazily down after her.

"Guess," she suggested.

Ileni blinked away tears and let out two short gasps. "Because you still want answers. About who I'm talking to, and why, and what they have planned."

"That's right," Karyn said. The menace in her voice was soft, almost casual. "I do. And you're going to tell me."

"Why would I?" Ileni managed. "You'll kill me anyhow."

Karyn's smile was almost as terrifying as the drop below. "And you think you won't tell me just to gain another few seconds of life? Another minute before you fall?"

Ileni couldn't speak. She had never known that fear could be as intense as pain. Karyn was right. She would say anything, anything at all, to stave off that fall for as long as she could.

Karyn's smile widened as she leaned forward—and then it disappeared. She looked over Ileni's shoulder, her posture rigid. After an agonizing moment, Ileni twisted her head to follow Karyn's gaze.

The sun shone straight through the clouds in a curtain of faint white light, softening the mountain peaks behind it. Three figures hovered directly in the curtain of sunlight, one with waist-length black hair whipping about her body. They were too far for Ileni to make out their expressions, but they were unnaturally still, nothing moving but their hair and the hem of one girl's flame-red dress.

Ileni's heart lifted—then plummeted as she realized they weren't moving toward her. They were just watching. She felt a rush of anger. And then another rush, this one of realization.

Maybe all they had to do was watch.

Karyn's lips were pressed together tightly. Ileni said, "Are you going to kill me in front of them?"

If Karyn had been an assassin, she wouldn't have hesitated. If she had been the master, she would have summoned Cyn and told *her* to kill Ileni, and Cyn would have done it.

But this was the Empire, and Karyn did hesitate, glancing from the watching students to Ileni.

Ileni's heart froze in her chest. Beneath her, the ground yawned, terribly far away.

"No," Karyn said finally. "But I won't have to." She stretched into a standing position.

Karyn's flickering hand motion was by now familiar to Ileni, as was the sharp twist of the spell that accompanied it. So she was ready for the impact, the sickening lurch, and— this time, with relief—the blackness.

Once again, she knew where she was while her eyes were still shut. It was so familiar . . . the darkness, the smallness, the sense of oppressive weight pressing in above her. She was deep in the bowels of the earth again. She was back in the caves.

"Sorin?" Ileni cried, and the sound of her own voice— lost and hopeless—shocked her. She sat up. Blackness, blackness . . . she touched her eyelids with her fingertip to make sure she had really opened them. She had, but it made no difference. There was no light to see with.

She tried to call up a magelight, a futile attempt too instinctive to stop. She closed her eyes, because it made the darkness easier to bear, and flattened one hand on the ground beneath her. Stone, unnaturally smooth and straight. She got onto her hands and knees and slid one hand forward, then the other, making her way across the slick rock floor. When she hit a wall, she wasn't surprised.

She took off one of her shoes and left it on the ground.

Then, keeping one hand on the wall, she began to walk. The wall curved inward.

Her gait was awkward and uneven, but it was only a short while before her bare foot hit her shoe. So her prison was circular and very small.

No. It wasn't a prison. Prisons had beds. And food. And water.

Perhaps Karyn hadn't wanted to kill Ileni in front of the others. But none of them would know where Ileni had been translocated to. And none of them would see when Ileni finally died, alone in the dark.

She crossed the room slowly, hands out in front of her, until she hit the far wall. She did it again and again, crisscrossing every inch of the stone ground, but the cavern was empty. There was nothing in here.

Nothing but her.

She stretched up on tiptoe, reached her hands above her head, and her fingertips brushed the flat rock above her.

She couldn't keep herself from reaching for magic again, digging frantically, ripping at her insides. But there was nothing. Nothing inside, nothing outside, nothing, *nothing* she could use to escape.

That was when she began to scream.

● ● ●

In the total darkness, it was impossible to keep track of time. At first Ileni could pay attention to the hollow ache in her stomach as it slowly intensified; she could track the worsening of the dry pain in her throat. But then both went away, and everything was endlessly the same.

She thought she slept a lot, but she couldn't be sure. There ceased to be a clear distinction between sleeping and waking. One slipped into the other. Eventually, she supposed, they would slip a little further, into death.

Instead of frightening her, the thought filled her with a vague, fuzzy discomfort.

Once, she opened her eyes and saw Sorin, his eyes blacker than the darkness. She said, "You can't be here."

"I can be wherever I want to be. Haven't you learned by now not to underestimate an assassin?"

"I mean it's not safe."

"It's not safe for *you*. I've come to take you back."

"No. I need to be here. I need..." She couldn't remember what she needed, and the effort pushed her into a doze. Some indeterminate amount of time passed before she roused herself and said, happily, "I'm on your side now."

The cavern was empty. Sorin hadn't been there at all.

He couldn't have been. And if he had, he would not have left her.

Another time it was Karyn, and by then all Ileni's pride was gone. She said, "Please."

Karyn smiled with cool disdain.

"You're ashamed to kill me," Ileni whispered. "That's why you're doing it secretly. But the others will find out. . . ."

"No," Karyn said, "they won't." Her eyes glittered, pinpoints of bright malice, and Ileni drifted into darkness again.

She should have been more careful. She should have stood there, among the people waiting for slaughter, and pretended she thought it was perfectly reasonable.

If something like this had happened among the assassins, she would have been killed at once—brutally, publicly, with no need to explain anything to anyone. Perhaps murder was worse when it needed to be hidden.

When she opened her eyes again, the pale girl knelt over her, clutching a baby to her chest. "You promised to save her," she whispered, as her magic flowed out of her and vanished into the stone around them. Her blond hair floated around her head. "You promised."

"I'm sorry," Ileni tried to say, but the woman vanished and she had no one to say it to. No one but herself. She was going to die, and because of that, she was never going to keep that promise.

The realization roused her, a jab of frustration piercing her lassitude. She wanted to do something *good*—something simply, purely, unmistakably good. In all her time in the Empire, she had made only one promise she could keep without guilt or shame, and made it to a girl whose power she had stolen. Here in the darkness, that promise seemed more important than the fate of the Empire or the plots of the assassins.

A part of her was glad that soon she wouldn't have to think about those things anymore, wouldn't have to untangle the tightly woven threads of good and evil that shifted with every new step. But she wished desperately that she could have saved the blond girl's baby before she died.

It hurt to think, like pushing her mind through a fog of needles. It was so hard to fight—and what, really, was she fighting for? What was worth all this pain? All she wanted was to slip back into the peaceful blackness.

So she did.

CHAPTER
19

Whehen she woke again, she woke fighting. Ileni did not recognize the figure looming over her—she didn't know if she was really awake, or really alive—but a sense of danger shot through her, real and sharp as pain. She surged upward, her back against the wall, hands up and curled into claws.

"Well," Arxis said, "I think she's feeling better."

Ileni snarled at him, even as she noted that she *was* feeling better. Her body was slick with sweat and grime, her eyelashes coated with gunk, her limbs trembling—but they were working, and so was her mind.

She realized that Arxis wasn't talking to *her* a moment

before she registered the faint light of a glowstone, and the figure holding it stepped close enough for her to see him.

Evin.

The tension drained out of her, and the trembling weakness in her legs took over. She slid to the stone floor. "What—" Her voice didn't work. It took her two attempts to manage more than a raspy whisper. "What are you doing here?"

"Rescuing you," Arxis said. "You're welcome."

He reached for her, and she struck at him with all her strength—which wasn't enough for him to bother noticing. He grabbed her wrist, pressed a finger to her pulse, and nodded. As soon as his grip loosened, Ileni jerked her hand away so hard her elbow thudded into the wall behind her.

"Someday," Evin said, "one of you is going to have to tell me about your history. It must be an interesting story."

Arxis laughed, but Ileni was too occupied with the pain ricocheting up her arm to respond. She gritted her teeth, waiting for it to pass. Evin moved forward to stand beside Arxis.

"I'm sure you won't be happy to hear it," Evin added, "but you sort of owe Arxis your life now."

His voice carried its usual light tone, and he stood in his

usual half-slouch, but there was something . . . off . . . about it. Like a hastily assumed disguise. Ileni frowned at him.

"Karyn told us she had banished you from the Academy, and you had gone back to your people," Evin said. "But Arxis told me once that you would never go back. We've been searching for you for days."

"You were half-dead when we found you," Arxis added. His eyes were deep in shadow, the planes of his face blurred by darkness. "Evin's been dribbling broth into your mouth for nearly an hour."

"You did the rest," Evin said.

That was when Ileni realized he was holding a lodestone in his other hand. She closed her eyes, just for a second, as magic flowed through her skin. Her mind was clear, and when she rolled her shoulders back, they moved without complaint. She had a vague memory, now, of working a healing spell, of Evin gently urging her on.

"Why?" she said to Arxis.

"Why what?"

"Why did you save my life?"

Arxis shrugged. "Evin insisted."

Trying to think made her lightheaded. She scrubbed her eyes with one hand. "Where am I?"

"We're in the Academy," Evin said.

"But—*where* in the Academy?"

Evin and Arxis exchanged glances. Then Evin closed his eyes, clenched his fists, and opened his mouth.

No sound emerged; his moving lips screamed the spell into nothingness, and the magic engulfed the sound as he spoke. Ileni had worked spells this powerful before, but never on her own, without a preexisting spell anchored to a solid object. Yet Evin was holding nothing, using nothing but his own power. He squeezed his eyes shut, face twisted with effort. A trickle of sweat ran down the side of his neck as he released the spell.

The walls shimmered and were gone, and sunlight flooded through the sides of the room, making Ileni flinch. She covered her eyes and concentrated on the sun beating at her skin, warming her bare forearms and her hair.

When she slowly uncovered her eyes, the brightness made her blink back tears, and rainbow shimmers danced across her vision. Then they cleared, and she walked slowly over to one of the now-invisible walls.

Empty space stretched ahead of her and plummeted to a ground she couldn't see from this angle. A Judgment Spire soared upward across from her, stark gray against a brilliant blue sky.

One Judgment Spire. She stretched up an arm to brush her fingers against the solid rock ceiling above her, and understood. They were inside the other spire.

"How did you know I was here?" she asked. When she turned, the sunlight warmed her shoulders and back.

"There's a bespelled key that allows entrance and exit from the spire cells," Evin said. "Karyn left it on her desk."

Each of those sentences demanded a million questions. Ileni chose, rather randomly, "What were you doing in Karyn's room?"

"Trying to find out what she had done to you."

"But wasn't that dangerous?"

"I'm incredibly brave," Evin said. "Haven't you noticed?"

"I don't . . ." She struggled to think. "I don't understand. Why would you risk so much to rescue me?"

"I'm not risking much."

She couldn't tell if that was true. "But you don't even like me."

Evin cocked an eyebrow. "Actually, I like you quite a lot. You're confused by the fact that *you* don't like *me*."

Her face burned. "That's—that's not—"

"It's all right." Evin shrugged. "I don't require people to like me before I decide to like them. That would be giving too much weight to their opinion of me."

"You are a very strange person," Ileni said slowly. "I assume you know that?"

"It's been mentioned. Usually people have the courtesy to do it behind my back."

Arxis rolled his eyes. "Ileni's not big on courtesy."

"I know. It's one of the things I like about her."

"How nice for both of you," Arxis said. "Before this becomes predictable, I propose we find out if Evin can use this spell to get us *out* of here."

"You don't know?" Ileni said.

"I'm almost sure I can do it," Evin said. "There's no way to know for certain until I try."

"*He's* almost sure," Arxis said. "My certainty is at a far lower level than *almost.*"

Ileni looked away from Evin, which was a relief, to focus on Arxis. "Then why did *you* come and risk being trapped here?"

"The confidence you both have in me is truly inspiring," Evin said. His habitual half-smile was back, his eyes light and dancing. "If you would be quiet a moment and let me concentrate, I'll do my best to exceed it."

Before Ileni could apologize, Evin held out a large silver key and focused on it.

He clearly didn't need to concentrate too hard. He lowered his hands, and the key floated in midair before him, ordinary looking but humming with power. Evin murmured a single word, then released that power with a casual motion of his hand.

Ileni felt the spell unleash, a sizzle that shot through her body from scalp to toe, making the world dissolve into chaotic fragments. Then her feet hit solid ground, and she lurched forward, hitting her hip on the corner of a desk that hadn't been there a moment ago. When she reached out blindly to break her fall, her hand knocked over a stack of papers. They flew sideways and scattered, a frantic flutter of white sliding across the stone floor.

"Don't vomit!" Evin said. "We can't leave any sign we were here."

The warning was just in time. Ileni clamped her lips shut. She fought her instincts, kept her mouth closed, and—with a whimper of revulsion—swallowed. The bile burned its way down her throat.

"A little late for that, don't you think?" Arxis said as the last paper fluttered against the far wall.

"We can clean that up," Evin said. "Karyn is disorganized. If they're out of order, she'll assume it was her fault."

That didn't sound like Karyn, but Ileni was in no state to argue. Her mouth hurt. Power tingled in the air, tantalizingly distant, and she reached for it and drew it in. Karyn's office must be just close enough to the testing arena. She could use magic to . . .

No. She stopped herself. Not *this* magic. Never again.

But she remembered the helplessness of falling through the air, of lying trapped in the dark, and she didn't let the magic go.

They were in a square, windowless chamber, its white rock walls lined with an assortment of bookcases, boxes, and large statuelike objects whose purpose Ileni couldn't begin to guess at. Boxes and papers and food-stained bowls were piled around the walls and filled much of the floor space.

"I'm sorry," Evin said. "Transportation is exhausting, even for me. I should have made it smoother."

Ileni swallowed hard before attempting to speak. Her mouth tasted foul. "Since your transportation spell also saved my life, I'll forgive you."

He grinned, which sent a surge of unexpected gladness through her. "I assume that comes with an offer to help clean up? We have some time, but not much—Karyn is in the city fixing the sandstorm shields."

Arxis was already collecting and stacking papers, with the same efficiency assassins used to spar—or kill. Evin joined him, slow and lumberish by comparison. A zigzag pattern of glowstones near the ceiling lit the chamber brightly. High on one of the walls, across from Karyn's desk, hung a large parchment map.

Aware that it was rude not to help clean up, Ileni walked to the map. There were no words on it, and she couldn't tell what the symbols meant, but she could see that it covered a vast territory. The Empire?

She lifted a hand toward the map, then snatched it away when the parchment's surface shimmered and changed. Another map, filled with curving lines and angles that seemed oddly familiar, covered the parchment.

The sudden stillness made her aware that the cleaning had stopped. She wasn't surprised when Arxis stepped up beside her. But there was something so predatory about his movement—as if he had dropped his mask—that only her fascination with the map kept her from stepping away from him.

"What is this?" Arxis asked. His voice was light and nonchalant, at odds with his grim expression.

"I don't know." Evin, still behind them, couldn't see

the fierceness in Arxis's eyes. He sounded as casual as the assassin was pretending to be. "The first map is the Empire, of course. This one shows whatever specific area Karyn's been looking at most recently."

Of course. Those curves, those lines—they were familiar to Ileni because she had memorized them, once.

It was a map of the Assassins' Caves.

Karyn had mapped them when she was there. And now she was using what she knew to plan an assault.

This map was of the *inside* of the caves, not the mountains around them. Karyn must have gotten farther into the caves than anyone had realized, back when she had been posing as a trader.

But Sorin knew about the river entrance now, which meant he would be guarding it— or, more likely, had blocked it off entirely. Whatever attack Karyn had planned was no longer feasible. *I'm right back where I started,* she had told Ileni.

Karyn hadn't given up, clearly. She was still searching for a way in. Still readying an attack.

How soon would it come? Ileni's heart pounded. Her choice lay in front of her, stark and clear. She could prevent this attack. With the Academy in ruins and the lodestones buried—with Karyn dead—this plan would die stillborn.

"I don't think you have much choice," Evin said.

Ileni half-turned, tearing her eyes from the map. "What?"

"Karyn will realize you've escaped. The only way to stay out of her reach is to go back to your own people. I know you don't like the idea. . . ." He hesitated. "I don't like it, either. But in the mountains, you'll be safe."

Would she?

For a moment the prospect was unbearably tempting. She could go back to being a Renegai, wrapped in empty dreams of someday—*someday*—making a difference.

But those dreams were gone, and she could never get them back. When she had believed she could learn the truth and make her own choice, she hadn't realized that truths could not be unlearned, that knowledge would rob her of choices as well.

She turned her back on the map, just in time to see Evin hold up the silver key and mutter a quick spell. The key sparkled briefly, and Evin placed it on top of one of the towering piles of paper on Karyn's desk.

Ileni blinked. "That's where you found it?"

Evin shrugged. "Karyn's messy."

"And busy planning a war," Arxis added. A hint of steel pierced his voice, then vanished, and he slouched against the white stone wall. "Which is probably distracting."

Ileni opened her mouth, then shut it. *She* was part of Karyn's plan for that war. She didn't believe for one second that Karyn would have been careless with the key to Ileni's prison. Not if Karyn really wanted her to die.

Karyn had intended for Evin to find the key.

A long shudder ran through Ileni. There was nothing heartwarming about this revelation. If Karyn didn't want Ileni dead, it was only because she still had some use for her. She still thought Ileni might be turned against the assassins, might choose the Empire, even after what she had seen.

Was she banking on Ileni's need for power? Did she really think Ileni would turn her back on everything she believed so she could keep using magic?

Or had she planned for *Evin*, specifically, to rescue Ileni? Was she hoping Ileni's gratitude would keep her from doing anything that would hurt her rescuer?

And was she right?

Ileni's head hurt. She missed Sorin. He never had doubts. If he was here, maybe he could convince her not to have doubts, either.

Sorin would say they all deserved to die.

But she was not Sorin, and she didn't have to play by his

rules. She could use the shattering spell, bury the lodestones—but warn the others first. Evin, especially, deserved that from her. Cyn, too . . . even Lis. She would get them out somehow, protect them.

Sorin wouldn't like it, wouldn't even understand it, but that was too bad for him.

"We need to get out of here," Arxis said, "before Karyn comes back."

Evin nodded. "Ileni, if you tell me where to transport you—"

"I can't go back." Ileni said it as fast as she could, in an attempt to make it hurt less. "I have no magic of my own, and my people don't steal magic. If I go back, I'll be powerless."

"There is more than one type of power," Evin said.

Easy for you to say. She shook her head. "I was the most powerful sorceress of my people, once. But there was . . . they made a mistake." It hadn't been a mistake. *They designed me to kill you.* "My power started fading, when I got older, and it faded until it was gone. And then I came here, and I couldn't . . . I couldn't resist it. If my people knew what I did here, the sort of magic I used, the way I used it . . ."

"But you can't stay here," Evin said. "Is there anywhere else you can go?"

"Maybe." Ileni didn't dare look at Arxis. "But I can't leave yet. There's something I have to do here first."

Arxis's voice was sharp and smooth. "And what's that?"

Ileni hesitated.

"If what you need to do here is a secret," Arxis said, "it's going to be harder for us to help you with it."

Ileni choked down a laugh. They both focused on her, and she bit her lip hard, using the pain to hold back her growing hysteria. She didn't know which side was right, or even less wrong. She didn't know if destroying the Academy was an act of heroism or of murder. But she knew one small thing that was simple and right, one choice she could be proud of.

"I made a promise to a dying girl," she said. "I have to keep it before I go."

CHAPTER 20

The knife thudded into the target with a force that made the man-shaped cloth swish against the stone wall. Another knife followed it, and then another. All three knives quivered, inches apart, exactly where the man's heart would have been.

"Impressive," Absalm said.

Sorin walked over to the weapons rack and pulled out a blade. The slight hitch in the sorcerer's breathing told him that Absalm knew which knife he had drawn.

He flipped it up in the air. The blade twirled, a deadly circle of steel, until he caught it by the hilt.

"Shouldn't you be careful with that?" Absalm asked. He

had recovered his usual gentle cadence—what Sorin thought of as his wise teacher tone.

"Should I?" Sorin said. "Can't the Renegai heal poison?"

"Not *that* poison."

Sorin threw the blade up again, spun on his heel, and was facing the sorcerer when he caught it.

"So if I nicked myself," he mused, "I would die. And what would *you* do, then?"

"Not heal you," Absalm said. "Because I can't."

"I believe you. I meant, after I died." Sorin's arm tensed, wanting to fling the knife up again. *Restraint,* the master's voice whispered, *is more impressive than courage.* "Who would become the new leader?"

Absalm tugged his earlobe, watching Sorin warily. "There is no obvious candidate."

"No, there isn't, is there? It was always going to be me or Irun. And Irun is dead." He ran one thumb down the spiral design on the knife hilt. "So there would be chaos. Several hundred killers, trained to follow orders, with no orders to follow. Who do you think they would turn on?"

"I understand your point," Absalm snapped. "I need you. So? You need me, too."

Sorin moved like lightning. The sorcerer didn't have time

to utter the first word of a spell before the dagger's edge was against his throat, so close it must feel like it was brushing his skin.

"Actually," Sorin said, "I'm not sure I need you at all."

Only Absalm's mouth moved. "But are you sure you don't?"

Sorin laughed, low and soft, then twisted sideways and threw the poisoned dagger. It landed in the center of the other three.

"No," he said. "That's why you're alive. But if you ever contradict my orders again, I will change my mind."

"I don't know what you—"

"You met with Bazel, before he left on his mission."

Sorin saw the sorcerer consider lying and decide against it. Absalm tugged his earlobe again. "How do you know?"

"You're not asking questions right now, Absalm. You're answering them. *What did you tell Bazel to do?*"

Despite Sorin's best effort, his voice hardened, just a bit. It wouldn't have given him away to most people, but Absalm had lived in the Assassins' Caves for years. His gray eyes narrowed. "I think you know."

Anger is a weakness. Sorin had to work to keep his face cool.

"You told him," he said, "to kill Ileni."

"Only," Absalm said, "if he believes she's going to betray us."

"Bazel hates Ileni. I think he'll find that easy to believe."

"He's an assassin. He won't let personal feelings interfere with his mission."

Sorin allowed his anger to show, and told himself it was a calculated decision. "How very subtle."

"It was the master's intent," Absalm said. "To kill her if she wouldn't go along with his plan. He didn't leave loose ends."

"She won't betray us," Sorin said. "She will see the truth about the Empire, and she will help us destroy it. She's not a loose end."

"If you're so sure," Absalm said, "why are you recruiting people to convince her?"

Recruiting, not *sending.* Sorin's expression didn't change, but Absalm looked satisfied anyhow. "Oh, yes. I know about the Renegai boy."

"I'm reminding her who she is," Sorin said. The edge in his voice made the sorcerer flinch, but not step back. The air between them felt hot. "But I'm not worried. She's on our side."

"In that case," Absalm said, "she'll be in no danger at all."

CHAPTER 21

The front of Death's Door was far more respectable than its side entrance. A façade of pink-veined white marble stretched beside a narrow street, occupied only by a trio of slouching young men, a mangy dog, and an old woman squatting next to a basket of apples. None of them seemed startled when three sorcerers popped out of thin air in front of the imposing building.

They did glance over when Ileni pitched forward onto her hands and knees and vomited on the dirt street. But only for a second.

"Oh, good," Arxis said. "That's inconspicuous."

"Too many translocation spells," Evin said. "I wish I had Karyn's silent-spelled boots—they're the only thing that would make them easier. But you understand why I couldn't put in a request."

"I'm fine," Ileni said through gritted teeth. Sourness burned her mouth, her face muscles hurt, and she was more chagrined than she wanted to admit that Evin was seeing this. Without thinking, she used a trickle of magic to clean her mouth and breath. As she did, the blond girl's desperate eyes floated through her mind, reminding her what she was using. Where this power came from.

She got to her feet. Evin flicked his fingers at the small puddle of vomit, and it vanished.

An auspicious beginning. Cheeks hot, Ileni faced the front entrance of Death's Door. Ironically enough, it consisted of *two* doors, austere and imposing, both built of heavy dark wood and inscribed with symbols she didn't understand. Nothing like what hid behind them, the lines of beds with their suffering victims, waiting to be tortured and killed.

"What now?" Evin said.

Ileni squared her shoulders. "We go inside and ask where that woman's child is."

"Ask who?" Arxis drawled.

The silence stretched. Ileni frowned at Evin. "Don't you know?"

He shrugged. "I've never been here before."

"But you knew where it was."

"Sure. I've heard of it. But I've never had a reason to come here."

Of course not. That way he didn't have to see the beds, hear the cries, truly understand where the Academy's lodestones were coming from. "Fine. We'll just have to figure it out as we go."

"That should be easy," Arxis said. "We'll explain to them that you want to rescue a baby, but you haven't the first idea what its name is or where it might be."

"She," Ileni said. "It's a girl."

"Oh, good. That should narrow things down considerably."

"You said you promised her mother," Evin interrupted, before Ileni could retort. "What do you know about *her*?"

"That she's dead, and she died at Death's Door." Ileni couldn't resist adding, "She died to give her magic to the Academy. She traded it for her child's care."

Evin nodded. "Then the Black Sisters will take care of her child. If we can find her."

Disappointment dropped right through Ileni's throat and into her stomach. She wasn't sure why. Had she really thought that Evin might not know? Or if he knew, that he would care?

"Of course," Arxis said, "that brings us right back to the *finding her* problem. If neither of you have any idea where to start, may I suggest—"

"Actually," a familiar voice behind Ileni said, "I believe I can help."

Ileni whirled. One of the wooden doors was now partly open. Bazel stood in the entrance, wearing a white robe and a large blue belt.

"Welcome," he said. "Please enter."

Absolute silence. Bazel glanced over Ileni's shoulder at Arxis. Not a trace of recognition on either face, of course. No matter his weaknesses, Bazel was assassin-trained.

"Someone you know?" Evin said.

"Just someone I met last time I was in the city." Ileni smiled at Bazel. "It's wonderful to see you again."

Bazel stepped back into the hall and swept his hand out in a welcoming gesture.

Arxis strode in, passing within inches of Bazel. Every muscle in Ileni's body tensed, even though the two didn't touch or even exchange a glance.

"Coming?" Arxis inquired.

"Ileni?" Evin's voice was soft, his brows furrowed.

If Evin had picked up on her tension, the assassins certainly had. Bazel's eyes were blank and steady, but Ileni detected—thought she detected—a hint of mockery in their depths. Since it was Bazel, she was probably right. He wasn't as good as the others at anything, including hiding his intent.

But what *was* his intent?

I'm here to show you something. He had said that last time, and brought her here, and made no attempt to harm her. But last time, her body hadn't screamed *danger* at her.

"We don't have to go in." Evin stepped up beside her. "I can take you somewhere else. He *is* wearing a blue belt."

Which meant what, exactly? But this wasn't the time to ask. Ileni pushed her unreasoning fear away and shook her head. "Thank you. But I do have to." She met his long-lashed brown eyes. "You—you don't have to. If you don't want to."

"Ileni." Evin sighed. "Don't you know anything about me by now?" His hand closed around hers, hesitantly. She pulled away. "I never do anything I don't want to."

She laughed, and the corners of Evin's eyes crinkled. She

walked ahead of him through the large door, into a long hall lit by glowstones.

The hallway was starkly clean, lined with evenly spaced doors, and absolutely silent. Sound-dampening spells were woven into the thick wooden doors, shutting out the groans and cries from downstairs.

"Do you know who keeps the recent records?" Evin asked Bazel. "We're trying to find the child of a woman who died here recently."

Bazel opened his mouth to reply, and one of the doors creaked open. A tall man with gold-streaked white hair strolled down the corridor toward them. "Who are these people?" he demanded.

"They're from the Academy," Bazel said. "I'm helping them."

The man nodded and walked past. He opened another door, and through it came, for a moment, the sound of a woman screaming. Then he shut the door behind him, and the hall was silent again.

Ileni drew in a series of shallow breaths, hoping that would be less obvious than a single deep one. So Bazel had infiltrated Death's Door, was known and trusted by the people here. No surprise. That was what assassins did.

But had he done it just so he could show her this place, open her eyes to the source of imperial magic? Or did *he* have a target, too?

You thought I would never leave the caves. She could still hear the pride in his voice. Oh, yes. The only mission an assassin would be proud of was one designed to end in death.

But whose?

Evin touched her lightly on the shoulder, reminding her that she, too, was an infiltrator. Known and trusted by the people she was meant to kill. "Maybe you should rest," he said. "That many translocations can leave you dizzy for a while."

Bazel's gaze snapped to the point of contact between Evin's finger and Ileni's tunic. His mouth curved in a small, smug smile.

A mistake no other assassin would have made. Ileni recognized the anticipation in that smile.

And she knew who Bazel was here to kill.

She moved without hesitating, pulling in magic, gasping out the words of the most powerful shield she knew. She moved faster than thought, because she didn't need to think.

She knew when she was prey.

Bazel's dagger streaked toward her, and she got the shield

up barely in time. The dagger stuck in thin air, its point inches from her eye.

Arxis screamed, very convincingly. Bazel flung out a spell, wild and chaotic and immensely powerful. Ileni's shield shattered with a force that drove her against the wall, and Bazel was across the hall in seconds. He slammed into her, pressing her to the wall, and his dagger whispered cold and sharp on the side of her neck.

"I'm so glad I get to do this," he hissed in her ear, and sliced the blade across the front of her throat.

It shattered into a hundred pieces.

Bazel dropped the broken dagger hilt and wrapped his hands around her throat, ribbons of blood crisscrossing his face. Ileni's throat had been stone a second ago, but a wild spell from Bazel turned it back to flesh. Ileni had forgotten how much power he had.

And someone had been teaching him how to use it.

But someone had taught her, too. She threw her weight backward, slid two fingers under his thumbs, and brought her knee up into his groin.

It was the first fighting move Sorin had ever taught her, and it worked. Bazel had expected magic, and was not defending against physical attack. His grip loosened, he staggered back, and Ileni could draw in enough breath for a spell.

Before she had even taken that breath, a thrust of power from Evin threw Bazel away from her. The assassin crashed against the far wall of the hallway and hung there, pinned.

Bazel lashed out with magic, which Evin brushed away. He strode forward and, with a viciousness Ileni had never seen in him, slammed his fist into Bazel's cheek. Bazel's head jerked to the side, cracking against the wall.

The hall was quiet and empty. All anyone would have heard, through those heavy doors, was a faint thud.

"Assassin," Evin snarled. It wasn't a question. "What do you have against Ileni?"

Bazel spat out blood. "What we have against her is that she is useless. Our master has no use for broken tools."

Our master. It took Ileni a moment to realize: that was Sorin, now.

It was worse than watching the dagger come at her. Her breath froze in her throat, an ice-cold shard that sliced and burned. Then she saw the gloating malice in Bazel's eyes, and she straightened.

She didn't believe it. Sorin might have sent Bazel to influence her—but not to kill her. Not even if it seemed that she was going to make the wrong decision.

No. The person who had ordered Bazel to kill her if she was "broken" was the same person who had taught him those spells.

Absalm. The Renegai Elder who had molded her life and destroyed her hopes. She hadn't turned out the way he had planned, so he was eliminating her.

"What is he talking about?" Evin said.

"I have no idea," Ileni said without thinking. Then she did think—about Evin discovering that she had lived with the assassins, about Karyn discovering that she was here to kill for them—and panic spurted through her. She couldn't let Bazel be questioned.

But she couldn't let him go, either. He was an assassin on a mission. Nothing would stop him from coming after her if he was free.

And alive.

She knew what she had to do. She knew she could do it. She had wanted to do it, once, in a small stone room, with a dagger in her hand and blood in her hair. She would have killed Bazel then, if he hadn't run, and she would have done it gladly. She lifted her hand, and Bazel's eyes focused on her, recognizing her as a threat.

So many spells she could use to kill. She remembered, briefly, that she shouldn't be using magic anymore. The thought vanished swiftly, drowned by the pounding of her heart. She chose a simple spell Cyn had taught her and spread her fingers wide.

And hesitated.

It was different now, with this vast quiet all around them, with Evin's eyes on her. It was different when she was making the sorts of cold calculations that Karyn, and the master— and Sorin, now—must make all the time.

She had thought, in the Assassins' Caves, that she had learned to kill. That she understood killers. But she hadn't, not really. She had only learned to kill in moments when the choice—kill or be killed—was stark and clear.

Bile rose in her throat. She swallowed, coiled the magic within her, and began to chant.

"Ileni?" Evin said sharply. He recognized the spell.

She released the magic with a hiss, and a band of blue light shot from her fingertips. At the last moment she altered its direction, so that instead of coiling around Bazel's throat, the glowing blue light wrapped around his body. It pinned his arms to his sides and squeezed.

In her mind, Sorin sighed and shook his head.

I know what I'm doing, she thought fiercely. Out loud, she said, "We have to bring him to Karyn. She'll get answers from him."

Bazel sucked in air through his teeth. But the pride in his eyes was almost frenzied when he said, "You think so? Assassins are trained to withstand torture."

She tightened the band, enough to hurt. "So they are. But somehow, I suspect you're not the best of assassins."

She flicked a glance at Arxis and saw his eyes narrow. The other assassins had never respected or trusted Bazel.

A flare of magic from Bazel sliced the blue band in two. It reconnected almost instantly, but even the least of the assassins was fast enough to take advantage of that *almost.* Bazel flung out his hand.

The blue band snapped it back to his side, ruining his aim, and his dagger hit the wall to the left of Ileni's head.

At the same moment, Arxis lunged sideways and slid a dagger across Bazel's throat.

It was swift and clean, as Ileni had known it would be. Blood spurted out in vast quantities, drenching Bazel's tunic. His head dropped forward into the blood, lolling again his chest.

Ileni met Arxis's eyes briefly, then let the blue band go.

Bazel's body slid to the ground and slumped against the wall. His chin and mouth were stained a shockingly bright red.

"He had another dagger," Arxis said curtly. He should have tried to sound as if it bothered him more, Ileni thought. "And he was calling up magic. He was about to kill her. I had to do it."

And that was true. Not the details, but the basics. Bazel would have killed Ileni eventually, if he had lived.

But maybe not before he spilled some of the assassins' secrets to Karyn. Which was why Arxis had done it.

Exactly as Ileni had known he would.

Weak, Sorin whispered in her mind. What difference did it make whether she killed Bazel with her own hands or arranged it so Arxis would? Did that make her better, that recoil, that cowardice? Did it matter that she was ashamed to kill, and Arxis wasn't? This death belonged to both of them.

Evin stood silent. Bazel's dead eyes were wide open above the red mask that covered the bottom of his face. Arxis's dagger—not a spiral-hilt assassin's dagger, just a standard knife—was stained the same dark red.

"Karyn will hear about this," Evin said finally. His

voice was carefully calm. "She'll be notified as soon as the body is found. We have to get Ileni out of here before she shows up."

"But—" Ileni said, then stopped, not sure what she was objecting to.

Evin was already striding toward the front door. "We won't get any answers here, anyhow. Not once they discover that Death's Door was infiltrated by an assassin. It will be chaos. We need to be far away when that happens."

Arxis's eyes glittered. He wasn't bothering to hide his expressions from Ileni anymore. It *would* be chaos, yes, and terror. A reminder that no place was safe from the assassins.

Bazel's body lay still in a way that was nothing like sleep, his face blank and empty. Memories flashed through Ileni: Bazel in her training room, one of twenty assassins, his round face fearful beneath his auburn hair. Bazel leaning back on white rock, grinning and raising a mug, the black river sliding past him.

She shook off those memories, replaced them with another: the dagger point thudding to a stop inches from her eyes. She forced herself to stop staring at the corpse, and only then realized that Evin was watching her.

She couldn't read his expression, couldn't shake the

feeling that, somehow, he suspected what she had done. She said, "What now?"

"First," Evin said, "let's get out of here."

"And go where?" Arxis inquired.

Evin slammed the heavy doors open with a surge of power, and they all followed him toward the sunlight. "I have an idea."

CHAPTER 22

"All right," Evin said, when they were several streets and stairways away from Death's Door. Here, the streets were wide and empty, lined with large elegant buildings decorated in marble. "Here's my plan. Ileni, how old is the baby?"

"I'm not sure," Ileni said. She was slightly surprised at how easily Evin seemed able to put Bazel's death behind him—but then, Bazel was an assassin, one of the enemy. And Evin *was* a soldier, even if he wasn't very enthusiastic about it. He had seen people die before. He had killed many of them himself.

She focused. "Her mother died of childbed fever. So I suppose . . . two weeks at most."

"Well, that's something to start with. An abandoned baby would probably be taken to the Sisters of the Black God to see if anyone claimed her." Evin leaned against the side of a pale yellow building and announced, in the tone of one presenting a masterpiece, "We can ask Girad to find her for us."

Nobody said anything. Somewhere not far off, a horse neighed shrilly.

"That's your plan?" Ileni said finally. "Ask a five-year-old for help?"

"Girad is six."

"Oh. Well, that's entirely different."

"I have a suggestion," Arxis cut in. "Why don't we just choose any random baby in the orphanage and help *her*? They're all equally in need of it."

"Because," Ileni said, through gritted teeth, "that's not what I promised."

Arxis shrugged. "The mother is dead. She won't know. And instead of spending your time searching for one particular baby who is exactly like all the others, you could save any of them. You could even choose the one who needs saving the most."

"No," Ileni said.

Arxis's lip curled. "Then you don't really care what

happens to any of them. All you care about is that it not be your fault."

Ileni clenched her fists, but could think of nothing to say. The sickening swirl deep in her stomach was familiar. This was exactly what arguing with Sorin felt like.

"I'm a Renegai," she said finally. "That means I keep my promises."

It sounded weak to her, but the expression on Evin's face was pure admiration. It sent a shiver of gratification through her, which she ignored.

Arxis's reaction was the opposite. Not even contempt: amusement. "How noble of you. Racing around after a baby, ignoring your true goals—whatever they are." Ileni flinched. "Do you know how many babies die, or are abandoned, in this city? Hundreds. And throughout the Empire, tens of thousands. Do you think you can save them all?"

Ileni opened her mouth, then closed it. The familiar sense of helplessness swamped her.

Evin snorted softly. "We're not trying to save them all," he said. "We're trying to save this one." He ran a hand through his hair, leaving it sticking up in brown tufts. "Let's go find Girad."

"So we're committed to the rely-on-a-six-year-old plan," Arxis said. "Excellent."

"Girad is more observant than most adults I've met. Once he—"

"Don't," Arxis interrupted him. "I'm not sure what I want to hear less: stories about how remarkable Girad is, or drivel about how superior the Renegai are."

"We'll try to split it evenly, then," Evin said.

Ileni spun on her heel. "Come on. Let's go talk to this six-year-old genius."

In the Renegai training compound, students had been strictly divided by age. As a result, Ileni had never spent much time around six-year-olds; and while she had a vague memory of *being* six years old, she didn't recall it being quite so . . . loud.

The orphanage of the Black Sisters was a rectangular building with an interior courtyard, which several dozen children were using as a play area. It was like being inside a storm of shrieks and wails. Evin, immediately upon their arrival, waded into the mass of children. Arxis and Ileni stood with their backs to the building wall, and the slightly wild-eyed expression on Arxis's face made Ileni feel an odd kinship with him. There had been children in the Assassins' Caves, too, but they had been silent and focused and disciplined.

"I don't know what you hope to gain from this ridiculous excursion," Arxis said. "If you were smart, you would return to your people while you still have your life."

The tingle of empathy vanished. "Since when do assassins care about life? You don't even care about your own. I find it hard to believe you care about mine."

"Of course I don't," Arxis said.

"So what you really want is for me to leave." Behind her, three children crashed into each other, and all three began screeching at once. "Am I interfering with your mission? How, I wonder, am I doing that?"

"Not interfering." Arxis raised his voice slightly to be heard over the wails. "Inconveniencing."

"Why did you help rescue me, then? Why not leave me to die?"

Arxis snorted. "I would have been more than happy to. But the master sent you. Besides, Evin would never have spoken to me again."

"And why is *that* important to you?"

A ball whizzed at them from somewhere within the crowd. Ileni ducked instinctively, but Arxis caught it and threw it back with a twist of his wrist. "Are you under the impression that if you keep asking the same question over and over, you generate some sort of force that requires me to answer it?"

Ileni's breath hissed through her teeth. "Don't you understand that things have changed? That your mission has to change, too? That map in Karyn's room . . . it was of the caves. She's planning an assault."

"No," Arxis said, utterly calm. "If she was planning an assault, there would have been markings on the map. She's planning something else."

Evin emerged from the sea of children, towing Girad by one arm. Girad did not appear happy to be called into service. He kicked Evin's ankle, twisted free, and raced back into the melee. Evin lunged after him.

"I was about to *win!*" Girad howled. His thin arms and legs flailed. "You're ruining everything!"

"Sorry," Evin said insincerely, and deposited him on the ground in front of Ileni, both hands firmly on the boy's shoulders. "This is more important than your game. We need your help to find somebody."

Girad glared at Ileni as if it was all her fault—which, to be fair, it was.

"Um," Ileni said. "We're very grateful. You're doing something *very important*. Someone's whole life might be changed."

Girad looked at her dubiously, and Ileni flushed. "We'll, uh, we'll also give you candy if you help us."

Girad glared up at his brother. "You had better not be in love with *her*."

Evin kicked him, not very subtly, in the calf. Girad kicked back. Arxis sighed and said, "Just ask the question, Ileni."

Ileni's flush had now knitted itself permanently to her cheeks. "We're looking for a baby," she said. "Newborn, probably brought here two weeks ago. Can you help us find her?"

"Sure," Girad said, rolling his eyes. "I could have done it after the game, too. Follow me."

Evin reached down and tousled Girad's mop of brown hair. Girad ducked away, scrunching up his nose, and a pang went through Ileni.

Once, she would have done the same—been confident enough of affection to avoid it. She found herself fixated on Evin's hand as it slid off Girad's head and came to rest on the boy's shoulder.

Girad slid away, pulled open a narrow black door, and headed into the interior of the building. The rest of them followed.

Inside, the walls were painted starkly white, dotted

regularly with doors and large open windows. Through the windows, Ileni could make out rooms with beds, rooms with tables, and rooms with desks and chairs. Every single room was stuffed to bursting with children, and every single child seemed to be shouting. The noise echoed back and forth between the walls, making her feel like she was inside a very loud, very badly played drum. But there were also a fair amount of adults—all women, all wearing bright yellow or orange robes. Ileni couldn't resist asking, as they turned a corner, "Are they the Black Sisters?"

Evin nodded distractedly.

"So why are they called the *Black* Sisters?"

Judging from Evin's look, that was a stupid question, but he was too kind to say so. He opened his mouth just as a wave of children turned a corner and descended upon them in a running, screaming mass.

Girad whirled, and Ileni was surprised to see real fear on his face. Without thinking, she reached for him, and was even more surprised when he lifted his arms to her. She hoisted him onto her hip.

Two thin arms wrapped around her neck. In a small voice, Girad said, "Those boys are mean to me."

"Well," Ileni said, "if they're mean to you *now*, I'll freeze them all with a spell." With magic she had sworn not to use anymore. Why was it so hard to remember that?

Girad rested his head on her shoulder and closed his eyes. "I tried that already. It just made them meaner."

What was she supposed to say to that? Ileni settled for tightening her grip until the older children were past, at which point Girad wriggled out of her arms as if her holding him was an indignity.

He led them around that corner into another hall, where a group of toddlers were all crying at the tops of their lungs while an orange-robed woman tried to coax them into moving forward. By the time the four of them entered a small, yellow room filled with wailing babies, Ileni's head felt like it was being battered with hot rocks.

The wailing was something else, though. It was more than annoying. It made her muscles vibrate.

There were ten babies in the room, in rows of roughly hewn wooden cradles. In the corner, a woman dozed in a large chair. How she could sleep through all that crying was beyond Ileni, but her eyes were shut and her chest heaved rhythmically up and down.

"This is the temporary nursery," Girad said. "It's

where they decide which babies they'll keep."

Ileni bit her lip. "What do they do with the babies they don't keep?"

Girad shrugged. "There are three new ones. In the corner, over there."

Over there was near the sleeping woman. Ileni started to cross the room. The woman's eyes immediately snapped open, and she fixed Ileni with a glare.

"Um," Ileni said. "Hi."

Even through the crying, she could hear Arxis snort.

"We're from the Academy," Evin said. She hadn't realized he was right behind her, and his voice—crisp, martial—made her jump. "One of these babies' mothers donated her magic. Her child will remain with the Sisters."

"Right." The woman sounded like she was still asleep, or would strongly prefer to be. "Which one?"

Silence—except, of course, for the crying.

"Um," Ileni said, and bit her lip. "One of the recent arrivals. A girl."

The woman lifted her hand barely an inch and gestured at the three cradles against the yellow wall. "They're all girls."

Of course they were.

With an effort, Ileni bit back another *um* and approached the cradles. Two babies looked back from tiny bright eyes; the other slept soundly, eyelashes resting on red cheeks. Aside from that, there was no difference between them. She couldn't have said which was the dead girl's if that baby had just been pointed out to her two minutes ago.

Arxis's gaze burned into her back. Maybe he was right. What difference did it make which one she saved?

"Couldn't you keep all three?" she asked.

Evin stepped on the side of her foot. The woman straightened the tiniest bit. "Why would I do that?"

"Because I'm not sure which one—"

Evin stepped harder, and Ileni broke off with a yelp. The woman shook her head. "If you don't know, why are you here? Her mother should have marked her. Too bad for her if she didn't."

"Wait," Ileni said, as the woman's eyes slid shut. "I do know. I mean, I will. I can . . ." The woman peeled her eyes open and examined her balefully. Ileni took a deep breath. "They're not identical. There must be a difference between them."

The woman let out an aggrieved breath.

"One of them cries a lot," Girad said.

"What?"

Girad stood next to Evin, his small hand clasped in his brother's. His round face was intent and serious. "I had to help out in the nursery last week, as punishment for . . ."— his eyes slid toward Evin—"something. One of them cries *all the time.*"

"Babies cry," Evin said.

"Wait," Ileni said. "Her mother died of childbed fever. She probably couldn't nurse her. Was one of them hungrier than the others?"

"That one." The woman nodded at the sleeping baby. "Wouldn't take to the wet-nurse at first, either. It was like she'd forgotten how to eat."

"Then that's the one," Ileni said.

The woman looked unconvinced. "You're sure?"

"Yes," Ileni said, with every ounce of confidence she could fake.

"All right, then." The woman levered herself out of the chair and lumbered forward. She drew a piece of chalk from somewhere in her dress and smudged a black line across the baby's forehead. Then, with far greater speed, she backed into her chair and settled into it again.

The baby didn't move. Ileni wondered if she would live after all. If her mother hadn't been able to feed her . . . but apparently, now there was a wet nurse. She didn't know enough about babies to know what that meant.

One of the other babies let out a little mewling cry. Ileni looked at her, at her splotchy red face and tightly shut eyes, at her broad wrinkled forehead unmarked by a chalk line. The baby's arms were crossed over her chest, tiny fingers curled under her chin. Ileni didn't move until Evin took her by the arm and pulled her out of the room.

"Well done," he said approvingly as soon as the four of them were back in the hallway.

"I don't even know if it was the right baby," Ileni said.

"Shh," Evin hissed. "Even if it wasn't. You did a good thing."

A good thing. She should have been happy; it was what she wanted. To do something unmistakably good. But it was so paltry and insignificant. She had saved one baby. She, who could do so much more.

Her palm hurt, and she realized that her fingernails were digging into her skin. She forced herself to relax her hand. Things *would* be better. She would get back to the Academy, she would open the portal, and she would tell Sorin she was ready. The Empire *wasn't* indestructible. They would find that out soon enough. She would make sure Evin and Cyn and Lis were safe, and then she would shatter all those mountain peaks and bury the lodestones in rubble.

And the rest of them? The beginner and intermediate students? Why should she save her friends and let them die? They were all equally guilty. *She* was as guilty as any of them. She had used the magic, too.

We face the truth, Sorceress: not that they deserve to die, but that their deaths serve a greater purpose.

She could see the wisdom in that, now. Better to think like an assassin, and live with the truth of what she would do, instead of trying futilely to convince herself she had nothing to feel guilty about.

"Ileni?" Evin said, and she looked at him sideways. It occurred to her, suddenly, that soon he would hate her forever. It surprised her how much that hurt.

She kept looking at him, frozen by the realization. He looked back, his brown eyes steady.

"I'm all right," she said, because she couldn't bear the concern in his eyes. "Everything will be fine."

"Yes," Evin agreed, because he didn't know what she

meant. His fingers brushed her hand—by accident, she thought—and he tilted his head down toward hers. "Yes. It will be."

That was when they emerged into the courtyard and found an army of sorcerers waiting for them.

CHAPTER 23

The fountains arced and swayed, crescendoing curves of water soaring and descending into mist. Behind the white lines of water, behind the invisible walls, were two lines of sorcerers in red-striped white tunics. Karyn stood in front, glowing with a blinding white light.

Ileni stopped in her tracks. Behind her, Girad said, "What?" then uttered a word Ileni was pretty sure a six-year-old shouldn't know.

Karyn raised a hand. The fountains went still. A series of graceless splatters filled the silence, and then there was nothing but a flat rippling pool separating them from the sorcerers.

The silence was so absolute Ileni could hear her heart thudding against her chest. A quick glance at Evin revealed that he was as wild-eyed and panicked as she was. She had no idea what Karyn was going to do.

Behind her, Arxis laughed, a low, satisfied sound. The danger shifted. For a moment, in the set of Arxis's face and the sharpness in his eyes, Ileni saw Sorin.

"What's *funny?*" she snapped.

He tilted his head slowly, and the resemblance broke. Sorin had never looked at her with that edge of cruel disdain. "That this ridiculous little quest of yours has finally given me what I need to complete my mission."

Evin blinked, but didn't turn to his friend. He still didn't know where the real danger lay.

"And what," Ileni said, as steadily as she could, "is that?"

Arxis smiled, a triumphant and contented smile.

"An audience," he said, and moved.

But not toward Evin.

Understanding rushed over Ileni all at once. She dashed past Evin, throwing herself in front of his brother.

She wasn't fast enough.

The knife meant for Girad pierced Ileni's shoulder, a bolt of searing pain. Her healing spell was instinctive, but the shield she tried to throw up was not, and it was a shade too slow. The second stab went under her arm, with deadly accuracy, and Girad screamed.

No! Ileni put her hand on Girad's small chest, and blood poured between her fingers. His eyes were wide and uncomprehending, and he was no longer screaming. That was a bad sign, wasn't it?

Arxis grabbed her arm. Evin snarled a spell, and Arxis was flung away. Behind her, a hard thud and the crack of bone, though the assassin didn't make a sound.

Ileni threw a healing spell at Girad, then another, digging frantically to remember what she had been taught. Half of healing was knowing what to fix, and the Renegai didn't focus on knife wounds; she could feel that things were wrong, that there was blood where there shouldn't be blood, rips in what should be whole, but she couldn't tell what precise spells would do the most good. Another random healing spell, and another—and then nothing. She had drained her power.

Girad's brown eyes closed, and Ileni choked down a sob before she saw his chest rise and fall. Her hands, when she lifted them, were dark with blood. It was under her fingernails, and the thick, metallic smell was in her throat.

She couldn't tell if she had saved Girad, but at least he was breathing. For now.

There was blood on his face, too, smeared across his cheek and forehead. So much blood—how much could a tiny body lose?

Evin dropped to his knees beside her and reached for his brother, making a noise that didn't sound like him—that barely sounded human. He gathered the small body into his arms, and finally Ileni turned.

Arxis was a crumpled heap against the far wall, and she didn't have to check to know he was dead. She had felt the power Evin unleashed against him. A ward shimmered around them, and outside it, Karyn was shouting orders. The ward was also Evin's work.

Four of the imperial sorcerers linked hands, and magic burst from them in a spray of violet light. Ileni braced herself, and she was ready when the world tilted around her. She landed on her hands and knees on a cold stone floor, stomach heaving.

She wasn't quite ready for the realization that she had landed there alone. But it made sense. Girad would need a healer, and Evin . . . Evin would need to be with Girad.

She, on the other hand, would need to answer for what

had happened today. She had known a killer was among them, and she had said nothing. Until it was too late.

When she got to her feet, she left bloody handprints on the gray stone.

It was half an hour before Karyn walked into the small stone room—enough time for Ileni to compose herself, steady her stomach, and force herself to think. When Karyn thrust the door open, Ileni said quickly, "Is Girad all right?"

Karyn slammed the door behind her and leaned against it. "He's alive."

A rush of relief went through Ileni. She closed her eyes, then opened them and focused on Karyn's hard face. Girad would live. Now Ileni had to concentrate on whether she would.

"For now," Karyn added, between her teeth. "He hasn't woken yet. The healers aren't sure he will."

"He's alive because of me." Ileni kept her voice mild, not defiant. She didn't have to prove this. Twenty sorcerers had seen her throw herself in front of Arxis's dagger.

"How long," Karyn asked, "have you known there was an assassin among us?"

Ileni had already decided there was no point in lying. "Since I first saw him."

"Why didn't you tell me?"

"You had just kidnapped me. Remember?"

"But Girad hadn't."

Ileni flinched. "I didn't . . . I thought his target was Evin."

"Evin," Karyn repeated flatly. "And he did deserve to die?"

This is war. But now was not the time to argue. She had to concentrate on getting through this, on convincing Karyn to let her live. Ileni shook her head.

Karyn stepped toward her, a slow, deliberate motion Ileni recognized. That of a predator sensing weakness. "But you weren't going to stop it. You were going to let Evin die rather than betray your assassin lover."

She hadn't just been going to let him die. She had been considering killing him.

"You know they won't stop," Karyn said. "The assassins never let someone go, once they are marked for death." Sorin had told her that once, proudly. "They will send someone else after Girad. Probably soon, while he is weak and helpless and easy to kill. And if the next person fails, they'll send another. And another. You might have saved him today, but Girad is dead."

"No," Ileni said. The protest was instinctive, but she meant it.

"And then they'll send someone after Evin," Karyn said. Whatever reaction she saw on Ileni's face made her lips compress. "And then, I am sure, after you. I assume you're more willing to help us now?"

Ileni stepped back. "I want to see Girad. Maybe I can heal him. I ran out of power before, but there might be more I can do."

Karyn's face tightened. "You think I'm going to let you keep drawing on the lodestones? After *this*?"

"I don't want to draw on them," Ileni said. She meant it, though she couldn't tell if Karyn believed her. "I don't want to use this magic anymore. But if I can help Girad. . . ."

Karyn pursed her lips, and for a moment Ileni thought she was going to refuse, just out of spite.

Instead she said, "I'll take you to him."

Girad was in a small round room with a bed in its center, so large it dwarfed its tiny occupant. Around the bed, several wooden chairs were arranged on the gray rock. Evin was slumped in one of those chairs, holding his brother's hand, eyes half-closed. But when Ileni walked in, he started upright, power coiling in his upraised hand.

No need to ask what he had been dreaming about. "It's all right," Ileni said. "It's me. I just wanted to make sure . . ."

Evin lowered his hand. His eyes were red and hollow. "He's doing better. I think . . . I think he's going to make it." It sounded like hope, not belief. "Thank you."

"Don't thank me," Ileni said.

Behind her, Karyn stepped out into the hall and closed the door. No doubt she was using magic to listen in on them anyhow.

Ileni walked over to Girad and reached out with her power. She couldn't feel anything wrong within him—at least, nothing she was skilled enough to detect. If he had simply lost too much blood, there was no spell to give it back. It was one of the few things Renegai magic couldn't fix.

She had done everything she could when the knife went in, and she had known then that it might not be enough.

"Ileni." Evin started to get to his feet, then sagged back into the chair. "I don't understand exactly what's going on. But I know you saved my brother's life."

And had put it in danger in the first place, by keeping quiet about who Arxis was.

Evin clasped his hands in his lap. He was holding a small wooden toy carved in the shape of a dog. "It was the bravest thing I've ever seen. I can't . . . I don't even know how I can thank you. But if there is ever something I can do for you, *anything*, all you have to do is tell me."

Ileni couldn't meet his eyes. "You saved my life, too, you know. More than once. You don't owe me anything."

"He's my brother. I owe you *everything*."

Was it possible to literally shrivel up from shame? She kept seeing the knife, impossibly huge in that thin chest, the wide-eyed incomprehension on Girad's round face, the blood everywhere. The smallness of his body as Evin gathered it up.

In the caves, news would have come of this child's death, and there would have been dancing.

She had danced with them, once. And she hadn't asked the age of their victim.

She swallowed hard. "Arxis was an assassin. From the caves. Girad was his target all along."

"I realized that. But I just . . . I don't understand." Evin turned the wooden dog over and over in his hands. "Why would they kill a child?"

He really didn't understand. Once, she wouldn't have understood either. The words of explanation were on her lips, words she had heard from Sorin: necessity, the greater good, the purpose served by murder. But she remembered how they had danced, and she knew that if she tried to speak, she would choke.

Evin finally looked away from the wooden dog, but still not at her. He fixed his gaze on his brother's face. "They really hate us that much."

So maybe he did understand, better than she did, for all the rational arguments she had stored in her mind.

"Yes," she said. "They really do."

Karyn wasn't outside the door when Ileni left—which did not, of course, mean she hadn't been listening in. Apparently, Ileni was free to go wherever she wanted.

For now.

Ileni went to her room, because there was nowhere else to go. She shut the door, leaned against it, and closed her eyes, feeling that she should cry. But no tears came.

She straightened and walked, steps leaden, to the oval mirror in the corner of the room. She flattened her palm on the cold glass.

The spell in the mirror thrummed against her hand, spanning the distance between her and Sorin. Passing through both sets of wards. She could bring it back to life—she was sure of it. She could look Sorin in the eye and ask if he was going to order the killing of a child.

She could ask if he had ordered Bazel to kill her.

She reached for power—not doing anything with it yet, not even readying it, just knowing it was there. She could. She didn't know if she should, and she didn't know if she wanted to, but she knew that she could.

The glass turned black.

Ileni leaped away from the mirror, power sizzling painfully through her palm.

This can't be good.

She pulled a ward around herself. The mirror was already becoming less black, the shadows inside it swirling into shapes, the shapes taking on form and color. It was a room, square and bare and stark, its floor covered with a chalk pattern that gleamed with silver light. A tall figure sat in the center of the pattern.

Ileni barely breathed as she watched the images solidify. Even though she knew what she was seeing, she couldn't grasp the final piece, couldn't believe it, until the figure rose to his feet.

His face was familiar, despite long absence. She knew every inch and angle, every mood of those eyes, every expression those thin lips could twist into.

She doubled over slightly, as if all the air had been driven out of her body with one swift blow.

She met his sky-blue eyes.

"Hello, Tellis," she said.

CHAPTER 24

They both stood frozen, eyes locked on each other. Tellis's eyes were wide and blank with pain, riveted to her face as if he couldn't believe what he was seeing. Ileni felt blank inside, too, but not from pain. It took her a moment to realize what she felt.

Nothing.

That was almost worse than pain. It was staggering. How could she have loved him so much, and now feel *nothing*? She could still remember how her heart had once leaped every time she saw him, how desperately she had wanted to be near him.

She remembered it, and still she felt nothing.

"Ileni," Tellis whispered. "He was telling the truth?"

"Who was telling the truth?" Ileni said. "Tellis—how did you—"

"I'm here to help you," Tellis said. "Elder Absalm opened the portal just enough for you to see me. But together, we can open the portal fully, and you can come through."

Elder Absalm? "Where *are* you?"

He shuddered slightly, which was answer enough. "Don't worry. I'm all right. I was just brought here to talk to you, and to help you escape."

"I don't need to escape," Ileni said. He blinked at her. "I'm not trapped here." Although that wasn't entirely true. "I'm—it's complicated. But I know what I'm doing."

That was entirely *not* true, but Tellis nodded, trusting her. He leaned closer, reaching out a hand, as if he could push it through the spell and touch her. He probably could, if he wanted to. He was more than powerful enough.

"Ileni," he said, and his voice caught on her name. "I miss you."

"I—" Ileni began, and then couldn't think of what to say. *I miss you, too?* She had shattered her heart against memories of him a million times. But now . . . now she was no longer the girl who had loved Tellis so uncomplicatedly and wholeheartedly.

She missed being that girl more than she missed Tellis.

"I knew I would," Tellis said. "But I didn't know . . . I didn't know it would be so hard. I didn't know, when I told you to leave, that I was making a mistake."

The thought crept into her mind, stark and inescapable: *I'm going to hurt him.*

Once, she would have been savagely glad of that. *He* had hurt her, after all, so badly she hadn't known how she would survive it. But that felt like so long ago. She *had* survived it. She had come out on the other side. And she no longer cared enough about Tellis to want to hurt him.

"Thank you," she said, and immediately hated herself for how stupid it sounded—for not coming up with something better. The intensity on Tellis's face made her heart twist. But she forced herself to meet his eyes, letting her own face show . . . whatever it showed. And she forced herself not to turn away when he searched her face, the hope in his eyes slowly dying. His throat pulsed, and he was the one to finally drop his eyes.

"So you're a weapon," he said.

"I—what?"

"The assassin leader said . . . he said you had a way to destroy the imperial sorcerers. Is it true?"

"What on earth were you doing with Sor—with the assassin leader?"

"It's a long story," Tellis said. "But he wanted me to talk to you. To find out what you were doing. What was stopping you from proceeding with the plan."

Curse you, Sorin.

Ileni had thought she understood what it felt like to be the betrayer, to become loathsome in the eyes of everyone she knew. Now she had an inkling of what it would truly feel like. Her insides clamped shut, shrinking into a thick, agonizing knot.

"It's . . . not that simple," she said, hearing and hating the weakness in her voice.

Tellis blinked at her, not angry as Sorin would have been, merely confused. "You're in the *Empire*. They drove us into exile, they kill by the thousands, they pervert magic. Why is it not simple?"

For a moment Ileni couldn't remember why. What Tellis was saying was true. Everything else was just complications.

She opened her mouth, then closed it. There was no point. She understood Tellis perfectly; she had *been* him, just a year ago. With no idea of how much she didn't know.

Suddenly she couldn't bear it anymore. She didn't want him to know what she had become. Not because she was ashamed—or not only because she was ashamed. But because someone should still be apart from all the death and the compromises and the terrible choices. Some part of the world should still be simple and pure.

Even if that part couldn't be hers anymore.

"Tellis," she said. "Are you trapped there? In the caves?"

"No," Tellis said. "The assassin leader said I can go back as soon as I talk to you."

"Then go," Ileni said fiercely. "Go back to the village, right away. Promise me."

"I will. Of course. But—"

She drew in magic, hoping Tellis couldn't sense it through the portal, and said, "There's no time. The portal is closing. Tellis—"

He leaned forward, but she hadn't planned an end to that sentence. She cut it off by slamming the portal shut, using all her strength and all her skill.

The last thing she saw, before the room went black and vanished, was Tellis's face. There was no horror on it, no anger, no betrayal. There was only bewilderment.

● ● ●

Ileni was almost too tired to cry.

Almost. But not quite.

She tried to be angry at Sorin, but the feeling got lost in the ache inside her. How did he know her so well? How did he know that sending Tellis to talk to her would cut so deep —would bring back everything she had once believed, and make her ashamed of what she had become?

And not because he was Tellis, but because he was *her*, what she had once been. She had grown up wishing daily for the destruction of the Empire, and now she had the chance to actually accomplish it. This wasn't about betraying Sorin, or Tellis, or the Renegai. It was about betraying the person she had thought she was.

When she finally fell asleep, tears still tracking down her cheeks, she dreamed of the girl at Death's Door. Blond hair blew across blue eyes that were wide and desperate and without hope. *I want the Black Sisters to take her. You can have my life if you promise me that.*

The girl had slit her own throat, but that didn't change the fact that she had been murdered—she and thousands like her, systematically and methodically, all through the Empire. And it would go on forever, death fueling power fueling death, unless someone did something.

Unless she did something.

She was a weapon forged to strike the Empire a killing blow, and that weapon could be used now or never.

Her mind whirled and spun, and her thoughts kept curving back to Girad's blood spilling over her hands, his wide uncomprehending eyes, to Evin's almost inhuman howl of grief. Sorin had explained it to her once, without a hint of regret. *One death in exchange for avoiding hundreds.*

She forced herself to wait until the sky outside her window was stained pink before she left her room. Outside the door to the sickroom, she heard soft voices murmuring. Two voices.

Girad? Her heart leaped almost painfully in her chest as she pushed the door open.

But Girad hadn't woken. It was Karyn in the room, talking to Evin in low tones, across the room from Girad's still figure.

Ileni froze, suddenly afraid. Yesterday, she had been more than ready for Karyn to take her magic away; it was magic she shouldn't be using. Today . . . she still believed that. Yet dread rippled through her body, making her reluctant to step forward and catch Karyn's attention.

She watched from the doorway—not Karyn, not the body in the bed, but Evin. Her heart hurt at the slump of his shoulders, the defeated set of his face. He looked ten years older than he had the day before.

No. She couldn't care about him. She couldn't care about any of them.

She couldn't forget that she was an assassin, too.

"Evin." Karyn's voice was soft, falsely so. "You can't sit here all day."

"If he wakes—"

Karyn met Ileni's eyes over Evin's bowed head. Ileni reached out, with a nudge of power, and pushed the boy's restless sleep into something deeper and more healing. She wasn't skilled enough to fix him, but she could do that.

She didn't think, until after she did it, about the fact that she had used power from the lodestones. Again.

"He won't wake," she said. "Not for several hours. You should sleep, Evin."

Evin's laugh was broken. "I can't sleep. I keep seeing . . . over and over . . ."

"Then prepare," Karyn said.

They both looked at her, Evin with bleary confusion, Ileni with sharp dread.

"You know we are preparing to attack the assassins," Karyn told Evin. "We will kill their leader and scatter them, and then they won't be able to do this to anyone, not for a long time. You can be part of accomplishing that. You could even lead us."

"Yes," Evin said. Just the word, but Ileni's dread spread through her body.

"It's the only way to save your brother." Karyn walked across the room and placed one hand on the headboard of Girad's bed. "If the assassins are left intact, they will keep coming after him until one of them succeeds. If you want to save Girad, if you want to put an end to the assassins—you will have to be better than you have been."

Evin nodded. He rose, facing Karyn, and Ileni couldn't see his expression. "I will be training, then." He turned. Now Ileni could see his face, but she barely recognized it.

"Evin," Ileni said. "Wait."

He clenched his jaw, his long mobile face made alien by the grimness around his mouth, the hardness in his eyes. She thought he wanted to say something, but instead he walked out of the room.

Ileni was left staring across the stone floor at Karyn. Girad breathed slow and deep.

"You . . ." Ileni tried to gather her thoughts, the reasons for her fury.

Karyn laced her fingers over the headboard. Ileni thought of a spell Cyn had taught her that would slam that hand off Girad's bed. "In times such as these, someone with Evin's power cannot waste it weaving pretty colors together."

Once, Ileni had thought almost the exact same thing, with the exact same edge of scorn. Once . . . about a week ago. It felt like much longer. "Evin doesn't want to use his power to kill people."

"Anyone can want to kill, given enough motivation."

Ileni could hardly argue with that. She swallowed hard and said, instead, "Why haven't you blocked me from the lodestones yet?"

"Because I think," Karyn said, "that you're ready to choose a side now. Do you really want to save Girad's life? Betraying the assassins is the only way to do that."

Ileni couldn't move, couldn't breathe, and—despite all her agonizing, all the thoughts that had worn grooves into her mind—couldn't think of a thing to say.

So instead of saying anything, she went after Evin.

She caught up with him at the beginning of the bridge, where he was walking instead of flying, his steps slow and heavy. She ran the few steps to catch him, making the bridge sway wildly beneath them, and grabbed his arm.

"Evin, wait—"

He whirled, eyes wide. "Is Girad—"

"No! Girad is sleeping. Still."

Evin let out a breath, and Ileni stood staring up at him, trying to think of something to say. The moment stretched on and on.

"Don't cry," Evin said.

She hadn't been aware, until he said it, that she was crying. She tasted salt on her lips.

"I mean—I'm sorry. What a stupid thing to say. Of course you can cry." Evin reached out and, with his thumb, blotted a tear on her cheek. His other hand was still clutching his brother's wooden dog. "I'm going to change it. I'm going to make sure they never kill again."

"No." Ileni tightened her grip on his forearm. "*Don't.* Nobody can change the way things are." *Nobody but me.* "Girad needs you, and you—you shouldn't have to be something you're not."

"If I change," Evin said, "that will be what I am."

And it would be. No one could force themselves back into innocence. She searched Evin's eyes for a hint of the wry, careless humor she had once despised.

She would never forgive Sorin for killing *this*.

"Don't worry," Evin said. "I'll still be the best at whatever I end up being." His smile was small and forced, but in it, Ileni saw a flicker of his old self.

Above them, a sound, so faint it might have been the wind.

Evin followed Ileni's gaze and sighed. He stepped back. The bridge tilted beneath them.

Lis dove headfirst and straightened when she was hovering beside them. She put one hand on the rail and said to Evin, "I'm sorry."

Bleakness settled on Evin's face, wiping away that brief glimmer. "Thank you. He will—I'm sure he will be all right."

But he didn't sound sure at all.

Lis drew in a breath, and her face twisted with an expression Ileni recognized.

Guilt.

I know exactly who Arxis is, Lis had said.

Ileni met Lis's eyes, and Lis whirled so fast her hair whipped audibly through the air. She leaped upward, arms tight at her sides, and streaked across the pink sky.

"I should go," Evin said. He lifted his hand toward

Ileni's face, then let it drop. "I should train."

"Yes," Ileni said. She curled one hand around the railing. "I shouldn't have—I didn't mean—I—I have to go, too."

"Wait. I want to ask you—" He looked down at the wooden dog in his hand, and held it out to her. "Can you give this back to Girad?"

Ileni took the dog, knowing that wasn't what he had meant to say. She nodded, then turned and ran.

She caught up to Lis on the ledge near the beginning of the bridge. When Ileni grabbed her arm, Lis jerked away, almost throwing the two of them off the mountain. Ileni used a thrust of magic to push herself closer to the gray mountainside.

Lis didn't. She crouched near the edge of the abyss, her heels at the very rim of the drop. As if she didn't care whether she fell.

She could fly, of course. But still, unease lodged in Ileni's throat, choking off her accusation. She recognized that sort of despair.

"What?" Lis said wildly. "What do you want? Do you have more useless warnings to throw at me?"

"I didn't have to warn you," Ileni said slowly. "Did I? You already knew what he was."

Lis laughed, and something about it made Ileni want to

back away. She pressed against the mountainside.

"Oh, yes," Lis said. "But unlike you, I know what *we* are."

"And what are we?" Ileni said.

"We're killers, too." Lis straightened, but didn't step away from the edge. "I kept Arxis's secret because he was *right*. It's that simple."

It's never that simple. But Ileni had once thought it could be. That *right* was a simple concept, that she could make a choice that didn't take into account who she was and who she loved and what she wanted.

"Arxis was just using you," Ileni said. "You were his way to Evin, who was his way to Girad."

"You don't know anything," Lis snapped. "I was far more important to the assassins than that."

To the *assassins*?

It all came together with a click, so fast Ileni wondered if some part of her had already known. Lis and Arxis, heads bent together. His taunt. *The assets we already have here.*

And the question she had never managed to answer.

Ileni gaped for a moment, then found her voice. "That's how Sorin knew I was here. You're a spy."

Lis smiled, arch and smug. "So tell Karyn. Do you think she'll believe you? Think you're better off than I am?

I know what Karyn has planned for *you*."

"How did you even know I was in the Academy?" Ileni demanded. "When Karyn brought me here, nobody—"

"Karyn told me." Lis laughed. "Evin and Cyn were putting down a riot, and she needed my help to set up extra wards around you."

"*Your* help?" Ileni said, and heard a moment too late how much she sounded like Cyn.

Lis flushed, dark red. "Yes. *Mine*. I'm not as worthless as my sister thinks. Karyn told me not to tell anyone about you . . . and I didn't. Not anyone *here*."

"How did you tell the assassins? I thought the wards—"

"The wards are quite effective, yes. In the Academy." Lis shook her head, hair swinging back and forth. "But when I go to battles . . . or riots . . . to harvest the wounded, there are no wards there. And it's easy enough to send messages to the caves."

Ileni's feet were fused to the rock. "But how—how did you—"

"The master sent Arxis here for two reasons." Lis's eyes shone with a worshipful fervor Ileni had seen before. Obviously, no one had told her the master was dead. "The first was to recruit me."

Ileni flinched, involuntarily, at the mention of the master. It didn't surprise her that he had known, from his black caves high in the distant mountains, that here in the Academy a girl was angry and disillusioned and ripe to turn on everyone she knew.

It didn't surprise her that Lis had been manipulated, expertly, from the very start.

"And the second reason," Ileni hissed, "was to kill Girad."

A muscle twitched in Lis's cheek. "Yes."

"And you don't care."

"I've seen lots of people die. I've harvested their power myself, to feed it to the Empire. I know what the assassins are fighting against." Lis was shouting now. "There is no room for pity in war. Arxis knew that."

"You're a tool," Ileni spat. "You don't know anything about the people you're serving. Arxis didn't need a *reason* not to care. He just didn't. Not about anything. He thought that was a *virtue.*"

Lis's jaw clenched, her face a stolid mask.

Ileni thrust quickly, looking for something that would hurt enough to keep that mask from closing. "He didn't care what his death would do to you. He didn't care about you at all."

"He was willing to make sacrifices," Lis hissed. "He did what was right, even though he loved me."

Ileni heard her own laugh, with an edge to it that would have made a sane person back away. Lis stepped closer.

"He *loved* me!"

"Oh, did he? Would he have stayed his hand if you asked him to? Let Girad live?"

"I didn't ask him to!" Lis shouted. Hair blew across her face. "I didn't know it would be Girad. He never told me . . . and even if he had, I wouldn't have stood in his way. He did what had to be done. This the only way."

"It's not," Ileni said. "It's not the only way."

"Oh, really?" Lis sneered. "You have another one? You think if you look long enough, you'll find a perfect shining solution and fix everything without getting your hands dirty?"

"No," Ileni said, and heard her own voice: small, defeated. "No. I don't."

"Then who are you to judge his sacrifice? Arxis knew what his life was worth, and what he was willing to trade it for. He was braver than any sorcerer in this Academy." Lis's hair hung in a tangle of threads over her face, lit into strands of silver by the sun behind her.

"None of them care about their lives," Ileni said. "There

will be another one to replace him. To kill Girad where he failed. Did Arxis ever tell you about the Roll of Honor? Because he might not have feared death, but I assure you, he feared not having his name carved on that column. And it won't be. Not now."

Lis's face twisted, and guilt stabbed Ileni. This cruelty wasn't all meant for Lis. Some of it was meant for herself.

Which didn't mean Lis didn't deserve it. Ileni saw again Girad's tiny body, heard the startled cry as he fell.

"Maybe you can fall in love with the next one, too," she said. "Since you enjoy being miserable so much."

Lis slapped her.

Ileni had been expecting that, and her block was instantaneous. Lis's hand froze an inch from Ileni's face. She struggled to break through, but Ileni held her off easily.

Lis snarled at her. Then she stepped backward off the ledge and dropped from sight.

Ileni didn't move. A moment later, a slim figure rose in the sky, black hair blowing wildly around her.

Ileni stood there long after the sky was empty again, not moving, the mountain firm against her back. The clean slashes of the mountaintops were smudged. She blinked fiercely and swiped at her eyes with the back of her hand.

She had also once thought that she was on the side of good—that she would do something wholly, unmistakably right. She missed that belief more than she missed Sorin, more than she missed her magic, more than she missed not wondering every morning if she would die that day.

For a moment, she envied Lis. She wished she, too, believed in something strongly enough to kill for it without hesitation or doubt.

She turned her back on the empty sky and ran.

CHAPTER
25

Ileni ran straight to her room, and straight to the mirror, and she pulled power from lodestones as she ran. She dropped to her knees and drew patterns on the floor with dangerous haste, her chalk strokes steady despite her shaking arms, pulling in yet more power through her skin. By the time she unleashed all that power on the mirror, sweeping her arm at the glass and shouting the spell, she had more than she could safely control.

And it wasn't even necessary.

The portal slid open easily, and behind the breach in the wards, someone was waiting for her. She knew it, sensed his presence, even before the mirror erupted into a rainbow whirlwind. When the colors faded back into the glass, he was there.

As if he had been waiting for her.

"Did you know about it?" Ileni demanded, before he could say a word. Her throat was so tight it hurt, but the words slid out easily.

Sorin's face didn't so much as twitch. He stared at her unflinching, not denying it.

Sorin. The two of them had stood together beneath the earth and faced death. They had lied to each other and betrayed each other and loved each other through it all. Her heart shattered slowly, a hundred agonizing hairline fractures.

"The boy? I didn't order that," Sorin said. His voice was calm, even. "Our assassin was placed there over a month ago. It was the master who sent him. You know that."

His cheekbones were sharp as blades, his eyes dark coals. She couldn't look away from him. Her heart pounded so hard she could hear it.

Sorin leaned forward, very slightly. A tuft of blond hair fell over his forehead. "What do you really want to ask me, Ileni?"

She sucked in a harsh, painful breath, and said, "Have you ever killed a child?"

Sorin's face hardened, and the dangerous slant of his eyes wiped away any hint of vulnerability. When he finally spoke, his tone was measured. "I've only been on one mission. I killed a nobleman. You know that, too."

"But you're . . . in charge now." She couldn't bring herself to say *you are the master*. "You must have sent people on missions. Since I . . . since I left."

"Yes."

She flinched despite herself. But she had always known he was a killer. She forced the next question out. "Were any of the targets children?"

He looked at her for a moment—a long moment, considering how dangerous it was to keep this portal open. His eyes had never seemed so impenetrable. Ileni braced herself, heart thudding.

He said, "No."

In the complete silence that followed, Ileni felt not relief, not joy, but an odd whirling . . . disappointment?

Because he's lying to me. But she didn't really believe that. And a moment later he added, "But I will if I have to. And someday, I will have to."

No. He wasn't lying.

"Arxis's mission was necessary," Sorin added.

Racing through the corridors, running this conversation through her mind, she had planned to be furious. She *should* be furious. Instead she was suddenly, deeply sad.

"No," she said. "You didn't have to kill Girad. You could have found another way. You *wanted* to kill him. You wanted to kill him because he's a child and because killing children inflicts the greatest possible pain."

"Yes," Sorin said, utterly calm. "This was about inflicting pain. We accept that necessity."

Her voice was still working, despite the pain in her chest. "You accept it far too easily."

"It's not easy," Sorin said, but for the first time, his gaze wavered.

This time, he was lying. It *was* easy. Their goal, their lives, their purpose, was to kill. Of course it was easy.

She was still holding Girad's wooden dog, so tightly her hand hurt.

"The Empire kills children, too," Sorin said. "In a dozen ways. By sacrificing their parents in its wars and then allowing them to starve. By waiting until they're too ill to recover and then taking their power when they die."

"Yes. And you kill them by selecting them as targets and slitting their throats with knives."

He lifted one shoulder. "What does it matter? The children are just as dead."

It does matter, Ileni thought; but if she said it, he would ask her why, and she had no answer that would convince him. These were the rules of this unending war, the rules the assassins had played by for centuries.

Sorin hated rules . . . or she had believed he did. But maybe all he had ever wanted was to be the one making them.

"You knew I was here," she whispered. "You knew why. I could have ended all of this. Why kill a child when I might be about to end the entire war?"

Something flickered across Sorin's eyes, something she had seen so often—from the assassins and the imperial sorcerers both—that she recognized it instantly.

Pity.

Are all Renegai as deliberately simpleminded as you?

She had forgotten—had allowed herself to forget—what the assassins were.

That they didn't look for reasons to avoid killing.

Would he still be a killer, she had wondered once, *if this war didn't require it?*

How stupid she was. He would always be a killer. He didn't want to be anything else.

"You need to come back," Sorin said.

She stared at him as if he had started babbling ancient poetry.

His face was still expressionless, but his voice was low and urgent. "You're in danger now, more than before. You need to come through, back to—to the caves."

"I can't," Ileni said.

"Then open the portal farther, and I'll come through to you. You have to, Ileni. They're going to kill you—torture you, and then kill you. Now that they know you could have told them about Arxis—"

"Arxis failed," Ileni said. "I stopped him."

Sorin said nothing. Maybe he had already known. His face was still the impenetrable mask it had been months ago, when they first met. She couldn't guess what was behind it.

A hysterical laugh rose in her. "Are you going to kill me for that?"

She knew it was stupid to ask. But she wanted to break that mask, to make him show some sort of emotion.

She wanted him to be something he wasn't.

And it worked. For a moment the mask vanished, and his face burned. Pain and longing and love, all directed at her— at *her*—with an intensity that scorched everything else away.

He said, "No. I'm not going to kill you."

She couldn't breathe. She certainly couldn't say, *So there's one person in the world you can't kill.*

It's not enough.

And she knew, suddenly, why a part of her had wanted to hear a different answer, when she'd asked him if he had killed a child. She had been disappointed because, if he'd said yes, that would have been the end. It would have been over. The knowledge would have broken her free of him, forced her to go through that pain and see if she came out on the other side.

If she didn't love him, everything would be so much easier.

"I can't kill you," Sorin said, almost steadily. "I know I should. But I can't."

"But you'll kill him," Ileni said. "Gi—the child. You'll send someone else after him. Won't you?"

He didn't respond, which was answer enough.

Ileni searched his face, looking for a trace of . . . shame? If he were an imperial sorcerer, that would have been the reason for his silence. But he wasn't a sorcerer. He was an assassin, and all she saw on his face was resolve.

Her chest hurt. Her eyes burned. She whispered, "I love you."

Sorin opened his mouth, and she drew the power back. Then the mirror was just a mirror, and she was staring at her own stricken face.

The emptiness in her chest was even worse than the ache of lost magic. The emptiness had teeth, and would never let her go. But Ileni reached through it and clung to the memory of how she had stood here earlier, looking at Tellis and feeling nothing.

If she had felt that way about Tellis, one day she would feel that way about Sorin, too.

It helped, but only in a vague, distant way. She wanted to close the connection between them—to slam it shut, so he would be leagues and leagues away and have no way to talk to her ever again.

But she didn't. She held the portal open, delicately—not wide enough to let someone through, just enough to keep it from closing entirely. It required every ounce of her Renegai training. It almost slipped from her, twice, but each time she managed to hold it back.

She dropped to the floor, snatched up one of the broken pieces of chalk, and drew a swift pattern over the one that was already there. She took the time to check the overlay of the two patterns, then placed Girad's wooden dog in its center and placed both hands on it. It had been worn smooth, and felt almost like warm glass. This was a toy that had been much-handled, deeply loved by a child.

But there was nothing else at hand she could use. *I'm sorry, Girad.*

She ran the words of the spell through her mind once, then began tapping her fingers along the toy in patterns she had memorized long ago. Halfway through, she got her finger pattern mixed up, and the building power shuddered and vanished. She gritted her teeth in frustration and began again.

The second time, she faltered over a word.

Focus. If she had been in the Renegai village, two tries would have been all she got; her teachers would have insisted she stop and replenish her strength. But here, she had an endless supply of power. She closed her eyes, took a deep breath, pressed her fingertips into the wood, and began again.

The third time, she got it right. As soon as the magic spiraled into the end of the spell, she let out her breath and opened her eyes. She let go of the wooden dog, and it rose into the air, undulating faintly.

Behind it, the mirror was dull and lifeless, the magic torn from it and instilled in the toy dog. The toy, now, held one end of the portal.

The other was still in the caves.

She couldn't bring herself to touch the wooden dog. She let it hover in the air in front of her when she was done, let it float before her all the way down the narrow hallway and the narrower ledge and across the swaying bridge.

Karyn and Evin were on the plateau, colored lightning zigzagging over their heads, frantic bursts of savagely beautiful lights. When Ileni stepped off the bridge, the brilliant zigzags disappeared before she could get a close look at them. But she knew what Evin was doing. Turning art into combat magic.

This place ruins everything it touches.

It was her last chance to hesitate, but she didn't. She walked straight over to the center of the plateau, past Evin to Karyn, the wooden dog hovering in front of her.

"I think," she said, her voice shaking only the tiniest bit, "that this is what you want from me."

CHAPTER 26

The plateau was completely silent but for the rush of wind around them and the cry of an eagle somewhere overhead. The sky stretched vastly blue over the harsh gray plateau and the soaring twin pillars of the Judgment Spires.

Karyn reached for the wooden dog, and so did Ileni. Ileni's hand closed around the small toy first, and she pulled it back.

The wind whistled around them, then went still. The residue of Evin's spell hovered overhead, faint glittering sparkles of color.

"Ileni?" Evin said.

"It's a way through the assassins' wards." Ileni kept her focus on Karyn, whose hand was still out, fingers curved. "A way into the caves. This was your plan for defeating them, wasn't it? For me to turn traitor and let you in."

Karyn curled her fingers slowly into a fist and drew her hand back. Evin murmured under his breath, and the remnants of color above them vanished, leaving the air clear and featureless.

"That's why you have a map of the caves in your room." Ileni tightened her grip on the dog. "You don't need a map unless you're thinking about getting inside. That's what this is about. It's what it's always been about. You let me stay, you let Evin rescue me, because you thought I had a way into the Assassins' Caves."

"That's all we need," Karyn said. "A way in. And we can put an end to their murders forever."

"Well," Ileni said. Her fingers shook only slightly. "Here's your way in. I just spoke to Sorin. That portal is still open, and it goes right through the caves' wards. I'm sure you can find a way to send people through it."

"Oh, yes," Karyn said, and her eyes were alight in a way that reminded Ileni of Sorin. "Yes, I can."

And then what? The caves were a warren of passageways, of

narrow stairways and sharp turns, and—most importantly—of vicious trained killers. The imperial soldiers would be slaughtered.

But Karyn had been in the caves. She had even mapped them. She knew that.

She must have another plan.

Karyn slid one foot forward and reached for the wooden dog. Ileni waited until the last moment before pulling it close, curving her arm around it.

"You can have it," Ileni said. "But I want something from you first."

Karyn's arm twitched. "What's that?"

Promise not to kill him. But she wasn't that stupid. Sorin was the leader of the assassins. Karyn would never make that promise, and if she did, she wouldn't keep it.

Besides, Sorin could take care of himself.

"I want you to leave Girad alone," Ileni said.

Evin made a sound she couldn't decipher, not without looking at him. She felt his eyes on her, but kept her gaze locked on Karyn's face.

"We wouldn't harvest his power." Karyn sounded genuinely shocked. Whether she truly was, Ileni couldn't tell. "We'll do our best to help him recover."

"I meant *if* he recovers. Don't force him into the Academy."

"We need Girad," Karyn said. But she said it slowly.

"As much as you need the assassins weakened?"

A moment of silence.

"Besides," Ileni said, "if you don't do this, you'll lose Girad anyhow. To the next assassin, or the one after that."

Not a sound from Evin. She had to force herself not to glance at him.

Karyn said, "All right."

Evin drew in a breath. Still, Ileni didn't break her focus.

"Is that all you want?" Karyn asked, with exaggerated patience.

"Hardly," Ileni said, and a sharp pain went through her. She, who was supposed to have the power to change the world, could now barely extract one tiny concession, for the fate of a single child. "But that's all I'm going to ask for right now."

She placed the wooden toy in Karyn's waiting hands.

Light flared in Karyn's dark eyes, fierce and hungry, and doubt shivered through Ileni. Karyn caressed the dog with one hand and murmured a brief spell—too brief; the bulk of it must have been prepared before. Ileni's stomach twisted. Karyn had been *ready* for this—

But it was too late for second thoughts to make a difference. Magic poured into the wooden dog and leaked into the air around it.

"Now," Karyn said. Her eyes were alight, almost madly so. "Let's take care of our little assassin problem."

"Now?" Ileni gaped. "You think—you're just going to go through? Right now? Into the caves? You'll be dead before you can take a step."

"Oh, no." Karyn leaned forward. "The caves are a death trap. You know that, and I know it. That's why no one is going there. *He's* coming here." Her teeth flashed white. She reared back and threw the dog—not just with her arm, but with her power. It arced across the bright blue sky, tumbling over and over like a falling bird, and settled lightly atop one of the Judgment Spires.

Karyn was smiling—or rather, hinting at a smile, as if the two of them were sharing a private joke—but the rest of her face made cold dread swirl in Ileni's stomach. "Call him."

"What?"

Karyn lifted both arms above her head and brought them down. Dizziness ran through Ileni's body, followed by a swift wave of nausea. She didn't need to reach for the lodestones to know her magic was gone. She didn't need to, and she *didn't*, though it cost every ounce of willpower in her. She focused on Karyn's face, on the sorceress's glittering, predatory eyes.

"You won't get the magic back," Karyn said. "I'll never give it back, not unless you prove you're on our side. Call him."

"You think he'll *come*? Like a dog at my call?" Ileni tried to laugh, but what emerged was a sob. "Don't underestimate him."

Karyn's whole face was as sharp as her fierce, triumphant smile. "If he thinks you're in danger, he'll come."

"No." As if this refusal would change the fact that she had already betrayed him. Ileni swallowed hard, past the solid block in her throat. "I've given you what you need to win this battle. I won't lure him to his death."

"Because you love him?" Karyn sneered.

Evin jerked, and despite herself, Ileni glanced at him. Then quickly away.

"I won't do it," she said. And she was talking to Evin, as much as to Karyn, when she added, "I'm sorry."

Karyn laughed.

"No need to be," she said. "Your answer, while disappointing, is not entirely unexpected. He's already been told you need saving."

Understanding rushed over Ileni.

"You know." She stepped back. "You know Lis is sending messages to the assassins."

Karyn stroked a finger against her cheek. "Of course I know. She honestly thought she was fooling me." Her lip curled. "Lis always was a stupid girl."

Which was how Karyn had known Sorin was the new master. Because she could tell Lis's messages were going to someone new, even if Lis herself wasn't skilled enough to realize it. But if Karyn knew, why hadn't she stopped Lis . . .

Ileni took another step back. Karyn hadn't stopped Lis because she could use her. To send false messages that Sorin would believe.

I know what Karyn has planned for you, Lis had taunted her.

You're in danger now, Sorin had said, *more than before. Open the portal farther, and I'll come through to you.*

"You told Lis I was here, back when you first brought me, because you *wanted* Sorin to know." Ileni forced herself to stop moving. There was nowhere to run, not anymore. "And you told Lis I was in danger. That you planned to torture and kill me. So she would pass it along."

Karyn laughed. "Oh, yes. Right after talking to you, she flew away from the Academy so she could communicate with your lover. I'd imagine he's ready to play the hero."

Ileni didn't doubt it. She didn't doubt it even before the air around them wavered, the ripple of power making her whole body vibrate.

"No," Ileni said. Above the spire, the sky was solid and heavy. She screamed, "Sorin, *don't!*"

But he was already there.

He stood atop the Judgment Spire like a bird poised for flight, a powerful and graceful creature, slim and taut against the fierce blue sky. He kicked the wooden dog over the side, and it fell, tumbling through the air and banging against the side of the spire.

Ileni met his gaze across the vastness of the space between them. His eyes were black and fathomless. And there she stood, on a windy plateau, alone with two imperial sorcerers.

Only two. Because Karyn hadn't dared wait long enough to summon the others. She needed Sorin to think it was Ileni, on her own, opening the portal.

So he wouldn't suspect there was a trap waiting for him.

Ileni began to laugh, high and wild. Both sorcerers stared at her, but she didn't care. For a moment, she didn't even care which side she was on.

Karyn had made a fatal mistake.

Ileni felt the sorceress's trap being sprung, a surge of magic that twisted and zigzagged across the vast space between the plateau and the spire, headed for Sorin. She didn't bother to shout a warning. She just watched.

There was nothing to watch, not until the last second. The spell was invisible.

So was the shield Sorin had prepared.

It was all silent menace and still blue sky, and Sorin, motionless, a dark shadow with white-blond hair. Silent as a picture, until the spell hit the shield and the world erupted.

Light flared between them, all around them, so bright Ileni threw her hands over her eyes. When she peeked between her fingers, there was nothing but the light, blazing white, covering Karyn and Sorin and the space between them. Ileni sensed the two sources of light pushing at each other, one trying to overpower the other, but there was no visual sign of a fight. Just the light, vast and burning.

Then it exploded, so bright it wasn't even a color, and Karyn screamed.

Ileni didn't turn, not until a thud—and Evin's horrified gasp—jerked her attention from Sorin. Karyn lay crumpled on the ground, eyes closed, unmoving. She wasn't dead, but it would take her a while to recover from the backlash.

Ileni wondered how long it would take Karyn to understand her error, in assuming Sorin wouldn't be prepared for a trap sprung by Ileni.

He did love her. But he wasn't stupid.

A flicker of motion made her whirl back to the spire. Sorin lifted his hand, and a blurred black line flew across the blue sky. Not magic. Just a dagger. It flashed right past Ileni, passing inches from her shoulder.

This time, Evin's gasp ended in a choked scream.

This time, Ileni leaped for him when she heard the thud.

She wasn't in time to catch him. He fell backward, his body hitting the plateau hard. Ileni skidded across the few steps between them and dropped to her knees, right into the pool of blood spreading across the gray stone.

Evin's eyes were wide and dark with panic. Ileni grabbed his hand and couldn't help reaching for the magic, desperately and hopelessly. The lodestones were so close, and they might as well not have been there at all. She couldn't heal him.

"Evin," she whispered, and saw a drop of water hit his cheek before she realized she was crying. He blinked and tried to lift his hand toward her, but his arm fell back to the ground. He shifted his head slightly, so it rested against her leg.

"Ileni," he gasped, and let his magic go. His eyes met hers. "It's yours."

At first, as the power flowed into her, Ileni didn't understand what was happening. And then, as Evin made a gurgling, groaning noise, she did. She had felt this before, at Death's Door—but not like *this*. Not the power of a full sorcerer.

It was real and alive, nothing like the power trapped in lodestones. It belonged to her. Her skin tingled, her hair brushed her face, and the world was a living, beautiful place. She was conscious of every breath of air, every prickle of her skin, every surge of her heart that pounded happiness through her.

Evin gasped in air, and she jerked and stared down at him. He was watching her, a faint smile on his face, as if even in dying he was happy for her joy.

While she, in her joy, had not even thought about him.

But she did now. She met his murky eyes, glazed with pain, and her heart stopped. The world was bright and beautiful, and in just a few seconds he would no longer be in it.

And she knew what she had to do with her power. With his power.

The magic connected them, letting her feel his death as well as his life, the faltering of his body. What was wrong inside him. She knew exactly what to do. She slapped one hand over the gaping hole in his shirt and the other on his forehead. The spell poured out of her as if she had last practiced it yesterday.

And the power flowed with it.

Evin screamed once, his back arching and his eyes squeezing shut. Then he thudded back to the ground and his eyes opened wide, black lashes glistening. He stared at her as if he had never seen her before.

With a great effort, he lifted his hand and closed it around hers. Their joined hands rested on his chest, still slick with blood. His heart pounded, hard and steady, against her palm.

Ileni looked away from him at the spire. Almost at once, her eyes met Sorin's. He stood staring at the two of them, his expression frozen. She couldn't read his face at all.

Not his face, but she saw the twitch in his shoulder, and knew he was reaching for another weapon.

She'd had a number of vague, desperate ideas—plead with him, go with him. *Go with him.* But Evin's head was still on her lap, and her hands were sticky with his blood, and Sorin was reaching for another knife.

"Evin," she gasped. "He won't stop. You have to—"

Evin lifted his head and managed a short, curt spell.

Power lashed across the sky. Sorin flew backward, off the spire and into the empty air. His hand opened, and Ileni recognized the object that fell from it—a standard assassin's dagger, turning over and over as it plummeted to the ground.

Evin muttered something, barely intelligible, and a ball of fire burst into the air above Sorin.

Raise a ward, she had been going to say. But Evin was nearly dead, and Sorin was the man who had almost killed him, and both of them were soldiers. There would be no *wards* in this fight.

A plea caught in her throat as Sorin fell. The ball of fire chased him down the sky, hissing and roiling, orange and white against the brilliant blue. All she could do was watch.

He didn't scream as he plummeted. It was almost graceful, the way his body twisted and arced, aiming at the impact far below. The fire flickered at his heels, spitting out tendrils of flame.

"Evin," she gasped. But before she could form the impossible plea, a surge of power exploded through the emptiness below Sorin. The air rippled and opened. Sorin fell into the opening and was gone.

Ileni recognized the shape of that spell, its intricate weavings, and knew at once a Renegai Elder had formed it.

Evin struggled to a sitting position. His breath hitched, and Ileni felt another surge of power burst from him—an imperial spell, blunt and vicious and vastly powerful.

"He's already through," she cried, and then realized that Evin wasn't trying to close the portal. He was holding it open for a few seconds longer.

Long enough for the ball of fire to follow Sorin through.

The air rippled violently, again, and a wave of heat surged over Ileni. Then the sky was bright and clear and empty, and Evin's head sagged back against her legs. He closed his eyes.

"Don't die," Ileni said, and for a dizzying moment she wasn't sure who she was talking to. Evin's eyes opened a slit, and his hand moved, weakly. She tightened her fingers around his.

He tried to smile, but only managed a half-curve of his mouth—more a grimace than his usual grin—before his eyes closed and she was alone.

She sat for a long time, unable to move or think. Evin's heart beat steadily under her hand. It was the only thing she could focus on. He was alive.

She couldn't bear to think of who might not be alive anymore. Who might be dead because of her.

But if Absalm had opened the portal, he could have defended the two of them against fire. A fire shield was relatively simple, and could easily encompass two people . . . if Absalm wanted it to. If he didn't see it as a chance to get rid of Sorin.

"I'm sorry," she whispered, even though the one she was talking to would never hear her.

And wouldn't have forgiven her even if he had.

CHAPTER
27

Karyn didn't wake until morning, which gave Ileni a long, long night to think about what she had done. She spent most of it staring into the mirror—just a mirror now, a pane of reflective glass—trying to figure out who she saw staring back at her.

Traitor. Killer. Coward.

But none of those were right. What she saw in the mirror was the person she had always, until very recently, believed she was.

The girl who would change the world.

Not, as it turned out, in some distant imagined future.

And not in one dramatic act. But slowly. Slowly, and laboriously, and without any certainty that she would ever succeed.

The girl in the mirror smiled at her, bright and luminous despite the tear streaks on her cheeks. The smile of someone who was no longer lost.

Finally, hours after nightfall but hours yet before dawn, she trod down the dark corridors to the room where Girad lay. Evin was there, of course, leaning over his brother's bed. When the door opened, he straightened, his eyes bright.

Ileni's heart stuttered in her chest, then leaped when she saw the reason for his joy. Girad's eyes were open.

She walked over. "How are you feeling?"

"Like I need candy," Girad said.

She laughed out loud, which offended Girad. He narrowed his eyes at her.

"Be nice," Evin said. "She saved your life."

Girad rolled over, turning his back to them. "Why does that mean I have to be nice?"

Evin laughed. It felt like years since she had heard him laugh. Then he gestured, and a chair near the wall slid across the rock floor and stopped next to his.

"Well," Evin said, as she sat. His voice was rough. "This

makes twice that I owe you more than I can possibly repay."

"You don't owe me anything," Ileni said, and swallowed hard. She tried not to think about how powerful he was as she said, "I knew Arxis was an assassin."

The silence stretched. She didn't dare look at him. She kept her eyes on Girad, who appeared fast asleep, which meant he probably wasn't.

"And you loved him anyhow?" Evin said finally.

Her stomach formed a familiar knot, but this one was jagged, pierced by its own sharp edges. "No! I mean—not *him*. But—" She gulped in a draught of air and finished, weakly, "It's complicated."

"Sounds it," Evin said. "Perhaps you should tell me another time, when Girad isn't listening."

Girad let out a loud and very fake snore.

Ileni risked a glance at Evin. His brow was furrowed, but he didn't look angry. Yet.

"You saved Girad's life," he said finally. Not to her so much as to himself. "You didn't know what you were doing when you put him at risk. But you knew what you were doing when you saved him."

It was partly true. She didn't quite have the courage to say, *I thought it was your life I was risking.*

"They're fighting the Empire," she said instead. What did it matter if Girad heard this? He, of all people, should know the truth about this fight. "I've seen where imperial power comes from. The entire Academy is fueled by death. You know that, don't you?"

It came out savage. Evin shrugged. "Of course I know. I still don't see being conquered by the assassins as a better alternative."

"But there's another way." She realized she was squeezing the armrest, and loosened her grip. "You gave me your magic, and I used it to heal you."

"Thank you again."

"Don't you realize what that means?" She swiveled in her chair to face him. "It means the ill, the dying—they don't have to give their lives to the Empire. They have another option. Once people realize *this* is possible, why would anyone release their power into a lodestone? When they know that same power, given to a sorcerer, could be used to heal them?"

"Ah," Evin said neutrally.

A shiver of doubt ran through Ileni. Evin was part of the Empire, and always would be. It was the only world he knew. Perhaps she shouldn't tell him she had planted the seed of its destruction.

But she knew, now, that doubt didn't mean she was wrong. It just meant she had considered that she might be.

"And I," Ileni said, "will make sure they know about it."

Evin lowered his head slightly, eyes searching her face. "How?"

"I haven't worked that out yet." Ileni sat back against the hard wood of the chair. "But most basic healing isn't difficult. Even low-level sorcerers can be taught. If there are enough healers, and if the word is spread . . ." The enormity of the undertaking—and its slowness—overwhelmed her. She remembered, suddenly, the scorn in Evin's voice when he'd said, *I have great and noble ambitions. I want to save the world.*

She stopped talking.

Evin waited, patiently, for several seconds. Then he said, "Sounds like you could use some help."

For a moment Ileni couldn't breathe. "Probably."

He reached for her hand. Ileni fought her first impulse, which was to pull away. His fingers curled protectively around hers.

Hope could hurt as much as fear. She forced herself to say, "You don't owe me anything. I told you."

"All right, then." Evin shrugged. "I suppose *you'll* have to owe *me.*"

He looked back at Girad, and so did she. She watched the small body curled in the bed, each breath making his torso rise and fall.

Thinking would have disturbed this moment of peace, this odd creeping happiness, so she let her mind smooth into exhausted blankness.

She was still holding Evin's hand when she fell asleep.

CHAPTER
28

The black room was heavy with smoke and ashes. Shards
of rock lay strewn across the ground, and in the corner,
the master's chair had been reduced to a few blackened
fragments of wood. But in the center of the room, a jagged
chalk pattern surrounded a smooth black circle unmarked
by destruction. Absalm had drawn his protection spell just
in time.

Sorin knelt in the center of the circle, crouched over
the mirror on the floor. It, too, had been protected by the
spell that had kept him—and Absalm—alive. It was flat and
shiny, unbroken.

He stood, leaned back, and smashed his foot into the center of the mirror.

Glass shattered outward. One shard hit Sorin right below the eye, and a trickle of blood ran down his cheek. He stamped on the largest piece. It cracked loudly, tiny slivers cascading across the floor.

Careful. But there was no one to see him. Absalm had raced off to control the fire, as best he could, and check the damage to the rest of the caves. Sorin should be with him. Not that he could do much to help, but he should see the destruction that had resulted from his foolishness.

His muscles were so tight they hurt. He got to his feet and walked to the small square window. Black soot covered new hairline fractures on the stone windowsill.

From here, he could see the path winding through the hazy mountains. For a moment, he fancied he saw a slim figure walking down that path, away from him, her brown hair swinging against her hood. He blinked, and there was nothing but the road, long and empty, stretching to the horizon and beyond.

And that was as it should be. He dug his knuckles into the sill and let go of his unworthy desire. A pang went through him, so sharp it seemed like physical pain.

But it wasn't pain. It was relief. She had been a vulnerability, nothing more. He saw that now. And finally, that weakness was gone.

I'll be here, he had told her. *When you do come back.*

But she was never coming back.

He turned away from the window and headed toward the door. A large broken glass lay in his path. He ground the heel of his shoe into it, rubbing it back and forth until the crunching sounds stopped, and then he kept walking.

He hesitated, for just a second, at the threshhold. His shoulder twitched, as if he was about to look back.

Instead he started down the stairs, deeper into the interior caves, and kicked the door shut softly behind him.

CHAPTER 29

Ileni's eyes snapped open to the sight of Karyn looming over her. The sorceress's eyes were black, and blue-white light crackled between her fingers.

Ileni jerked upward in the chair. Her hand had dropped out of Evin's while they slept, and she clasped it now around the armrest, steadying herself.

Wake up, she thought at Evin. But his lashes rested against his cheeks, and his breaths were soft and even.

"Come with me," Karyn said.

Both Evin and Girad were peacefully slumbering. Ileni swallowed. "I don't think so."

Karyn curled her fingers together. Light sputtered between her knuckles. "Why not?"

"Because," Ileni said, "I've noticed an interesting thing about you imperial sorcerers. You don't like to kill when people are watching."

Karyn let out a breath. She opened her hands and spread them to her sides. The blue-white light stretched between her palms, becoming more and more translucent, then disappeared.

"You really need to stop assuming," Karyn said, "that people want to kill you."

"No," Ileni said. "Actually, I don't think that would be a good idea at all."

She reached for her magic—still gone, of course— then kicked the side of Evin's chair. His body slumped over sideways, but he went on sleeping.

"I just want to talk to you." Karyn's voice was silk sliding over steel. "Without interruption. Things yesterday did not go as planned, and I want to know why."

"Mostly," Ileni said, "because your plan wasn't a very good one."

"Really." Karyn crossed her arms over her chest.

"Really. What would killing him have accomplished?" Her throat almost closed up when she said *killing him*. She forced herself on. "I already killed their leader once. It didn't stop them."

"Because another leader was ready to step up, and they all knew who it was." Karyn shook her head. "That's not the case this time. It will take them years to regroup."

"But they'll do it," Ileni said. "You don't know them. Even if he was dead, it wouldn't end this forever."

Karyn gave her a pitying look. "Nothing will end it *forever*. But for now, they wouldn't be a threat."

Ileni didn't know if Sorin was dead—she didn't want to have to hope he was. But she knew what kind of devastation that fire must have wreaked in those dry, narrow stone passageways. Many of the other assassins must be dead, and their stronghold nearly destroyed. Even if Sorin was alive, it would be years before they were at full strength again. Years before they could resume their missions.

Which meant for now, Girad was safe.

Karyn's lips thinned. She brought her hands together and clasped them in front of her chest. Ileni braced herself.

A low, clear laugh rang through the room.

"Well," Cyn said from the doorway, "nobody can say the Renegai aren't brave. Stupid, yes. But that's an entirely different argument, don't you think?"

She was leaning against the doorpost, wearing a fluttery bright green dress. Her hair shadowed one of her eyes, but the other was faintly narrowed.

"What plan were you talking about?" Cyn went on, as calmly as if Karyn wasn't looking daggers at her, as if the air around the sorceress's hands wasn't sizzling with power.

Silence. Cyn tilted her head to the side.

"We had a chance to trap and kill the master of the assassins," Karyn said finally. "But he was prepared. Someone warned him."

Cyn's face went very still, and Ileni wondered if she knew—or suspected—her sister's true allegiance. Cyn knew about Lis's entanglement with Arxis. And by now, everyone knew what Arxis had been.

Yesterday, Ileni would have been glad to see Lis punished for this. Even if it wasn't her fault, so many other things were. But now, watching fear transform Cyn's face, she hesitated. Then she threw her head back and, very deliberately, laughed.

It sounded fake and wooden, but it got their attention.

"No one warned him," Ileni said. "He is *always* prepared."

"Even for treachery from someone he loved?" Karyn said.

Ileni managed not to flinch at that—though Cyn did,

so slightly that only the quivering of her hair gave her away. Ileni knew, then, that she was right. Cyn did know about her sister's treachery and was keeping silent about it.

"Especially for that," Ileni said. "That was your mistake yesterday. And if not for me, you would have died for that mistake. Sorin would have killed you while you lay there unconscious."

"That doesn't mean I'm going to let you stay," Karyn snapped, and the edge in her voice sliced through the air.

Ileni glanced swiftly, again, at Cyn. Then she focused on Karyn. "You'll let me stay," she said, "because I can teach your students something you can't. I can tutor them in healing."

"And why," Karyn said, "would I be interested in that?"

Ileni crossed her arms over her chest. "Because the assassins are no longer an immediate threat. So you won't need as much power any more. Will you?"

Karyn came to attention, and once again doubt stabbed Ileni. She took a breath. "Evin sent a fireball into the caves. The assassins will be rebuilding for a long time. And when Evin was dying, he gave me his power—"

"Evin appears rather not dead," Cyn observed.

Karyn was perfectly still. Ileni couldn't tell what she was thinking. So she spoke to Cyn. "That's right. He's not.

Because instead of taking his power, I used it to heal him."

Silence. Karyn's mouth tightened, the only sign that she understood. Cyn was still staring, not at Ileni or Karyn, but at Evin.

"It didn't even require all his power." The words spilled out of Ileni in a rush—not careful, controlled, the way she wanted to tell it. "Healing spells almost never do. And whatever I used, it's not lost to him forever. He'll get it back. His power will grow back, because it's *his*."

"Good to know," Cyn said. Ileni couldn't read her voice.

"I could do the same for others," Ileni said. "I could train other sorcerers to heal as well. We could *save* lives instead of ending them."

She threw it out like a challenge. *Go on, Karyn. Let your most important sorceress hear that it's their deaths you're interested in. That you don't care about lives.*

Karyn looked at Ileni, her fury almost palpable. The air around her sizzled—and then, slowly, went still. Karyn smiled, and the smile was more frightening than the power gathered within her.

"Well," she said slowly. "That's not entirely true, is it?"

Cyn flung out one arm and shouted, a short, savage spell. A beam of silver sparkles shot from her hands, whizzed past

Ileni, and exploded in an iridescent shimmer against Evin's slumbering form.

Evin jerked awake, eyes wide. He looked first at Cyn, then at Ileni, then at Girad, and then—finally—at Karyn. "What—"

"Ileni was telling us something interesting," Cyn said sweetly. "I thought you might want to hear it."

Karyn pressed her lips together. Evin straightened, ran a hand through his rumpled hair, then rubbed his bleary eyes. "Okay?"

"That was hardly necessary, Cyn," Karyn said. "I understand perfectly what Ileni is saying. And it's wonderful."

Ileni went very still.

"No one has to die," she repeated. But it came out uncertain.

"Of course not," Karyn said smoothly. "It was always regrettable, that people had to die to give their power to the Empire."

Evin tensed, as if he knew where Karyn was heading. It took Ileni a few moments longer, and then a slow cold dread settled in her stomach.

"I don't understand," she said.

But she did. She just didn't want to.

Karyn looked at her through hooded eyes, as if she knew Ileni understood, but would condescend to explain anyhow. "I am sure they would much rather give their power in exchange for their lives."

"No," Ileni said.

"You don't see how it would work?" Karyn wasn't bothering to hide her smirk. "It doesn't have to be *their* power that heals them, does it? It can be a simple exchange. Power into a lodestone, at the moment of death, in exchange for last-minute healing from a sorcerer. You told me once you could heal dozens of people with one lodestone. We would still gain far more power than we lost."

"That seems risky," Evin observed, his voice cool but nonchalant. "Waiting for the moment of death."

Karyn shrugged. "It's a chance to live. People will take it."

"No," Ileni said again. Her voice caught. "It's not—that's not what I wanted."

Karyn sighed. Her voice turned gentle—as if she was talking to a child. "It doesn't matter what *you* want, Ileni."

Ileni wasn't aware that she was moving until she heard the chair thud to the floor behind her. The passageways blurred around her as she ran, feet pounding and stumbling on the stone. She didn't stop until she was on the ledge outside the mountain, staring at the brilliant blue sky, at the spire where Sorin had stood, at the distant plateau where Evin had lain dying beneath her hands.

She should have known better than to think the Empire could be brought down by an act of healing. She should have taken the only chance she'd ever had to change things.

Sorin had been right. She never should have come here in the first place.

"It will be all right," Evin said behind her.

She faced him, putting her back to the drop, heedless of her lack of magic. She knew Evin would catch her if she fell.

"Don't be stupid," she said, with a savageness he didn't deserve. "Nothing will be all right. They're just going to keep taking magic from people, in exchange for healing them."

"It's still better, isn't it?" Evin said. "Better than killing them."

It was. Of course it was. But she had thought . . . she was suddenly ashamed to tell him what she had thought. That she would single-handedly change *everything*, make it not just better but actually good.

"Besides," Evin added offhandedly, "they need you to teach them to heal, don't they? It's not as if you have no power here."

Said by someone who didn't understand power. Even so, a glimmer sparked in Ileni—just for a moment—before it was buried under the knowledge of what she would be up against.

"Nothing is going to change," she said wearily. "It doesn't matter what I try to do. They're going to win."

"They're going to win some of the time." Evin grinned. "I bet we can win some of the time, too."

He said *we* so naturally, without even a pause. Ileni did hesitate, though, before she met his brown eyes.

"Actually," she said, "I'd bet most of the time."

"Well. You are the ambitious one."

Ileni swallowed hard.

"Yes," she said. "I am. But it's all going to be the same, for a very long time. The sorcerers will have all the power, and the assassins will eventually regather and start attacking again . . . and I haven't made any difference at all."

"Well," Evin said, "I think you've made quite a bit of difference to the people whose lives you saved. Speaking as one of them."

She stepped away from the edge, closer to him.

"Do you regret it?" he asked evenly.

His face was half-shadowed, but his eyes were bright and

piercing. Not wide with pain and devoid of hope. She felt again his hand, limp and helpless in hers. Felt it tighten as Sorin plummeted past the gray rock.

"No," she said. And for at least that moment, it was entirely true.

Because this, as it turned out, was her destiny. Not to be the powerful sorceress her people had been waiting for, not to be the ruthless killer the assassins needed. Her destiny was to save one person at a time, change things one tiny step after another.

It still hurt, a tinge of loss. Her life wouldn't be grand, or dramatic, or momentous. There would be no great choices to make, no moments when everything would change. It would make a dull story if she was ever called upon to tell it.

It hurt, yes. But it was also something of a relief.

"I think Cyn will help us," Evin said.

"So do I," Ileni said, though she wasn't entirely sure. And then, with more certainty: "Lis will, too."

Evin frowned doubtfully . . . but he didn't know Lis as well as he thought he did. And more crucially, he didn't know that Ileni had something to hold over Lis's head.

Ileni took a deep breath. "All right," she said. "Let's take it one person at a time. For now."

Evin smiled at her brilliantly, a smile so laden with hope that she looked away. Something inside her stirred, but it was something she wasn't quite ready for. Not yet.

Evin extended his hand to her, and her heart leaped unexpectedly. A smile spread across her face, and she bit her lip. Maybe she would be ready sooner than she thought.

She walked across the ledge toward him. His eyes brightened, and he took her hand in his.

She knew Evin thought she had chosen because of him. Because somewhere, deep down, she loved him. And maybe someday—if she did end up loving him—she would tell him the truth.

That it hadn't been about love.

It had, in the end, been about death. About who needed it, and who was ashamed of it, and who celebrated it. About who might, someday, move past it.

She leaned against Evin and closed her eyes, shutting out the precipitous drop below them and the vast sky above. And for a while, she concentrated on the sunlight on her face and his solidness at her back, and she didn't think about the Empire or the assassins or anything at all having to do with death.